"The ducks are [illegible] even move around."

"Geez! And they're serving this right here in Ranchero?"

"Yes," she answered quickly. "At a price that would water your eyes." She stopped, not sure she wanted to remind him how much she'd charged on the company card.

Egan leaned back in the chair. "This is going to ruffle a few feathers at Longhorn Prime Rib." He grinned, obviously pleased with his play on words.

"I was totally complimentary about the restaurant in general." Jordan thought about the Chocolate Decadence Cake that had doubled as breakfast that morning. "The desserts were phenomenal, and the service—fantastic."

Egan studied her face. "I had you pegged for a simple meat-and-potatoes girl. For the life of me, I can't figure out why you'd order this when you're obviously so outraged at how they get it."

Here it is! This was where she'd have to admit she was clueless when it came to fancy food. This was where he'd realize what a big mistake he'd made giving her the job. "The waiter recommended it. Said it was imported from Canada. Since I knew it was too expensive to ever try on my own, I went with it."

"I still find it hard to believe you'd even order the dish, knowing how you feel about it."

"I thought it was chicken," she blurted, looking away for a moment, imagining the pink slip falling from this week's pay envelope.

THE FIRST IN THE NATIONAL BESTSELLING
CANDY HOLLIDAY MURDER MYSTERIES

TOWN IN A Blueberry Jam

B. B. HAYWOOD

In the seaside village of Cape Willington, Maine, Candy Holliday has an idyllic life tending to the Blueberry Acres farm she runs with her father. But when an aging playboy and the newly crowned Blueberry Queen are killed, Candy investigates to clear the name of a local handyman. And as she sorts through the town's juicy secrets, things start to get sticky indeed . . .

penguin.com

M772T0910

FROM THE *NEW YORK TIMES* BESTSELLING AUTHOR OF *EGGS BENEDICT ARNOLD*

·LAURA CHILDS·

BEDEVILED EGGS

The ladies at the Cackleberry Club café are busy preparing for Halloween. But someone's jumped the gun on the tricks. As mayoral candidate Chuck Peebler leaves the café, he gets struck with a crossbow arrow and is killed instantly. When another murder occurs on the historical society's Quilt Trail, the Cackleberry Club needs to sniff out the bad egg—before he strikes again.

penguin.com

M782T1010

LIVER LET DIE

Liz Lipperman

BERKLEY PRIME CRIME, NEW YORK

THE BERKLEY PUBLISHING GROUP
Published by the Penguin Group
Penguin Group (USA) Inc.
375 Hudson Street, New York, New York 10014, USA
Penguin Group (Canada), 90 Eglinton Avenue East, Suite 700, Toronto, Ontario M4P 2Y3, Canada
(a division of Pearson Penguin Canada Inc.)
Penguin Books Ltd., 80 Strand, London WC2R 0RL, England
Penguin Group Ireland, 25 St. Stephen's Green, Dublin 2, Ireland (a division of Penguin Books Ltd.)
Penguin Group (Australia), 250 Camberwell Road, Camberwell, Victoria 3124, Australia
(a division of Pearson Australia Group Pty. Ltd.)
Penguin Books India Pvt. Ltd., 11 Community Centre, Panchsheel Park, New Delhi—110 017, India
Penguin Group (NZ), 67 Apollo Drive, Rosedale, Auckland 0632, New Zealand
(a division of Pearson New Zealand Ltd.)
Penguin Books (South Africa) (Pty.) Ltd., 24 Sturdee Avenue, Rosebank, Johannesburg 2196,
South Africa

Penguin Books Ltd., Registered Offices: 80 Strand, London WC2R 0RL, England

LIVER LET DIE

A Berkley Prime Crime Book / published by arrangement with the author

PRINTING HISTORY
Berkley Prime Crime mass-market edition / October 2011

Cover illustration by Sarah Oberrender.
Cover design by Ben Perini.
Interior text design by Laura K. Corless.

For information, address: The Berkley Publishing Group,
a division of Penguin Group (USA) Inc.,
375 Hudson Street, New York, New York 10014.

ISBN: 978-0-425-24404-3

BERKLEY® PRIME CRIME
Berkley Prime Crime Books are published by The Berkley Publishing Group,
a division of Penguin Group (USA) Inc.,
375 Hudson Street, New York, New York 10014.
BERKLEY® PRIME CRIME and the PRIME CRIME logo are trademarks of Penguin Group (USA) Inc.

PRINTED IN THE UNITED STATES OF AMERICA

10 9 8 7 6 5 4 3 2 1

To Dan, my real life hero since high school.
Without you beside me all the way,
I could not have achieved my dreams.
Te Amo.

ACKNOWLEDGMENTS

Since this is my first novel, there are a lot of people I need to thank. Please indulge me as I mention a few. I promise, like at the Academy Awards, when I hear the music, I'll stop.

First, to my wonderful agent, Christine Witthohn of Book Cents Literary Agency, who is a friend as well as a business partner. Thank you for always being there as a counselor, a therapist, a critique partner, a taskmaster when I needed it, and more importantly, a cheerleader who gets as excited about my books as I do. Most of all, thank you for believing I could take my writing to another level even when I doubted it.

To my fabulous editor, Faith Black, at Berkley Prime Crime. Thanks for making my first venture into publishing so painless. Your enthusiasm for my characters and their stories warms my heart. I only hope I live up to your expectations. And to all the talented people behind the scenes at Berkley Prime Crime, your dedication and hard work didn't go unnoticed.

To my critique partners, Joni Sauer-Folger and Shelly Kuehn, who never let me get away with anything. Thanks for always insisting on great instead of mediocre and showing me how to do it when I sometimes forgot.

To my real life siblings, Jack Roth, Don Roth, Mary Ann Nedved, Dorothy Bennett, and Lillian Magistro, who taught me how to love and laugh, so I could create characters who do the same. To Theresa Pollack, Chuck Roth, and Bob Roth, who left us way too soon. I know you're all smiling down from heaven with Mom and Dad.

To my Sangria Sisters, aka Bunko Babes, many of whom I've known for over three decades. Your belief in me never faltered, even when mine sometimes slipped. Take a bow, Tami Ramey, Judy Neal, Nancy Dunsmore, Marilyn Pyhrr, Jane Helms, Linda McCraw, Anna Nelson, Barbara Valentine, and Vaneesa Cohen.

To my fantastic beta readers, Chris Keniston and Sylvia Rochester, thank you for your honest comments and your contagious enthusiasm.

To Kari Lee Townsend, Barbie Jo Witek, Danielle Labue (my plotting pals), and all the Book Cents Babes, who are so amazingly supportive with each other, and to my fellow writers on the GIAM loop, my RWA and DARA chapters, my MWA and my SinC loops. Your advice and support means a lot to me. And to every writer out there still waiting to be in my shoes, be patient. Someday your dream will come true like mine did.

And lastly, to my children, Nicole and Dennis Bushland and Brody and Abby Lipperman, thank you for always being there to show me every minute of the day how important family really is. Special thanks to Brody for his eagle eye and for making me say this.

And then there are my grandchildren, Grayson and Caden Bushland and Ellie and Alice Lipperman. You put the fun in my life. I love you all so much.

And now I hear the music . . .

CHAPTER 1

Single white female stuck in a dead-end job who barely makes the rent on the closet she calls home—looking for tall, dark, handsome rich guy who loves . . .

Jordan McAllister jumped, slamming her finger on the Delete key when the shrill ring of the phone on her desk jarred her from her daydream.

"Personals," she answered.

"Ms. McAllister, this is Jackie Frazier. Mr. Egan needs to see you in his office."

Jordan frowned. She'd been at this job less than three months, and already she was being summoned to the editor's office. Since the administrative offices were on the second floor, she hadn't even met the man yet. "When?"

"Now would be good," Jackie said, inserting a touch of sarcasm and ramping up Jordan's paranoia another notch.

Hanging up, she leaned back in the chair, trying to guess where she'd screwed up. Other than allowing an ad to run several days past its contract, nothing popped into her mind, but she was still on probation, which meant they didn't need a reason to fire her.

Jordan glanced around the room at her co-workers, all either chatting with one another or busy at their cubicles. Since the only person who bothered to talk to her was the chubby guy in the mail room who hit on her every chance he got, there was no one to calm her fears.

Why was the editor summoning her to his office?

Yanking her purse from the bottom drawer of the desk, she powdered her face. If she was going to get tossed on her butt, she didn't want to have a shiny nose. Shoving her purse back in, she locked the drawer. She didn't know these people well enough to trust them with her lunch, much less her purse.

Jordan smiled. First of all, everyone stayed clear of her, acting like she was a leper after their jobs. And second, there was a grand total of $6.52 in her wallet. She knew this because when she'd paid for the crunchy chicken sandwich at the deli on the corner an hour ago, she'd sacrificed adding a latte so she'd have enough money to buy a package of bologna on her way home.

How pathetic was she? Big-city college graduate with dreams of becoming a sports columnist for a famous city newspaper, wasting away in a small-time newsroom writing personal ads for desperate people looking to hook up. Even more pathetic was that the one she'd been working on before the phone rang was her own.

She reached in the top drawer and pulled out a Hostess

Ho Ho, thinking this was the drawer that should be under lock and key. God forbid she go through a day without one or two of these suckers. Glancing around to make sure no one was watching, she unwrapped one and popped it into her mouth, closing her eyes as the chocolate immediately elevated her endorphin level. Common sense told her it couldn't possibly work that fast, but there was something to be said for the placebo effect.

Standing, she blew out a calming breath and shut the drawer. She'd save her last chocolate treat for when she was cleaning out her desk. She walked down the aisle to the other side of the room, feeling twenty pairs of eyes on her. The newsroom was small, and it was a given that everyone knew she was on her way to getting canned. Kind of like at NFL training camp when a player got called to the head coach's office and was told to bring his playbook.

Still, she kept her head high and tried to convince herself the editor was doing her a favor. Now she'd be forced to go out and find the job of her dreams.

Who are you kidding?

After Brett dumped her for the cute little weather girl with perky clouds of her own before she'd even had time to find gainful employment after the move to Dallas, Jordan had spent two months searching for this miserable job. Seems the metroplex had as many wannabe sports reporters as it did cowboys driving pickups. Her only shot at a career that didn't include flipping burgers had brought her to Ranchero, a small town north of Dallas. The short, squatty human resources director at the *Ranchero Globe* had offered her the "opportunity of a lifetime" writing personal ads until "something else opened up."

After a month on the job, Jordan realized "something else" was never going to open up. This was Ranchero, Texas, population 22,773—22,774 after she rolled into town with four suitcases and Maggie, her goldfish. Most of her co-workers had worked at the newspaper since high school, some even before. Unless someone got reassigned to the big newsroom in the sky, there would be no job openings anytime soon.

She stopped at the desk in front of the editor's office and got her first look at Miss Sarcasm herself. "Jordan McAllister. I'm here to see Mr. Egan."

Jackie Frazier looked up from a stack of papers, her eyes scanning Jordan before her lips curved in a half smile. "He's waiting."

With dark curly hair that looked like it had a mind of its own and small, beady eyes, Egan's secretary could have easily passed for Gilda Radner's alter ego Roseanne Roseannadanna.

Jordan took a deep breath, then pushed through the door to where Dwayne Egan sat behind a large desk piled high with newspapers and file folders. Expecting to see a tall, distinguished businessman, she was surprised to find the fortyish editor short with a receding hairline, looking more like Joe Pesci than the Michael Douglas she'd imagined.

Make that Joe Pesci with huge ears!

She stifled a giggle as she took a closer look. With his bushy eyebrows, dark mustache, and big ears, Dwayne Egan could be Mr. Potato Head's brother, minus the black top hat. She tried to concentrate on something other than his ears, but it was a losing battle. She wondered if he could hear the whispers of disgruntled employees from across the room.

"Sit down, McAllister," Egan said, pointing to a chair piled high with newspapers.

Moving the stack to the carpet beside the chair, Jordan did as instructed.

Egan waited until she was settled before he opened the file in front of him. "Says here you graduated with honors from the University of Texas six years ago. That true?"

Who lies on a résumé? And even if she had, would she be dumb enough to fess up now? "Yes."

"Says you worked as a copy editor at the *Del Rio Gazette*." He shook his head. "That doesn't make sense. Why would someone with your credentials do a job any Tom, Dick, or Harry off the street could do?"

She opened her mouth to lie, then thought better of it. If she was about to get fired, who cared if he knew her life history? "I moved with my boyfriend there where he worked as a sports intern at the local television station. With the economy the way it is, the only job I could get actually *writing* for a newspaper was in a town about two hundred miles north of Del Rio. I chose not to do that."

"Surely with all your smarts you could have stayed in Austin and written for one of the bigger papers."

She lowered her head. Talking about her personal life with a total stranger was getting uncomfortable. She swiped at the sweat beads forming under her collar. "I could have, but I hoped my job at the newspaper was only temporary. Unfortunately, they weren't lining up to hire a female sports reporter in a small town full of good old boys."

"So, you wanna be a sportswriter. Why'd you stay in Del Rio so long if you didn't think you had a shot at that position? And why move to Ranchero?"

Jordan tapped her fingers on the armrest. If he was going to fire her, she wished he'd get on with it. This twenty questions thing was starting to annoy her. She didn't need Dwayne Egan to remind her how shortsighted she'd been when it came to Brett. She'd put her own dreams on hold for over six years, only to find out his long-term plans didn't include her.

"My ex was offered an entry-level position in Dallas at one of the bigger TV stations, and I followed him."

Egan shifted in his chair, his eyes never leaving hers. "How'd you end up here? This is a pretty good commute from Dallas."

"We split up before I had a chance to start my own job search. I wanted as far away from big D as I could get." Okay, maybe that was a little lie, but Dwayne Egan didn't have to know his was the only offer she'd gotten. She was grateful his bionic ears were limited to hearing and not reading minds.

He eyed her suspiciously. "Got dumped for a newer model?"

Startled by the question, she tried to find the right words to tell him it was none of his frickin' business, then decided once again, who cared? "One loaded with bigger equipment."

She watched as he assessed her before smiling. "I like your attitude, kid." He leaned forward with his elbows on the desk. "So, you've been here about three months, right?"

She nodded, expecting his next words to send her to the unemployment line on the way home.

Instead, he opened another file. "Ever meet Loretta Mosley in those three months?" When she shook her head, he continued. "Loretta is our culinary reporter. Writes a popular weekly column called the Kitchen Kupboard." He stopped to take a drink from the cup on his desk. "Know anything about cooking?"

"A little," she lied, thinking about last night when she'd microwaved a TV dinner a tad too long and ended up sneaking it out to the stray dog that hung around in the alley behind her apartment building, filling up on chips and salsa instead.

"Well, Loretta went and broke her hip on Saturday. Looks like she'll be in rehab for six weeks. We need someone to write her column until she returns."

"Why can't she write it from rehab?"

Egan laughed out loud. "That's exactly what I asked before I found out she also broke her right arm. Apparently, there's a clause in her contract that says we have to pay her full salary for three months if she can't work. Do you really think she's going to make an effort?" He paused. "There are benefits to being the owner's niece."

He shoved a piece of paper across the desk. "So, do you want the job or not?"

Jordan stared at the contract. Was this her golden opportunity to finally eat something other than bologna sandwiches three nights a week? "How much of a pay increase will I get?"

His expression never changed, although she swore there

was laughter in his eyes. "Let's look at it as an opportunity to get your name out to a lot of households. Did I mention Loretta's column is very popular?"

She sighed. "I guess that means a very small one."

"Worse. I can't pay you anything extra since I have to keep paying her. And you'll still have to write the personals every day."

"Let me get this straight. You want me to take over this woman's job and still do my own without compensation?"

"Pretty much. You're the first person I've offered this to, but if you're not interested, I'm sure I can find someone who is."

Jordan pretended to mull it around in her head. Given she had zero culinary skills, she wasn't sure which scared her more, writing a weekly column about food or having her name in print for the whole world to see. Okay, maybe not the whole world, but at least the twenty-two thousand plus in Ranchero.

"I'll take it," she said, reaching for the contract. "When do I start?"

He cleared his throat. "Actually, tonight. I need you to run by a new restaurant that just reopened off Highway 82 and write a review."

Her hand stopped midway through her signature. "You never said anything about working at night. With my nonexistent pay raise, I can't afford fancy restaurants."

"That's the good part. Everything's on the newspaper. The restaurant caters to the Dallas crowd looking for dining by the lake. The locals can't afford it, so Loretta was looking forward to a four-star meal with all the fixings. That was before she hopped on one of those personal watercraft things, slammed into a buoy on Lake Texoma, and went airborne." He paused and slid a credit card across the desk. "Your job's simple. Chow down on a free steak and write about it."

Jordan looked away so Egan wouldn't see her facial expression. "It's a steak house?"

"Is that a problem? You're not a vegan or something, are you?"

"Ah, no," she answered too quickly.

The fact was, she hadn't eaten steak since her dad forced her to try a rare one when she was a teenager. She still had nightmares of the cow mooing as she bit into it. Ground beef was the only red meat she ate now and even that had to be burned to a crisp.

"You said it was reopening?"

Egan walked around the desk and reached for the contract. "Yep. About six weeks ago, one of the owners was killed in an after-hours robbery. The place was a crime scene for a long time, but the new owner is finally reopening with higher-quality food, supposedly."

"What'd you say the name was?"

"Longhorn Prime Rib."

She groaned, then coughed to cover it up.

"Have a great meal on the *Globe* tonight. The owner knows you're coming, so introduce yourself when you arrive. The service will be a lot better that way. I'll expect to see your review sometime tomorrow."

Jordan stood and walked to the door, hesitating briefly before exiting. Could she pull this off? She'd need a lot of help and a little luck. When she finally made it back to her desk, she plopped down on the chair, praying that Longhorn Prime Rib served chicken.

• • •

Jordan glanced at Rosie bent over a tray of jewelry. Rosella LaRue was the first person she'd met when she arrived at Empire Apartments three months ago. Fiftyish with long bleached hair worn in braids, Rosie was the last person Jordan expected to befriend.

The woman who lived in tie-dyed T-shirts and made her living selling handmade jewelry on eBay had taken her under her wing that first day. She'd introduced Jordan to the other residents on the first floor, who had helped carry her meager belongings up the front steps and into her apartment. Rosie even made sure her stomach was full before Jordan fell onto the couch exhausted.

She turned 180 degrees in front of the mirror to get a glimpse of her backside as Rosie approached with a jade and black necklace.

"This one is perfect. It'll bring out your eyes." She lifted Jordan's reddish brown shoulder-length hair and clasped the necklace.

"Isn't this the one you sold last week for big bucks?"

Rosie laughed. "I'm waiting for the check to clear before I mail it," she said, winking. "Think of this as you're breaking it in."

Jordan fingered the chunky stones, thinking they really did dress up the simple black jersey number she'd chosen for her debut as a food critic. "It's perfect." She hugged Rosie before turning again to the mirror. "What about the dress? Has all your great cooking settled south of my tailbone?"

Rosie huffed. "Honey, I've still got a lot of work to do to put some meat on your skinny butt."

Jordan smoothed the material over her thighs. Rosie was right. After her breakup with Brett, she'd been too upset to eat and had dropped a few pounds. If her mother were here instead of in West Texas, she'd be feeding her carbs every chance she got, just like Rosie was.

"Put these on," Rosie said, handing Jordan a pair of earrings.

"Girl, you're not going anywhere until we get a look at you," a voice bellowed from the living room.

Jordan turned quickly as Michael Cafferty marched into the room, his head nearly touching the top of the doorway. His partner, Victor Rodriguez, a good six inches shorter, squeezed past him.

"Whoa! You look hot," Victor said. "Too bad you're not my type." He winked at Michael. "You sure you're really going to a restaurant by yourself?"

"Hush. She's already nervous enough to puke." Rosie spun Jordan around so the guys from across the hall could get a better look at her. "Stay here. I'll be right back."

She hurried from Jordan's apartment, and when she returned, handed her a sparkly black clutch. "Now you're ready to knock 'em dead."

"Thanks, guys." Jordan swallowed hard as she shoved her lip gloss, ibuprofen, and a few tissues into the small purse. Since she had the credit card Egan had given her, she wouldn't need her wallet. After pulling out her driver's license and a five-dollar bill, she shoved the wallet back into her big organizer bag. "I'm ready."

"Looking like that, you might even get lucky," Victor deadpanned. "Then you might not end up an old maid with no sex life like Rosie here." He bent down and kissed the older woman's forehead.

"Speak for yourself, young man. I'll have you know I have an active sex life." She giggled. "Well, I will as soon as I run by Wal-Mart and get some new batteries."

"Good God, woman. I didn't want details! I was only . . ." He shrugged.

Jordan high-fived her friend. "I don't think I've ever seen Victor speechless."

"Okay, let's leave these women to themselves," Michael said, nudging Victor toward the door. "Too much information going on over here."

"Have fun, Jordan," Victor said over his shoulder, winking. "I can't wait to hear all about it."

When she was alone and ready to leave, Jordan took one final glance in the mirror, wishing she felt as brave as she was pretending to be. Heading down Main Street toward the restaurant, she scolded herself for being so jittery. Worst-case scenario, she'd have to eat a steak. Seeing her name on her own byline would make it well worth it.

Longhorn Prime Rib was located six miles west on the outskirts of Ranchero. Jordan pulled into the porte cochere, then changed her mind and drove to the back lot to park her Camry, a decision she second-guessed on the long walk to the front of the restaurant. But five bucks was five bucks, and she needed it more than the valet guy.

She took a deep breath before entering, again hoping

she could pull this off. "Jordan McAllister from the *Ranchero Globe*," she said to the maître d'.

After checking his reservation sheet, the distinguished-looking gentleman led her to a table in the center of the restaurant and handed her a menu. "May I get you a cocktail or a glass of wine?"

Not much of a wine connoisseur, she fidgeted with the napkin he spread across her lap. "What would you suggest?"

"The Viognier for starters. It's our finest white."

Jordan nodded, smiling up at him.

"J. T. will be here in a moment to take your order."

She opened the menu and nearly choked. The cheapest appetizer was twenty-eight dollars. Good thing she wasn't paying.

"Welcome to Longhorn," a masculine voice said, setting the glass of white wine in front of her. "I'm J. T. and I'll be your waiter. Can I start you off with an appetizer, or are you ready to order?"

Jordan looked up. This guy definitely didn't have to worry about sleeping alone. Tall, blond, with the darkest eyes she'd ever seen, his smile was a whole other subject.

Jordan stared at the menu wishing she saw nachos and mozzarella sticks instead of oysters and sushi. She leaned closer to J. T. "I'm cutting back on red meat," she whispered, noting there were no prices listed. "Can you recommend something else?"

"That's too bad. The filet here is the best I've ever tasted." He took the menu, glancing both ways before he pointed to an entrée. "Ordinarily, I wouldn't recommend this because it's way overpriced, and I've never tried it myself. This is one of the few items on the menu the chef won't let us try without paying."

"And you think I should try it?"

"Why not? See that guy over there? He comes in once a week or so and always orders this, never the steak. At that price, it must be worth it."

Jordan glanced across the room. The man was alone, sipping a glass of red wine, and he raised an eyebrow when he caught her looking. Quickly, she looked away, her gaze connecting with another man three tables over whose eyes seemed to bore into her. This one was dark and brooding, as if he'd just been told his pony finished fourth. She attempted a smile, but his expression never changed, and she quickly looked away.

"And you're sure it's not beef?"

After J. T. nodded, she leaned closer to him. "How much does it cost?"

"Sixty-five dollars without a salad."

Sixty-five dollars would buy a lot of bologna, she thought, then remembered she wasn't footing the bill. "Okay, I'll give it a try. What's it called?"

"Foie gras."

Sounded tame enough. "Foie gras it is, then." She leaned back and sipped the wine, which was so smooth it was easy to forget she was drinking alcohol. "Oh, and J. T., could you bring a salad, too?"

"Do you want to try the Strawberry-Mandarin Salad? It's a house specialty."

She frowned, thinking that sounded expensive, and she was already splurging on the foie gras.

Screw it. If Egan couldn't pay her any extra, at least he could spring for a side salad.

After J. T. left to fill her order, she gulped a big drink of the wine, convinced she could actually feel the alcohol drowning the butterflies in her stomach. For the first time since she arrived, she allowed her shoulders to relax.

Scanning the room, her eyes connected with the brooding stranger's again. He looked to be a little over six feet tall, and even from this angle, she could tell his eyes were light-colored, bringing out the blond streaks in his darker blond hair. Either he had a great hairdresser or he spent a lot of time outdoors. She'd bet money on the latter.

She raised her glass in a mock salute, and for a split second she saw a smile cross his face before it dissolved into brooding again.

A sixty-five-dollar entrée, a glass of excellent wine, and eye candy a few tables away. Maybe this wouldn't be so bad after all.

CHAPTER 2

"Bon appétit." J. T. set the covered dish in front of Jordan and lifted the lid before picking up her empty salad dish.

Jordan stared at the food. It definitely wasn't red meat, but it didn't look like chicken, either. Two slices resembled the dark meat of turkey, drizzled with reddish black syrup that oozed over the sides. Completing the entrée were two small blobs the same color as the syrup, decorated with red berries. They reminded her of the type growing on the hedges in front of her house in West Texas, the ones her mother had always warned were poisonous.

She gulped. "What exactly is this, J. T.?" She glanced up, hoping he didn't see through the fake smile and quivering lips.

He squinted. "It's a delicacy imported from a small town in Canada. I hear it's fabulous." He stared at the plate, hedging. "Let me know how you like it. I may have to break down and try it myself one of these days."

"Can you bring some bread?" she asked, resigning herself to an all-out carb fest. Thank heavens she'd at least had the salad.

As she waited for J. T. to return, she picked up her fork and poked at the soft meat, not quite sure she'd ever seen anything like it before. She glanced toward the man who always ordered it and saw him looking her way, his brow furrowed. She dropped her fork, catching the glass of wine a nanosecond before it sloshed on the tablecloth.

With as much dignity as she could muster, Jordan steadied the glass and took a sip, wondering when J. T. would return with the bread. Except for the small salad, she hadn't eaten since the chicken sandwich and Ho Ho at lunch. Her growling stomach was audible reinforcement that it was well aware of that fact.

Seeing her waiter approach, she had a sinking feeling she'd go home hungry tonight, but there was no way she could eat what was on her plate without knowing what it was. She prayed J. T. wouldn't tell her this was calf fries or something equally gross. Why Texas cowboys bragged about eating those was beyond her. And why call them calf fries when they were really buffalo testicles?

Eew!

J. T. placed the basket of bread in front of her. "You haven't tasted it yet?"

"You didn't tell me what it was."

He shuffled his feet a little then cleared his throat, pointing to the blackish red blobs and the syrupy squiggles. "The sauce is made from black currants."

"And the meat?" She was pretty sure she didn't want to know.

"Fatty duck liver."

"Fatty duck liver?" Jordan's head shot up, positive she hadn't heard him correctly. Noticing the stares generated when her voice rose a few octaves above normal, she leaned closer to J. T. "Seriously . . . fatty duck liver?"

With his face nearly the hue of the berries on her plate, he nodded. "Sorry. I thought it might be fun trying something you'd never order on your own because of the price. Do you want me to bring you something else?"

Feeling the weight of all eyes in the room, Jordan contemplated her dilemma. She could send the duck back, or she could take a few bites of it, then feign a poor appetite. A glance down at the entrée verified eating it probably was not an option, at least not without serious gagging—or worse. But what kind of message would leaving the duck untouched send about her qualifications? A food critic who preferred a Big Mac over a high-priced delicacy?

Jordan imagined the owner of the restaurant on the phone with her boss. She'd lose her byline faster than she'd gambled away her first paycheck playing the *Sex and the City* slot machine on a Louisiana casino boat.

She made a split-second decision. "No, thanks, J. T. This looks good." Surely, she wouldn't go to hell for lying about food.

Or would she?

His face lit up. "Can I get you anything else?"

"Maybe another glass of wine," she replied quickly, thinking it would take a lot more liquid encouragement for her to stomach the duck liver.

She stared at the plate long after he walked to the bar across the restaurant. The only thing standing between her being stuck writing personals for the rest of her life in this podunk town and seeing her name on her own column was this lousy gourmet dish.

And lousy it was! She picked up the knife and fork and cut off a small portion, suddenly feeling like a cannibal. With her mouth slightly opened, she raised the fork, her eyes tightly closed.

Just do it, Jordan.

Bringing the fork to her lips, she tasted the sugary black currant syrup.

Crap!

She placed the fork with the uneaten morsel back on her plate. She'd never eaten duck or liver, so what made her think she could suddenly pretend this was a chicken breast? She did a quick scan around the restaurant, and when she was sure no one was looking, she shoved the duck, berries and all, into Rosie's purse, absolutely positive her friend would kill her.

Convinced she'd just pulled off the greatest con in history, she tore off an end of the sourdough loaf in front of her and buttered it. Leaning back in the chair, she devoured it before reaching for a second piece.

By the time J. T. returned, she had polished off the entire loaf. "You liked it?"

"Loved it," she lied, hoping the devil wasn't getting her room ready down yonder.

"Are you sure? Because I could get you more bread." His eyes twinkled with glee as he pointed to the empty basket.

Jordan studied his face. "You saw, didn't you?"

"Yep." He grinned, leaning closer. "I probably wouldn't have eaten it, either." He handed her the dessert menu. "Nothing on this menu will end up in your purse, I promise."

It only took a few seconds to scan the sheet in front of her and choose the fantastic-sounding Chocolate Decadence Cake. With Huey, Dewey, or Louie stashed in her purse and nothing in her stomach except lettuce, bread, and wine, Jordan savored the rich chocolate treat topped with a liqueur glaze and fresh raspberries. The kind of sensation she experienced eating the sinful dessert usually only occurred after a few margaritas and a good massage.

She didn't realize she was moaning softly until she caught the eyes of "Brooder," as she now thought of him. His facial expression left no doubt he was enjoying watching her eat the dessert. Instead of being embarrassed at being caught, she smiled and licked the remaining evidence off her lips. His return grin told her the gesture wasn't lost on him. Then her saner self took over, reminding her that although flirting was fun, she had a column to write and no clue what to say.

After J. T. removed the dishes and scurried away for after-dinner coffee, she noticed "Ducky," as she'd dubbed the man who ordered foie gras every week, get up and walk over to the bar. If anyone could describe the entrée, it was this guy.

She dabbed her lips with the napkin, thankful she was wearing the all-day lipstick that didn't leave traces on the expensive-looking white linen, and then she stood up and headed across the room. Purposely passing Brooder's table to give the flirting another go, she was disappointed when he didn't look up.

Okay, that's another thing I suck at, she thought as she made her way to the bar, the irony of her day job taunting her along the way.

She stepped close to Ducky and tapped his shoulder. When he turned around, his face was scrunched with anger, and Jordan cringed.

Geez! How worked up could you get over a drink order?

"Excuse me," she stammered as his eyes bored into her. "I'm Jordan McAllister from the *Ranchero Globe*. I noticed you ordered the foie gras tonight. I was wondering if you could tell me how you liked it for my column this week."

Her column! It sounded so good rolling off her lips she forgot her initial fear of the guy.

"Who'd you say you were?" Ducky asked, visibly upset at being interrupted.

"Jordan McAllister. I also had the duck and I wanted to get a second opinion about it."

He whirled around, getting right in her face. "You had the foie gras?"

Again, she cringed as his six-foot frame loomed over her. "Yes, it was terrific. How was yours?"

He mumbled something she didn't catch then slammed his hand on the bar before turning back to her and attempting a smile. "As usual, the duck was cooked exactly how I like it, tender and succulent." He leaned in and whispered, "You ate the whole thing?"

Jordan flinched. Had he seen her shove it into her purse? "I may have left a little," she replied, not wanting to sound like a glutton in case he hadn't. "Can I quote you, Mr.—"

"I would prefer you didn't. Now, if you'll excuse me, I have unfinished business here."

Okay, then. She'd still use his comments with the information she'd get from Google to write a decent report even if he was a jerk.

Heading back to her table, her self-confidence returned. What could have been a disaster had turned out okay, and she didn't even have to taste the gross duck liver.

J. T. appeared with her coffee a few seconds after she sat back down. "Just for the record, your secret is safe with me." He bent down to whisper. "Do you want me to send you home with another piece of cake?"

A man after my own heart. "That would be terrific." She reached for her purse. "I have to dig my credit card out of all this goo." She giggled when he handed her a napkin.

Holding the purse under the table, she fished for the card, shuddering when her hand made contact with the squishy duck. When she finally found it, she wiped it off then handed it to J. T. "You deserve a big fat tip, but unfortunately my boss is already going to flip out over the cost of the meal. I'll never get away with more than fifteen percent. Sorry."

He met her gaze. "I'll settle for your phone number."

She tossed around his offer in her head. Maybe it was time she jumped back into the dating scene. He was adorable. "Throw in another loaf of that yummy bread with the cake, and you're on."

It was eleven fifteen by the time Jordan got home, too late to stop by and tell Rosie about her night. Her friend conked out right after the ten o'clock news every night and was up at the crack of dawn. That's when she was the most creative, she'd explained.

Jordan slipped off her heels and carried them to the bedroom, where she stripped, then hopped in the shower. With the warm water splashing over her, she thought back on her night, pleased with the way it had accidentally turned out. Not only had she completed her first restaurant critique, but she'd also met a cute guy in the process.

Before she'd left the restaurant, the owner had stopped by her table and introduced himself. Tall, olive-skinned, with salt-and-pepper hair falling just below his ears, Roger Mason was handsome in what looked like a tailor-made navy suit. She hadn't seen too many men in suits like that since she'd moved to the small town. Come to think of it, she hadn't seen too many men in suits, period.

She'd thanked Mr. Mason and assured him she'd found both the food and the hospitality to be excellent, wondering what he would think if he knew what really happened with the meal.

Oh no! She'd forgotten about the duck in her purse. In Rosie's purse! It must reek by now.

Quickly, she turned off the water and stepped from the shower. After toweling dry, she slipped into her Cowboys T-shirt and running shorts, her usual bedtime attire, and padded to the kitchen. Grabbing Rosie's purse, she put the stopper in the sink and dumped the entire contents, hoping the smell wouldn't gag her. Leaning over, she held her breath, just in case.

Disgusting! There was duck in the grooves of the lipstick tube, smeared all over Abe Lincoln on her five-dollar bill, and even oozing from the teeth of the zipper. No doubt her friendship with Rosie would be past tense.

First, she sprayed the money, then placed it on a kitchen towel to dry. Clean or not, it was tomorrow's lunch money. After rinsing off the rest of the items, she turned the purse inside out, taking more deep breaths to keep from upchucking. A tiny sparkle caught her eye as it clattered into the stainless-steel sink.

It was one of Rosie's rhinestones from her jewelry-making supplies. She rinsed it and threw it into Maggie's bowl, watching it skitter through the water and settle in the rocks at the bottom. Before she'd finished spraying the purse, five more fell out and were added to the fish's watery playground.

Tomorrow, she'd confess about the purse and make amends to Rosie. She'd probably have to break down and buy her a new one if the smell didn't go away by morning. That meant skipping lunch all week.

Jordan sighed, wondering how she'd gotten herself into such a financial mess. Her boss had been right. She could have gotten a better job if she'd stayed in Austin after she graduated, but she'd been in love and thought Brett was, too. All her friends warned her to let him go to Del Rio by himself for a year or two before following, but she hadn't listened. Now she was too embarrassed to go home with her tail between her legs and admit her stupidity.

Her eyes were drawn to Maggie swimming fast and furiously around the six rhinestones now glittering among the rocks at the bottom of the bowl. She sighed, thinking every female in the world loved bling. Apparently, girlie fish did, too.

CHAPTER 3

Jordan dropped her review on Dwayne Egan's desk and stepped back to await her fate. She'd spent the entire morning researching foie gras on the Internet and had come away outraged and ready to make a stand on the issue.

That was before Egan grabbed the report and lowered his eyes to read, and all her bravado dissipated. Shifting nervously and second-guessing herself, she tapped out the melody of a rock song along the side of her slacks with her fingers.

Too late to change her mind as Egan motioned for her to sit.

She eased into the chair behind her, eyes fixed on the editor while he finished the first page and flipped to the second. Her nerves were like aliens ready to burst through her skin.

"You actually ate this?" he asked, finally glancing at her over the top of his silver-rimmed reading glasses.

"Yes and no," she replied. "Mostly, no."

Egan had already turned back to the report, rereading the first page. "And this is how they get the duck liver?"

Her eyes lit up. Maybe he wouldn't scream at her after all. "Yes sir. They force-feed the animals to fatten them up." She paused, remembering how the pictures had sickened her, how seeing the tubes shoved down their throats had nearly made her gag. "The ducks are kept in tight cages so they can't exercise or even move around."

"Geez! And they're serving this right here in Ranchero?"

"Yes," she answered quickly. "At a price that would water your eyes." She stopped, not sure she wanted to remind him how much she'd charged on the company card.

Egan dropped the report on his desk and leaned back in the chair, hands behind his head, making his ears protrude even more. "This is going to ruffle a few feathers at Longhorn Prime Rib." He grinned, obviously pleased with his play on words.

Jordan shifted in the chair. "I was totally complimentary about the restaurant in general." She thought about the Chocolate Decadence Cake that had doubled as breakfast that morning. "The desserts were phenomenal and the service—fantastic."

Egan studied her face, his head tilted as if in deep thought. "I had you pegged for a simple meat-and-potatoes girl. For the life of me, I can't figure out why you'd order this when you're obviously so outraged at how they get it."

Here it is! This was where she'd have to admit she was

clueless when it came to fancy food. This was where he'd realize what a big mistake he'd made giving her the job. "The waiter recommended it. Said it was imported from Canada. Since I knew it was too expensive to ever try on my own, I went with it."

"I still find it hard to believe you'd even order the dish, knowing how you feel about it."

"I thought it was chicken," she blurted, looking away for a moment, imagining the pink slip falling from this week's pay envelope.

Egan threw back his head and laughed. And continued to laugh until Jordan finally gave in and smiled.

"So, let's see," he began when he was finally able to speak. "I have a culinary expert who has no idea what she orders at restaurants." He slapped the desk. "That's rich. Loretta would never see the humor in that, of course, nor would she be caught dead ordering anything but a thick, juicy steak." He leaned forward and lowered his voice. "And just between you and me, she wouldn't know foie gras from chicken piccata, either, even if it bit her on her overpaid butt."

"I'm sorry, sir. Maybe you should give this job to someone else."

His eyes bored into her. "Are you joking? This is going to grab the attention of every animal lover in Ranchero who probably has never even looked at Loretta's column before." He slid the papers across the desk. "Take this down to the copy room ASAP. I want it in tonight's edition."

Stunned, Jordan grabbed the report and headed for the door.

"Oh, and McAllister?"

She whirled around, expecting her little bubble of excitement to burst like a piñata at a birthday party with eight-year-old boys on a sugar high.

"From now on, you'll do two columns a week with recipes and food information. Fancy food like this. A couple of exposés would be great." He rubbed his hands together. "If my gut is right, with the exception of the restaurant owner, the good citizens of this fine town are going to love you."

"What about the personals?"

He smiled. "Look at this as a freelance opportunity," he said. "And the personals as your day job. Now go."

Jordan wondered how he could say that with a straight face, but she was too excited to care. She hurried out the door, surprised to see Jackie Frazier smiling. She'd obviously been eavesdropping. She imagined her, as Roseanne Roseannadanna, saying, *It's always something*, and she smiled back.

Who knew fatty duck liver could wipe the sarcasm off the secretary's face and maybe even jump-start her career?

"You actually scooped up the duck guts and shoved them into your purse?"

Jordan nodded, looking across the table at Victor Rodriguez before turning to Rosie, her eyes pleading with her not to be angry. "I'm sorry, Rosie. I'll buy you a new one. I tried to eat it, but I couldn't. I didn't know what else to do."

"Please, child, that purse is as old as Raymond here." She pointed to Ray Vargo, the retired cop and the oldest one in the group, who lived three doors down the hall. "No offense, Ray."

"None taken," he replied. "When you look as good as I do, age doesn't matter, right, honey?" He squeezed Lola's hand.

Lola Van Horn was the local psychic and tarot card reader who lived next door to Ray and shared more than a cup of sugar with him. "Ain't that the truth?" She lowered her eyes, the pink flush spreading across her cheeks.

"Criminy!" Victor said. "Can you two make it through dinner?"

Ray laughed and gave his lady an adoring smile. In her seventies with blackish red hair one shade shy of maroon, Lola smiled back, licking her plumped-up, flaming, red lips. A freebie from a plastic surgeon who couldn't make it through the week without one and sometimes two tarot readings.

"Come on, I'm starving. Jordan can tell us about last night while we eat," Michael Cafferty said.

Rosie stood, still grinning. "I would have loved to have been a fly on the wall to watch you cram that mess into the tiny purse in the middle of that fancy-schmantzy restaurant. Bet you got a lot of strange looks."

"Nobody saw me do it, except the waiter. That's why he sent me home with an extra piece of cake." Jordan giggled, suddenly remembering her goldfish and the rhinestones. "When I was cleaning your purse, several crystals dropped out. I put them in Maggie's bowl for safekeeping. You'd think I had given her chocolate the way she swims around them. I meant to bring them tonight but forgot. After we eat, I'll run over and get them."

"Sweetie, crystals went out of style two or three years ago. I'm into turquoise and big colorful stones now. Let

Maggie enjoy them." She headed for the kitchen with Lola following close behind.

Jordan leaned back in the chair and glanced around the table. Michael and Victor were bickering back and forth, totally oblivious to the others in the room. Michael was the local DJ at Ranchero's only radio station, and Victor had just opened an antiques shop downtown. They'd pooled their money and bought the apartment building a year ago, sinking every available penny they had into renovations. Empire Apartments had come a long way but still needed a lot of work. Apparently, something Michael said on the air about Victor's frivolous spending habits wasn't sitting well with his partner.

Ray, retired from the police force for several years, doubled as the maintenance man for the apartments and cooked a mean pumpkin pie. Despite his age, he looked like he could still take on a bad guy or two and come out on top. Religiously working out several times a week at the local gym with a couple of retired cops, he would roll up his sleeves when prompted and show off his "lethal guns." As a widower with no children of his own, he had taken Jordan under his wing that first day, and God help anyone who messed with her.

These people had adopted Jordan from the start and still doted on her. Friday nights were potluck get-togethers at Rosie's, followed by a serious card game of Screw Your Neighbor.

Since Rosie was the only one besides Ray who could actually cook, the others brought the fixings and pitched in on the meat. Jordan always stopped at the Food Warehouse on her way home from work and picked up a ninety-nine-cent loaf of hot Italian bread, which suited both her budget and her culinary skills.

"Come and get it," Rosie hollered.

Needing no coaxing, they surged to the kitchen, where Rosie and Lola had the dishes lined up, buffet-style, on the small countertop by the stove. Like Pavlov's dog's, Jordan's mouth began to water with one look at the steaming dish in the center. She'd skipped lunch to finish her copy, and other than the cake and a Ho Ho, hadn't eaten all day.

Okay, two Ho Hos.

Grabbing a plate, she scooped up a generous portion of the casserole and a small salad before heading back to the dining room table. When they were all seated, the chatter stopped as Rosie said grace before they pigged out.

"Mmmm, this is divine! What is it?" Victor asked. "I think I've died and gone to the great boutique in the sky."

Rosie smiled. "Potato Chip Chicken. It's one of my mother's favorites."

"And now, one of ours," Lola said, reaching for a second helping from the casserole dish Rosie had positioned in the middle of the table. Lola loved food and didn't mind anyone knowing it, covering her slightly overweight body in free-flowing caftans that swished when she walked.

Jordan finished hers in record time and also reached for a little more. "You outdid yourself, Rosie."

The older woman beamed. "Thanks, dear. Nothing I like better than sharing my food with good friends like y'all."

"I second that about the good food and good friends," Victor said, licking his fingers, narrowing his eyes before shooting Michael a look.

When the casserole was completely gone, Ray got up and went to the kitchen, returning with his signature Pumpkin Pie Crunch. "So, Jordan, you never finished telling us what your editor said about your review. Did he like it?"

Jordan shoved the last bite into her mouth and dabbed her lips with the paper napkin. "That's the best part, Ray. After I told him how they fatten the ducks, he went nuts."

"What do you mean nuts? Like 'You're ready for the big-time' nuts or 'Go back to writing personals only' nuts?" Michael asked, cocking one eyebrow.

Jordan laughed. "Don't get carried away. It was only one review, but I did get promoted in the process."

"Fantastic!" Victor reached over and high-fived Jordan. "No more bologna sandwiches for you."

She scrunched her face. "Not exactly."

Ray set a slice of the dessert in front of her. "Not exactly what, Jordan?"

She dodged the question. "Egan is convinced the people of Ranchero will be just as upset as I was about the inhumane treatment of the ducks. He thinks I'll touch a lot of readers with the story."

"Oh, you definitely will," Victor said. "I'm ready to go down to the restaurant right now and boycott."

"Don't be such a drama queen," Michael said tartly, still not ready to make nice with Victor. "So how much of a raise came with this promotion, Jordan?"

She lowered her eyes. This was going to sound way worse than it really was. "Egan can't afford to up my salary as long as he's still paying the woman who used to write the column."

"What?" Victor exclaimed. "Honey, I'm not trying to tell you how to run your life, but is this what you really want to do? Work harder for less pay?"

"Oh, leave her alone," Lola said, coming to her defense. "This job obviously means a lot to our girl if she's willing to do that. We need to be supportive." She paused. "Besides, Jordan loves bologna."

"Yeah, and I'll be writing two columns a week now instead of just one."

"Honey, that's terrific," Ray said. "Why the sour puss?"

Jordan thought about denying she was worried, then decided these people knew her better than any of her co-workers who were by her side forty hours a week. "I have to post recipes and write about fancy food."

"So?" Ray shrugged. "How difficult can that be?"

"Hello. Remember me—the queen of the 'I'll have fries with that' club?"

After a long pause, Michael finally verbalized what everyone else was thinking. "Yeah, that might be a problem."

"Does Egan know you're clueless in the kitchen?" Victor blurted, before slapping a hand over his mouth. "Sorry, Jordan. That didn't come out right."

"It came out perfect, Victor. I am clueless. I was so excited about seeing my name in the paper twice a week, I forgot what a fraud I really am."

"First off, you're not a fraud. You're one of the most genuine people I know. Besides, I think I have the perfect solution," Rosie said as all eyes turned her way.

"What do I love to do best besides making jewelry?" she asked. When nobody responded, she threw her arms in the air. "Cooking, you ninnies. I love to cook."

"How's that going to help Jordan?" Lola asked, her face showing her confusion.

Rosie leaned across the table toward Jordan. "What if you printed some of my recipes in your column?"

Jordan reached over and patted the older woman's hand. "You are such a sweetheart, Rosie, but as much as I love your food, I can't use it. Egan specifically mentioned fancy recipes."

"Okay, back to square one," Ray said. "Get your brains in gear, you guys. We've got to help our girl out."

"I got it!" Victor leaped from his chair with enough force to send it backward. Michael caught it just before it crashed to the carpet. "Budin de Papitas Fritas con Pollo." With all eyes looking at him as if he were on drugs, he added, "Potato Chip Chicken, an old-world recipe my grandmother brought over from Spain." He winked at Jordan. "Nobody has to know my grandmother came from a little village outside Mexico City. It's perfect."

Jordan barely had time to think about it before her friends erupted with glee.

"That's freakin' brilliant, Victor, putting a fancy name to Rosie's masterpiece," Ray said. "What do you think, kiddo?"

Jordan rubbed her forehead, her eyes moving around the table from one friend to another. They were all smiling as if the Cowboys had just won the Super Bowl. Maybe it could work.

"Budin de Papitas Fritas con Pollo. I like it!"

"Problem solved," Rosie said. "Now help me clear the table and let's get on with the card game. I have a fistful of pennies, and I'm feeling lucky. Let's see who's gonna get screwed tonight."

By the time the party broke up and Jordan returned to her apartment, she was twenty-two cents richer but exhausted. She decided she'd stay in bed until lunchtime tomorrow, errands or not. Another piece of Chocolate Decadence Cake to eat in bed in the morning would have made it perfect. She'd have to make do with a bagel.

On the way to the bedroom, she pulled the cell phone from her back pocket, surprised to see a voice message. No one ever called but her mother, and she'd already talked to her today. Listening to the playback, she was surprised to hear J. T.'s voice. She hadn't expected him to move so fast. Most guys went all macho and played the make-the-girl-wait game before the first few dates.

"Jordan, it's J. T. I'm at work now, but I have to talk to you. It's really important. I get off at ten, and unless you call back and tell me no, I'm heading your way." There was a pause. "Jordan, I really need to talk to you tonight."

How easy did he think she was? Did he seriously think an extra piece of cake entitled him to a late-night booty call? Did his mother never tell him girls liked dinner and a movie first?

She glanced at the clock over the couch. Ten fifteen. He should be there any minute. She'd let him know, in no uncertain terms, she was not the kind of girl he expected—or hoped for. Brad Pitt eyes or not, he'd have to at least feed her first.

She sprawled on the couch to wait and quickly fell asleep, dreaming of ducks with tubes down their throats.

The machine feeding them made a rip-roaring noise as it pumped down the corn.

"Police, open up."

What were the police doing in her dream? When the pounding grew louder, she sprang from the couch. This wasn't a dream. Someone was banging on her door.

She made her way over to peek through the peephole. It really was the police.

"You have ID?" she asked, suddenly apprehensive. A while back, she'd seen a TV show where a rapist had used phony police identification to gain access.

The officer pulled a badge and ID card from his chest pocket and held it up to the small opening. It looked genuine.

Slowly, she opened the door, keeping the chain intact. "What do you want?"

The cop was short and a little on the stocky side, not much older than her. "We need to talk to you."

A taller man about the same age emerged from the shadows, and Jordan jumped back in surprise, stifling a scream.

"Sorry, didn't mean to frighten you. We just need to ask a few questions."

She slid the chain latch and slowly opened the door. "What's this about? What time is it, anyway?"

"A little after one in the morning, ma'am," the short one said. "I'm Sergeant Calhoun and my partner here is Officer Rutherford. Do you know a gentleman named Jason Spencer?"

She thought for a moment. "No."

Both men eyed her suspiciously. "You're sure about that?"

"Positive. Why would you think I know him?"

"He had your name and phone number in his pocket," Rutherford said.

She thought harder. "I really have no idea who the man is, Officers. Maybe he was making a delivery or something."

Calhoun smirked. "At midnight?"

She was positive she didn't like what he was insinuating. "Look, I had a late night and I have a busy day tomorrow. So, if there are no further questions, I'd like to catch a few more hours sleep before my alarm goes off," she lied.

"Late night? Where were you?"

Jordan's annoyance level rose, but it didn't require an advanced degree to know getting cranky with the local cops wasn't smart. She'd probably get a speeding ticket every day from now until next Christmas. "I played cards with my neighbors until after ten."

"Then what?"

"Okay, I'm trying to be cooperative here, but you're going to have to tell me why you're asking all these questions—at two in the morning."

"Jason Spencer was found stabbed to death under the staircase outside your door on the first floor of this building tonight. It's a pretty big coincidence he had your name and phone number in his pocket, don't ya think?"

She gasped, ignoring the sarcasm. "Someone was murdered in this building?"

"Yes, ma'am, and he had your information on his person."

"Look, I'm telling you I have no idea who this man is."

Calhoun reached into his breast pocket and pulled out a

Polaroid. When he handed it to Jordan, she caught her breath. She'd never seen a dead man before, and if she were lucky, she'd never see another. The camera had caught rivulets of dark blood spreading over the concrete floor next to the young man. A closer look showed his eyes fixed in the same grotesque stare of death she'd often seen on cop shows.

"Ohmygod!" She dropped the picture and stepped back. It was J. T.

CHAPTER 4

Calhoun caught Jordan when she swayed and led her to the couch. "Sit," he commanded.

"That's J. T.," Jordan repeated, sure her face was as white as the other cop's notepad.

"So, you do know him?" Calhoun walked to the chair opposite Jordan and sat down. "And what was he to you? A colleague? A boyfriend?"

Jordan's eyes widened. "No," she protested. "I only met him yesterday." She paused. "Actually, two days ago," she added, glancing toward the ornate clock hanging above the opening dividing the tiny living room from the even smaller kitchen. Victor had given it to her only last week. Said it was collecting dust and taking up valuable space at the antiques store.

"Hopefully, this won't take much longer, ma'am," Calhoun said, noticing her gaze toward the clock.

"We'll finish up fast if you're honest and open and don't try to hide anything," Rutherford interjected. "Trust me, we'll find out if you're lying."

Calhoun shot him a warning look before turning back to Jordan. "Jason," he began, before correcting himself. "J. T. lived in McKinley and had a student ID card from Grayson County College in his wallet. You a student there?"

Jordan shook her head. "I'm a reporter for the *Globe*." She would never get tired of calling herself that.

Officer Rutherford took a step closer, writing madly on the notepad. Glancing up, he narrowed his eyes, turning his eyebrows into a V at the top of his nose. He reminded Jordan of a banana, tall and lanky, curving slightly at the top.

"You said you only met the deceased on Thursday. What exactly was your relationship to him?"

"There wasn't one." Jordan threw up her hands. "He waited on me at Longhorn Prime Rib. I didn't even know his name was Jason."

All three glanced toward the door when there was a sudden knock. Drawing his weapon, Calhoun motioned to Rutherford to move to the opposite side as he approached and slowly opened the door.

Rosie ran into the room, oblivious to the two automatic weapons pointed in her direction. "Oh, honey, isn't it just awful?" She eased down beside Jordan. "A mugging right here in our building."

Calhoun stepped closer. "What makes you think it was a mugging?"

"What else could it be?" Rosie answered, throwing the

officer a how-dumb-are-you look. "You can put away the canons now. This isn't an episode of *Law and Order*."

Rutherford glared, holstering his weapon. "Oh, I don't know, ma'am. Maybe Miss McAllister here had a quarrel with her lover. Maybe he broke it off, and she wasn't real happy about it."

Jordan straightened up. "I already told you I just met him." She slumped back into the sofa cushions as Rosie patted her hand.

"So, why would a man you only met a few days ago as a restaurant customer show up at your apartment at midnight with your name and phone number in his shirt pocket?" Calhoun curled his lips in a smile meant to put Rosie in her place for the sarcastic look she'd given him.

"Single women have been known to give their phone numbers to cute guys on occasion, Officer. Have you never asked a pretty girl for her number?" Rosie stared Calhoun down until he turned back to Jordan. The short, pudgy guy would never admit it if he hadn't.

"That's true. But most single women don't end up with a potential boyfriend under the steps of their apartment with a knife in his back."

At the mention of the gruesome murder, Jordan lowered her head, sniffing back the tears threatening to spill over. Who would do such a thing to a guy as sweet as J. T.? "He called earlier," she volunteered, sure they would find out anyway. "Said he had something important to talk about and would stop by after his shift at the restaurant."

"He never hinted at what was so important he had to see you at midnight?" Calhoun's smirk left no doubt he was not buying her explanation.

"I never spoke to him. I found his message when I returned to my apartment after playing cards."

"Did you erase that message?"

Shaking her head, Jordan pointed to her cell phone on the end table. Rutherford scooped it up, turned it on speaker and pressed Play. At the sound of J. T.'s voice, Jordan bit her lip to hold back the tears welling in her eyes, mad at herself for thinking the worst of him when he'd mentioned stopping by her apartment.

"What time was that message recorded, Paul?" Calhoun asked his partner as he glanced down at his watch.

"Nine fifty-five."

Calhoun turned back to Jordan. "And you never got suspicious when he didn't show up?"

"I fell asleep while I was waiting," she admitted, thinking she would kill for a Ho Ho right now. The chocolate treats were like Prozac to her.

Just then the door flew open and Ray rushed in with Lola on his heels, a leopard robe covering what Jordon knew was probably her birthday suit. It had slipped out one night during a card game that both Ray and Lola slept in the buff. All agreed that was way more information than they wanted.

"What the hell's going on here?" Ray turned to Calhoun, who now had his hand on his weapon. "Hey, Davey. How's your old man?"

Calhoun moved his hand away from his gun and stretched it toward Ray. "Good to see you, Mr. Varga. Dad's doing great, enjoying retirement. Spends most of his free time fishing out at Texoma."

"One of your colleagues knocked on my door looking

for you, Davey." Ray looked away and made eye contact with Jordan. "You okay, honey?"

She nodded as Ray moved closer. "You know anything about this?" he asked softly.

"No."

Ray turned his attention back to the officers, singling out Calhoun with his eyes. "So, Davey, you about ready to wrap this up? This young lady looks exhausted." His eyes darted around the tiny apartment while he spoke.

"I think so." Calhoun tried to get out of the chair and had to use both hands to lift his squatty body upright. "You *will* stay around and make yourself available should we have any further questions, right, Ms. McAllister?"

Before Jordan could answer, Ray darted to the kitchen, backing up against the counter near the sink and leaning back. "Of course, she will. Have your dad call me the next time he goes fishing. It'd be good to catch up."

"Will do, Mr. Varga," Calhoun said, motioning with a jerk of his head for Rutherford to head out.

The moment the door closed, Ray blew out a breath. "Calhoun's dad was the biggest screwup in the department, and it doesn't look like the apple fell far from the tree."

He moved away from the counter and pointed to the knife rack he and Lola had gotten as a gift for sitting through a time-share presentation somewhere in Arkansas. Since the two of them had more kitchen stuff than they needed, they'd given the set to Jordan as a housewarming present.

He cocked his eyebrow. "So, Jordan, where's the missing knife?"

Jordan jumped up from the couch. "What knife?"

"The one that should be right here." He pointed to the rack.

Jordan walked into the kitchen, confused. "I have no idea, Ray. Check the dishwasher."

Ray pulled the door down and a sour smell wafted up, wrinkling Jordan's nose. "Whoa! You need to run this now and again, princess. Even if you never use anything except glasses."

Ray pushed the door shut and straightened up. "Think, honey. If I spotted the missing knife two minutes after I walked in here, the cops won't be too far behind me." He paused. "Okay, maybe I'm giving them too much credit. I forgot it was Calhoun's son running the show."

"You all know I don't even cook." Jordan's eyes pleaded with them to believe her. "I only use the dumb thing to cut my bologna down the side before I fry it."

"Why in the world would you cut bologna, dear?" Lola inched up beside her.

For a split second, Jordan thought she was about to get a peek at things that would probably scar her for life as Lola's robe pushed open a little. Thankfully, the older woman grabbed the sash and retied it before actual skin showed.

"Because if you don't cut it, the bologna will curl up in the frying pan, right, sugar?" Michael said as he and Victor barged into the room.

"We just spent the last hour being grilled by a cop who looked young enough to be spending his nights preparing for the SATs instead of chasing killers," Michael continued.

"Yeah. All the old guys were forced to retire several years back when the city council discovered younger guys worked for less," Ray said. "Since the highlight most days for the youngsters rarely includes anything more dangerous than getting old lady Lozano's fat cat out of the tree in front of her house, their decision hasn't come back to bite them in the butt . . . yet." He paused. "Now they have to deal with crime scene tape. We'll see how these young bucks handle that," he added sarcastically.

"Isn't it dreadful about that young man? He isn't one of our tenants," Victor said. "Wonder what he was doing here so late."

"He's Jordan's waiter from the restaurant the other night," Rosie said. "The police act like she's a suspect."

"What? That's ludicrous."

Rosie reached up and pushed back a stray lock of red hair that had fallen over Jordan's eye. "I know. How silly is it to think our girl here could do anything that gruesome? Shoot, she couldn't even kill that mouse that made her crazy last month, putting a trail of crackers out her door for a whole week before the ugly thing finally got the message and moved on."

"I squashed that sucker," Ray interjected. "What?" he asked when Lola jabbed him in the side. "She should know why it never came back."

Jordan frowned. She'd worked hard getting rid of the mouse in a nonviolent way.

"Can it, you guys," Lola said, patting Jordan's hand. "Back to the knife. Think, sweetie."

"What knife?" Victor and Michael asked in unison.

Rosie pointed to the rack on the kitchen counter. "One is missing. Fortunately, Ray discovered it and threw his body across the counter before the police noticed."

"Oh my!" Victor shook his head. "Jordan, is there something you want to tell us?"

"Have you gone freakin' mad, Victor?" Ray snapped.

The younger man laughed. "Chill out, my friend. I meant about the knife's whereabouts."

"No, but I'm going to tear this place upside down to find it. I promise," Jordan chimed in.

"Good idea," Lola said. "But in the meantime, I'm going to call my friend Quincy and have him stop by and talk to you."

"Quincy Dozerly?" Michael whirled around to face Lola. "The guy who makes book out of the back room at that laundry by the mall?"

"It's Terlinga's Laundry, and Quincy is the lead counsel for them," Lola said with a huff. "He's a really nice man and a good lawyer."

"And why on earth would a laundry need a lawyer on its payroll, my dear?" Michael responded. "I heard the guy from Kansas City who lives on the third floor lost a bundle to him during March Madness last spring."

Ray ignored the comment and focused on his lady. "Why do you think Jordan needs a lawyer, darlin'?" he asked, standing behind her now and rubbing her shoulders.

"She probably doesn't, but it won't hurt to be prepared if it ends up she does." Lola shrugged out of Ray's caress and went to Jordan, grabbing both hands. "I read tarot cards for Quincy every so often. He's a little eccentric, but he's a good lawyer, and he'd do anything for me."

"Have they told Jordan she's a person of interest?" Michael asked.

"Cautioned her not to leave town." Ray rubbed his chin.

"My little apple dumpling may be right about this. I'm not crazy about Quincy Dozerly, either, but he was a pretty good defense lawyer in his day. Managed to get a lot of scumbags off on technicalities."

Rosie's face scrunched with concern. "Won't it look suspicious if Jordon hires a lawyer?"

"It might," Ray answered. "But I can tell you from my years in the Dallas Police Department, those cops will get our little girl in a room and pound away at her like you wouldn't believe. Before long, she'll be confessing to everything." He turned back to Lola. "Make the call, sweetie."

Lola smiled up at him in a way that left no doubt he would be rewarded later for siding with her. "I'll invite him to our card game this Friday," Lola said. "That way Jordan can check him out, and if it becomes necessary to seek counsel, at least she won't have to talk to a perfect stranger."

Jordan gulped. "Ray, do you really think I might need a lawyer?"

"You never know, honey," he responded, his voice nowhere near reassuring. "It's gonna hit the fan, though, when the police discover you're missing a knife from the set."

CHAPTER 5

The rest of the weekend passed without further drama. The police didn't question Jordan again, but they'd made it clear before they left that she was a person of interest. And they didn't even know about the missing knife. Early Saturday morning, Ray took the rack and remaining knives to a storage unit he kept a few miles down the road. Wondering how the cops would react if they tracked it there, Jordan envisioned her and her friends sitting in a jail cell down at City Hall.

On Monday, Jordan returned to work, still a little shaky over the whole experience but anxious to hear about the reaction to her scathing exposé of the foie gras at the Longhorn. The minute she walked though the door at the *Globe*, she knew something was up. Three people actually seemed pleased to see her as she crossed the newsroom to her desk.

"Egan wants to see you before you get settled," a middle-aged woman hollered from three cubicles over. "Great job on the article, Jaden."

Okay, so the woman didn't get her name right, but after the freeze-out she usually got from her co-workers, she didn't care what they called her.

"Thanks. Know what he wants?"

The plump woman shook her head.

Time to face the music.

When Jordan locked her purse in a desk drawer, she was tempted to pop a chocolate antianxiety treat but staunchly resisted. She tried to limit her indulgence to afternoons. She'd look like a blimp if she ate one every time she got jittery. Some days, she felt like an alcoholic, watching the clock until a minute after twelve.

Jackie Frazier wasn't at her desk when Jordan walked into the editor's waiting room, so she settled in a chair against the wall. Grabbing a magazine from the stack on the table, she thumbed through it mindlessly before giving up and drumming her fingertips on the cover photo of Matthew McConaughey, naked from the waist up on a Caribbean beach. She stopped tapping and slid her fingers over his abs, imagining how it would feel to actually caress him.

When the secretary's voice called her name, Jordan nearly jumped out of the chair. "What?"

"You can go in now. Mr. Egan's waiting."

She stood up, thinking if she didn't get a grip soon, there would be a straitjacket in her very near future. Big mistake not eating that Ho Ho to settle her nerves. Heading toward Egan's office, she noticed Jackie following close behind with a tray.

"Come in," Egan bellowed when she knocked timidly on the door.

When he saw her, he slapped his desktop, hard enough to rattle her bones. "My, my, my," he said, leaning back in his chair, hands behind his head. "Any idea how the good people of Ranchero reacted to your duck story?"

Here we go, Jordan thought. She glanced up to see the secretary still standing beside her.

"How do you take your coffee?"

Jordan turned, half expecting to see someone else in the room. When she didn't, her anxiety level skyrocketed. It was worse than she thought if Egan's secretary was serving her coffee.

A going-away present?

"One Sweet'N Low," she stammered, reaching for the cup along with the sweetener.

After Jackie left, Egan asked again. "Aren't you the least bit curious about this?" His eyes sparkled like he'd just drawn a straight with his River card up at the Indian casino across the Oklahoma border.

Jordan bit back her smile, remembering the joy she'd felt seeing her name in Saturday's edition. No matter what happened today, they couldn't take that away from her, even if it was only fleeting. "Did they hate it?"

"Hate it? Are you kidding me?" He turned his computer screen toward her. "See this?" He pointed to the inbox folder on his Outlook Express. "Over three hundred e-mails. You struck a nerve, girl, just like I knew you would."

Jordan swallowed. "Three hundred? And they all agree with me about how inhumane it is?"

Egan shook his head. "Not everyone. There are a few kooks out there who think you're one of those flaming liberals who throw red paint on mink coats. One guy even suggested your lack of a love life is what makes you so cranky."

"What does my love life have to do with anything?" she asked, stunned by the comment.

Egan sipped his coffee, prompting her to do the same. "No idea. The guy's probably one of those weirdos who gets his kicks at that ranch outside of town, killing feral hogs for sport. I can picture him now, dressed in camouflage that barely covers his beer belly, thinking he's saving the world with every wild pig he slaughters." He paused. "Anyway, what you are or aren't doing in the sack is your own business. But if he's right, then I say put on that chastity belt and keep writing these great exposés."

For the first time since walking into Egan's office, Jordan relaxed, letting the breath slowly escape her lips. The man must be reading her mail. She might as well be wearing a chastity belt the way her social life was going. "So, does this mean I'm still writing the column?"

"Oh, yeah. You've picked up a following now, for sure. The only ones upset with you are the printing crew. You messed up their bowling league Saturday night when they had to stay late and do a reprint. We couldn't keep up with the 7-Elevens clamoring for more."

"What about Longhorn Prime Rib?" Jordan hesitated, unsure if she should even ask. "Have you heard from them?"

Egan scratched his chin. "As a matter of fact, I have."

Jordan braced herself for what she knew was coming

next. Something to the effect of never letting that blankety-blank talentless fraud near the restaurant again.

"Roger Mason called bright and early this morning. Seems he had no idea how they fattened up the ducks." Egan huffed. "Like I believe that! Anyway, he wants another chance to prove his restaurant deserves four stars. He's invited you back tomorrow night, and this time it's on the house."

Jordan gasped. There was no way she wanted an encore at the restaurant, especially without J. T. to save her. At the thought of the waiter, she fought off a feeling of guilt. There was no J. T. at all. She still had a hard time believing he was dead.

"Did you know my waiter at the restaurant was found stabbed to death under the stairwell at my apartment building Friday night . . . well, actually, Saturday morning?"

Egan shot up in his chair. "You live at Empire Apartments? Why didn't you say so?"

She nodded. "He was on his way to talk to me."

"What?" Egan reached for the phone. "Jackie, get Harold Dobson on the line. Tell him he needs to talk with Jordan before today's edition goes to print." When Jordan looked confused, he added, "Harold's the lead reporter on that story. Anything you can tell him will help."

Jordan shrugged. "I really don't know anything. I'm not even sure why he was coming to see me."

"Doesn't matter. The fact he was coming to see you is a lead. Ranchero hasn't seen anything this big since old man Watkins shot those two drunken wannabe thieves trying to shove one of his cows up a ramp into the back of their pickup. Fortunately, it was only buckshot, but the two idiots ended up sitting on soft pillows for a while."

He moved his head in a slow circle as if to stretch out a kink, and Jordon could swear his left ear waved at her. She blinked to get the visual out of her mind.

"Back to Longhorn Prime Rib. Mason has it all set up for tomorrow night. You okay with that?"

She cleared her throat. "I think there's something you should know about me, Mr. Egan," she began. "I really don't eat red meat. That's why I tried the duck the other night. I'm probably the last person you should send out to review restaurants."

Egan shook his finger at her. "You don't give me nearly enough credit, McAllister. I knew that the minute you told me about your experience there. Why else would you pass up a forty-dollar filet at a restaurant famous for its beef?"

She stared, thinking now would be a good time to confess her addiction to fast food, too.

"I talked with Mason about this. He's agreed to have his chef prepare you a dish that used to be on the menu before it closed a few months back. Rattlesnake Pasta, it's called, and before you go getting all squeamish on me, it's not really rattlesnake. It's pasta with Cajun-grilled chicken, lots of vegetables, and Alfredo sauce. Said he was thinking about putting it back on the menu anyhow. So, you game?"

She closed her eyes, remembering the Chocolate Decadence Cake melting in her mouth. "And it's all gratis?"

"Absolutely."

Jordan tossed the idea around in her head for a few minutes. It might be the perfect opportunity to find out if anyone at the restaurant had any idea about why it was so important for J. T. to see her the night he was killed. Maybe he mentioned something to the other waiters or even to

Mr. Mason about her. Feeling a little bit responsible for his tragic death, even though she knew that was utterly ridiculous, she owed J. T. something.

"Make the call."

As Jordan stood in line at Mi Quesadilla, her mind flooded with the events of that morning. Not only did the article spark a lot of comments, she'd even received her first fan letter.

Dear Jordan, it read. *You're the bomb! Thanks for calling out the "quacks" in this town.*

Okay, so it wasn't thought-provoking and could have been written by a third-grader, but so what? It had been addressed to Jordan McAllister in care of the Kitchen Kupboard. That had a nice ring even though it was a far cry from her goal of being a sports diva.

"Ma'am, you okay?"

Jordan snapped back to reality as the skinny, pimply-faced kid stared at her like she was on drugs. When had she turned into a ma'am? She was only twenty-eight years old for heaven's sakes. You're not a ma'am until forty, at least.

"I'll have a Grande Chicken Quesadilla with extra cheese and guacamole, an order of queso and chips on the side, and a Diet Pepsi."

"I find it hard to believe you can eat like that and still maintain that girlish figure," a soft male voice said behind her.

Jordan turned, fully expecting to go off on someone about minding their own business, but she stopped short when she stared into eyes the color of a cloudless sky.

"Cat got your tongue?"

Jordan caught her breath as she recognized the man behind her as Brooder from Longhorn Prime Rib the other night. He seemed taller than she remembered, forcing her to look up. "What I find hard to believe is that you actually pick up girls with that line." She turned back to the skinny kid who was now tapping his long fingers on the counter.

Mentally, she scolded herself for not going to the restroom and fixing her hair before ordering. Mi Quesadilla was only two blocks from the newspaper, and she'd decided to walk. Although it was a gorgeous fall day with temperatures in the midseventies, the wind was blowing at a pretty good clip.

Instinctively, she reached up and combed her fingers through her hair, knowing full well it wouldn't tame the wild red mess she'd been "gifted" with at birth, as her mother always proclaimed.

Gifted, my butt!

She'd listened to "I'd rather be dead than red on the head" all her life, and one of these days when she had a little leftover money lying around, she'd see about getting highlights to tone it down.

"What good is inheriting fifty million bucks if you have a weak heart?"

Jordan had just taken a sip of her soda while waiting for change and spewed it across the counter.

"That's the line that usually works," Brooder added.

The skinny kid sent daggers toward her before grabbing a cloth and wiping off the counter. Embarrassed, Jordan threw her last dollar at him to compensate, picked up her lunch, and quickly walked to a table.

In a few minutes, Brooder straddled the chair across from her. "Since I made you laugh, the least you can do is let me join you for lunch."

Jordan held his stare. It was a free country, she told herself. He could sit wherever he wanted. It might even be fun talking to someone who didn't act like she had a contagious disease for a change, although it was amazing the way her co-workers' attitudes toward her had changed dramatically overnight. Four people had actually stopped by her desk to express their horror about the ducks and to congratulate her for being brave enough to write the article.

"Suit yourself," she said, finally. "I've got to be back to work shortly, anyway."

"Alex Montgomery," he said, extending his hand across the table. "Where do you work?"

She shook his hand, making a mental observation that he definitely didn't do manual labor for a living. His hand was as soft as hers. "Jordan McAllister. I'm a journalist at the *Globe*," she said, thinking journalist sounded way better than reporter. "And you?"

"I sit around all day drinking beer and watching reality TV," he quipped.

"What?"

"Did you forget about my fifty million already?" he added as she continued to look confused.

Jordan laughed. "So, you're not gonna tell me?"

His eyes lit up; he was obviously enjoying making her laugh. "I'm the assistant manager at the Ranchero Commerce Bank. I was transferred from the Houston branch a few weeks ago, and I'm just getting settled in." He paused and flashed that multimillion-dollar smile again. "Actually, I could use some help finding my way around this town."

He was so going to hell for lying. It had taken her all of a half day to navigate the town when she'd first arrived. But what would it hurt to play his game? He was definitely not hard on the eyes, and she'd always been a sucker for a guy who could make her laugh. She'd grown up with four older brothers, and though she'd never say it out loud, she missed their constant teasing.

"I think you're full of it, but my social calendar isn't exactly overflowing at the moment. I'll be glad to introduce you to Ranchero someday." She shoved the queso and chips toward him. "My eyes must have been bigger than my stomach," she said, wondering what in the heck that meant, anyway.

And since when didn't she finish off everything she ordered? Especially queso and chips, her favorite. Her dad always teased that she had the appetite of a lumberjack.

"Ah. My remark about keeping that pretty little figure worked. I get the leftovers," Alex said, reaching for a chip.

The heat crawled up her cheeks, making her wonder if it was a pre–hot flash.

"Gotcha," he said, obviously noticing the blush before both of them laughed out loud.

After what seemed like seconds but was actually a good ten minutes, Jordan glanced at her watch. "I've got to get back. Except for the part where you got to see Diet Pepsi shoot out of my nose, this was fun, Alex."

"Be forewarned. I never let a girl forget something like that," he countered. "Unless of course, they break down and agree to let me buy them dinner."

When he stood, Jordan couldn't resist a quick scan. She'd never walked into a bank anywhere and seen an employee built like this guy. The man could have stepped out of a *GQ* magazine with his charcoal suit and a baby blue shirt that matched his eyes. There was definitely a gym membership with his name on it somewhere in the Houston Metroplex.

Ordinarily, she expected several phone conversations before going out with a guy. That way she could pick up on whether he was a racist, all about himself, or simply a well-clothed jerk. Something about Alex blew all her caution out the window. "I'd like that."

She was rewarded with another dazzing display of perfect white teeth.

"What about tomorrow night? I could pick you up after work, and we could ride around while you show me the town before I buy you that dinner."

Her face fell. "Can't tomorrow. I'm on assignment."

"Can we at least have dinner?"

She shook her head. "Dinner is the assignment. I'm doing another report on the food at Longhorn Prime Rib."

As if a lightbulb had gone off in his head, Alex stared for a moment. "Jordan McAllister. I knew that sounded familiar. You wrote about the foie gras, didn't you?"

"That would be me," she admitted, wondering what side of the fence he was on about the issue.

"Good job, by the way. Do you eat there often?"

"Who can afford to?" She stopped herself before mentioning J. T. "I have to get back. You know how to find me." She scooted under his arm while he held the door open. Something told her not to, but she couldn't resist another quick glance before she headed for the office. He smiled back.

A block away, she paused. Was someone watching her? Turning to look in all directions and not seeing anything out of the ordinary, she passed it off as wishful thinking. The man was hot, and it wouldn't be all that bad if he was watching.

That Rattlesnake Pasta had darn well better be worth my giving up dinner with Mr. Hot Bod.

As she neared the office, she chanced one final glance over her shoulder, and was disappointed when she didn't see him. Just in case he was watching, she added a wiggle to her walk.

CHAPTER 6

Alex Montgomery settled back in his chair, hands behind his head, studying the image on his computer screen. He'd had a gut feeling the girl was somehow involved when he'd initially seen her at Longhorn Prime Rib. When his police scanner had first squawked the news of the murder at Empire Apartments, he'd hightailed it over and watched from down the street as the cops investigated. Having already checked out Jordan McAllister, he knew this was where she lived. Now all he needed to do was make the connection.

He'd driven by the apartment early the next day on a hunch and had seen Ray Varga hurrying from the building with something in his hands.

Since he'd checked out all Jordan's friends, he knew Varga

was a retired cop. Something about the way he'd acted made him forget about watching Jordan and he'd followed Varga instead. He'd been surprised at how easy it had been, thinking either the guy knew he was being followed—any ex-cop worth his salt could spot a tail—or the old man's skills had seriously deteriorated with age.

Maybe he'd been so intent on hiding whatever it was in his hands he hadn't paid attention. And what was important enough to take to a storage unit at ten in the morning?

Getting his hands on the video from the storage security cameras had been tricky, but he hoped it was worth the effort. He leaned in for a closer look, which clearly showed Ray looking over his shoulder before opening the unit. He'd been around long enough to recognize this as a red flag that something shady or illegal was about to happen.

A coincidence that Ray was hiding something only a few hours after a dead body had been found at his apartment building?

Alex thought not. Even if he believed in coincidences—which he didn't—this one was too obvious.

He thought back to earlier today when he'd followed Jordan to the Mexican restaurant. Sitting across the room from her at the steak house, he'd had no idea her eyes were that green or that her hair sparkled like diamonds dancing across a calm lake on a moonlit night.

Not until he'd stood behind her and she'd turned to make fun of his pickup line. He'd almost gotten tongue-tied himself watching her perfectly shaped lips forming the words meant to put him in his place.

Lavender. He'd never smell the flower again without

thinking of the way the fragrance had drifted from her hair and tickled his nose even before she spoke to him.

Under different circumstances, Jordan McAllister was the kind of girl he gravitated toward. Not too skinny, and from the way she'd chowed down on the Mexican food, not the least bit concerned about being paper thin. Guessing she was athletic, he remembered her calves, the muscles perfectly honed.

For a second, an image of her five-eightish frame in stilettos took over his brain until he quickly wiped that visual away. The last thing he needed was to get distracted from the real reason he was in Ranchero.

Yes, the girl was definitely a runner, he decided. The only thing fighting that wholesome, girl-next-door persona was the mass of wild red hair that fell into her face when she laughed. Another picture, this time a wild animal complete with reddish coat and glow-in-the-dark eyes, flashed in his mind, and he wondered which Jordan McAllister she really was.

Secretly, he hoped for the animal.

Exhaling noisily, he enlarged the picture on his computer screen, but that only distorted it. Grabbing a magnifying lens from the desk drawer and moving it over the screen, he concentrated on what Ray Varga had in his hands. Was that a block of something?

Son of a . . .

The retired cop was carrying a knife rack, and it looked like at least one knife was missing. The police had questioned everyone at Empire Apartments, but they'd concentrated mainly on the girl since the dead guy was found with her name in his shirt pocket. This photo of Varga didn't make sense unless he was the killer and was hiding evidence.

Alex moved the mouse and another image filled the screen. A picture of Jason Spencer sprawled on the tile-covered floor. Suddenly, it hit him like a two-ton brick building.

What if Ray Varga wasn't hiding evidence for himself? As if someone had just sucker punched him in the stomach, Alex doubled over. What if he was hiding it for the girl?

Now he had his connection.

Jordan pulled around back at Longhorn Prime Rib, unwilling once again to fork out five bucks for the valet. From the looks of the parking lot, the place was rocking. Fortunately, her six-year-old Camry, a graduation gift from her parents, could squeeze into spots bigger cars dared not go.

By the time she reached the front door, she'd made a decision to use the valet the next time she came, no matter what the cost. The smile she flashed at the doorman faded when she saw the standing-room-only crowd. No surprise, she thought, noticing there were almost as many people waiting as were seated in the bustling room.

"Jordan McAllister," she said, scanning the waiting area for an empty seat, anticipating at least an hour's wait.

The maître d' picked up a menu. "Your table's ready, Ms. McAllister."

Feeling the glare of every envious diner in the waiting area, Jordan was pleasantly surprised when he seated her at a table by the window with an awesome view of Lake

Texoma. Even though the lake was several miles away, she could see the last bit of afternoon offering a stunning display of shimmering light across the calm water as the sun disappeared over the horizon. Apparently, her status had risen in the world, or more likely, the owner was pulling out all stops to get a better review this time.

"Will you have a cocktail or a glass of wine before dinner?"

"I'll have a glass of that excellent Viognier you recommended the last time, please."

In record time a young man appeared with the wine. "I'm Kenneth. I'll be your waiter tonight." Jordan recognized him from her last visit. He'd been laughing with J. T. by the bar. Assuming they were friends, maybe he could answer some questions.

Shooting a quick look around the restaurant, she wondered who all these people were. They didn't look like Ranchero's down-to-earth residents, who were too thrifty to spend their hard-earned cash on an overpriced meal. One lady two tables over was even wearing a sweater with what looked like a mink collar. Unless it was fake, she was definitely not a local.

Jordan moved on with her scan, locking eyes with a man sitting alone several tables over.

Ducky! She recognized him as the guy who always ordered foie gras, the one who had been rude to the bartender. She wondered if he'd read her review in Saturday's paper. Probably not, or he wouldn't be smiling at her right now.

She nodded then quickly looked away. Something about him creeped her out.

"Mr. Mason said I'm to treat you like a VIP," Kenneth said. "Can I bring you an appetizer to start?"

"I've been called a lot of things, Kenneth, but VIP has never been one of them," Jordan said with a laugh. What was it about this place? This guy was almost as hot as J. T. Was Longhorn Prime Rib Ranchero's version of a Hooters for women?

She caught a whiff of his musky cologne. "Did Mr. Mason mention the chef is preparing a special chicken dish for me?"

"Rattlesnake Pasta," Kenneth replied. "I'm anxious to taste that myself."

"It's not really rattlesnake, right?" Jordan asked, needing reassurance her editor wasn't pulling a fast one on her.

A smile turned up the waiter's lips. "It could be," he said, a mischievous twinkle in his eye. "But that would add another twenty bucks to the price." When her face dropped, he added, "Don't worry. It's actually spicy Cajun chicken."

Jordan let out an audible sigh of relief. "Okay, then I'm ready when you are. And Kenneth, would you bring a Strawberry-Mandarin Salad, too?"

"Good choice."

He left her briefly, returning with the salad and a basket of bread minutes later. Jordan reached for a slice as soon as he was gone, remembering how good it was. All she'd had for lunch was an order of fries, purposely saving her appetite for the free dinner.

Her skin crawled as if all eyes were on her. There was nothing more conspicuous than a woman dining alone, she thought. She decided to concentrate on the people around her while slowly munching the slice of bread. Why did women hate eating alone at a restaurant when men obviously didn't have a problem with it? There were at least four tables with single men, none of whom looked the least bit uncomfortable. Her eyes connected again with Ducky's, and again she quickly looked away.

"Here it is," Kenneth said, setting the steaming dish in front of her. "I have to admit the chef fixed a small plate for me in the kitchen. I only had time to grab a quick bite, but enough to know it's delicious."

"I hope so, Kenneth. Thanks."

Picking up her fork, Jordan moved the food around on her plate. It looked yummy enough, and she was starving. She put a piece of the meat in her mouth, chewing cautiously. It definitely tasted like chicken, but she'd never tasted rattlesnake. It didn't help that weird delicacies were often described with the cliché "tastes just like chicken."

She never really got that. If it tasted like chicken, why not just eat chicken and let the frogs keep their legs?

She poked at the lightly coated vegetables before trying them. Still crisp, they complemented the bite-sized pieces of chicken that nearly melted in her mouth, and before long, two-thirds of the entrée was gone.

"What do you think?" Kenneth asked, setting another glass of wine on the table. "Compliments of Mr. Mason," he explained when Jordan gave him a questioning look.

She thought everything was compliments of Mr. Mason, but she was too embarrassed to ask. It could get ugly if Kenneth handed her a huge bill. Why hadn't she verified that before she inhaled the pasta dish?

"Thanks. Give the chef my compliments. This meal was definitely four stars."

"Did you leave room for dessert?"

At the thought of the Chocolate Decadence Cake, Jordan's mouth began to water. Embarrassing or not, she had to know if she'd have to give up eating until next week to pay for all this abundance. "Were you told I'm writing a review on this meal, Kenneth?" When he nodded, she continued, "And were you also told this meal is gratis?"

He laughed out loud. "No worries. You're a VIP, remember? Mr. Mason said I'm not even allowed to accept a tip from you."

She'd have liked to think she had enough integrity not to be swayed by the owner's obvious attempt to guarantee a good review, but she wouldn't bet her life on it. She could get used to fancy food that tasted like this and the special treatment that went with it in a hurry.

"In that case, I'll have a piece of the Chocolate Decadence Cake, please. And Kenneth . . ." She lowered her voice, deciding to skip the rest of the small talk and jump right in. "Did you know J. T. was coming to see me after work the night he was killed?"

After a quick glance over both shoulders, the waiter leaned closer and lowered his voice. "J. T. and I weren't good friends. I wasn't aware you had a relationship with him."

"I didn't really," Jordan said. "But he was killed in my apartment building. I'm trying to figure out what he wanted to talk to me about so late."

Kenneth shuffled his feet, stealing another glance toward

the kitchen. "I don't know, but he was upset before he left. He'd received several phone calls and even went out in the back alley once to talk when the boss shot him one of his looks."

"Who was he talking to?"

He shook his head. "No clue, but he talks a lot to a girl named Brittney Prescott. I thought he might be dating her, but around closing time on the night he was killed, some big dude came in screaming at him to stay away from her. I asked J. T. what it was about, and he said it was personal."

"And you have no idea what this big guy's name is?"

"No, but he was wearing a Grayson County College letterman jacket."

Grayson County College, a small private school, was located about ten miles away in Connor. Jordan remembered hearing Michael talk about how they'd nearly won the Division II championship the year before. They'd made it all the way to the finals only to lose a heartbreaker in overtime.

"You're not filling Ms. McAllister's head with petty gossip, are you, Kenneth?"

"No sir. She was just asking about J. T."

Roger Mason's eyes narrowed, despite his smile. "Shame what happened to him. But that's a subject better left to the police." He fired an unmistakable look Kenneth's way. A look that said he didn't pay the waiters to gossip with the customers. Kenneth got the message and bolted toward the kitchen.

Mason extended his hand. "I hope you found the food better than the last time, Ms. McAllister."

"Call me Jordan," she said, reaching for his hand. "And

yes, the Rattlesnake Pasta was heavenly. I'll make sure all of Ranchero knows it, too."

His eyes showed his pleasure, making Jordan remember why she'd thought he wasn't hard on the eyes the last time. Standing at about six one, Roger Mason was one of those classy-looking middle-aged men who always had a gorgeous woman on his arm. *He must live in tailor-made suits*, she thought, noticing the way the charcoal jacket emphasized his dark eyes.

For a small town, Ranchero had its share of cute guys and it seemed she'd seen them all today. First there was Alex, then Kenneth, and now the restaurant owner.

"I like the way that sounds," Mason replied. "Especially after your first story."

"I'm sorry about that," Jordan interrupted.

"Don't be. I have my sources checking out the processing plant in Canada, and if what you reported is true, we will no longer be serving foie gras."

Just then, Kenneth reappeared and set the dessert on the table.

"If you'll excuse me," Roger said, stepping back and bowing slightly. "Be sure and let Kenneth know if you want another piece of cake to go, like the last time."

Jordan's mouth dropped as he turned and walked away. She hoped J. T. hadn't gotten in trouble for that or, worse, had his pay docked. But that didn't matter much now.

She finished the dessert and reached for the take-out box Kenneth had placed on the table. "Are you sure I can't tip you?"

"No need to. It's not every day I get to wait on a lady as

pretty as you. Enjoy that cake," he said before disappearing.

On the way home, Jordan contemplated what Kenneth had said about J. T. and the big guy from Grayson County College. First thing tomorrow, she'd try to locate Brittany Prescott and see if she'd agree to talk to her. She wouldn't tell her J. T. had been coming to see her the night he was killed, just in case they were having a serious fling.

Empire Apartments was especially dark when she walked up the three flights to her apartment. She made a mental note to tell Michael and Victor the stairwell light was out again. Standing in front of her door, a weird sensation gripped her. Something wasn't right. For a second, she entertained the idea of knocking on Ray's door and having him stay with her until she was sure she was only being paranoid.

Remembering that he and Lola had gone to the late show to see the new Denzel Washington film, Jordan took a deep breath and chided herself for acting like a teenager after a spooky movie. Opening the door slowly and reaching for the light switch, her hand shot up to her mouth, her scream echoing through the hallway, resembling that of a wounded animal.

Her apartment was *totally* trashed.

The scream brought Victor and Michael running down the hallway.

"Holy . . ." Victor covered his mouth with his hand.

"Are you all right, Jordan?" Michael ran to her and enveloped her shaking body. "Victor, call 911," he said over his shoulder as he led her to the sofa.

"Dear God in heaven!" Rosie said, rushing into the room. "Jordan," she shouted. "Where's Jordan?"

"Right here," Michael said, motioning for the older woman to sit next to him.

Ignoring him, Rosie squeezed her body into the tiny space on the other side of Jordan, taking her from Michael. "Shh. Shh," she whispered, pushing the hair from Jordan's eyes and wiping the tears now sliding down her cheeks. "You're safe now, baby," she cooed.

"Ray isn't back from the movies yet?" Victor asked.

When Michael shook his head, Victor wandered over to the doorway leading into Jordan's bedroom. "Oh my, somebody was seriously looking for something."

Fifteen minutes later, Jordan was still staring in disbelief at the mess, unable to stop her lower lip from quivering. "Who would do this to me?"

"Don't touch anything," a voice from the opened front door shouted fifteen minutes later. Everyone keep your hands where we can see them."

The two familiar faces entered the apartment cautiously. "Looks like someone didn't like your story, Ms. McAllister," Paul Rutherford said, unable to disguise the smirk on his face.

"You think someone did this because of her duck story?" Rosie's voice elevated, and she glared at the police officer who had ticked her off the last time he'd been there. "Someone from the restaurant?"

By now, Jordan had stopped shivering, and she shook her head. "I was a guest of the owner at the restaurant tonight. I don't think this is about my story." She groaned when she glanced around her living room.

"What other reason would someone have?" Officer Calhoun said, sitting down in the chair opposite her despite the stuffing protruding through a long slit down the center.

"I don't have a clue," Jordan admitted. She had nothing of value unless you counted the autographed picture of Troy Aikman hanging over the couch. She whirled around, expecting to see an empty wall behind her.

Following her eyes to the picture still hanging there, Calhoun said, "Have you had a chance to see if anything's missing?"

Jordan shook her head. "That's the only thing I have worth stealing, and it's only of value to a Cowboys' fan."

Rutherford walked over to the picture. "I loved Aikman. Where'd you get this?"

"A present." It was one of the few things she'd kept from Brett after they broke up.

"No jewelry or expensive silverware?" Calhoun continued.

At the mention of silverware, Jordan's eyes moved to the kitchen counter before she remembered Ray had taken the knife rack away. The counter was empty except for Maggie, swimming mindlessly around the fishbowl like she hadn't noticed all the people invading her space.

"Did your story in the newspaper make anyone mad enough to do this?" Rutherford asked, finally tearing his gaze from the NFL Hall of Famer's picture.

"I . . . I don't think so," Jordan stammered. "The only one who might be upset over it is the owner of Longhorn Prime Rib." She paused, distracted when Calhoun flipped a page in his notebook.

"That would be Roger Mason?"

"Yes. But I had dinner at his restaurant again tonight, and he actually thanked me for bringing the story to his attention."

Officer Calhoun slammed the notebook shut just as Ray

and Lola barged into the room. With a nod to the retired cop and his lady, the policemen headed for the door. "The crime scene guys are on their way to check for prints, but I seriously doubt we'll get anything."

"What's going on, Davey?" Ray asked. "Who did—"

"We'll fill you in after the policemen leave, Ray," Rosie interrupted, clearly anxious for the officers to go.

Before closing the door behind them, Calhoun turned to the group all huddled around Jordan. "I don't know what's going on here yet, but I promise I'm gonna find out. I doubt this was a random B and E. In the meantime, I'd suggest you ask your landlord to install a security camera until we figure it out." He left, pulling the door shut behind him.

When they were sure the police car had pulled away, everyone began talking at once. Finally, Ray held up his hand. "Let Jordan tell me."

By the time she'd explained, Ray was shaking his head. "I'll have to bring the rack of knives back, honey. I'm already bordering on withholding evidence." When he saw her widened eyes, he added, "I said I would bring it back. It's up to the cops to find it."

"There's no way we can afford a security system," Michael said. "The renovations on the first floor drained our bank account, and we're still not finished. The crumbling tile floor upstairs needs replacing before the fire inspector codes us again."

Ray thought for a moment. "Let me work on it. I know a guy in Dallas who sells stuff like that. Maybe I can talk him into renting us one until you can get the money together to pay it off." He paused, glancing toward Jordan. "Or at least until they find out who's behind all this."

"Jordan, think. Why would anyone want to ransack your apartment?" Lola squished her expansive behind between Michael and Jordan.

Jordan shook her head. "I don't know. My social life isn't exactly hopping right now and usually, I'm home." She stopped abruptly as a small cry escaped her lips. "Oh Lord! What if I'd been here?"

Rosie tightened her grip. "You weren't, dear. Don't even think about that."

Easier said than done, Jordan thought, unable to get the horrible scenario out of her head. What if someone had been expecting her to be home? She shuddered, imagining what might have happened if she'd confronted a masked man bent on robbing her—or worse.

She wouldn't let herself believe someone was trying to harm her. Besides the people in the room, she barely knew anyone in Ranchero. The alternative was someone who'd known she'd be gone all night and had used the opportunity to break into her apartment.

But who?

Other than her friends, her editor, and the restaurant employees, she hadn't told anyone else she was going out. And who knew where she lived?

A wave of nausea rushed over her as she remembered that wasn't entirely true. She'd told one other person about her assignment at the restaurant tonight, and he'd had more than a little interest in her plans, especially when she mentioned Longhorn Prime Rib.

She felt like such a fool. She'd done everything but give Alex Montgomery a key to her apartment and carte blanche to all her things.

CHAPTER 7

As expected, the police didn't find any fingerprints at Jordan's apartment other than hers and her friends. Nor did they have any idea who was responsible since there were possible suspects but no apparent motive. Jordan and her friends had worked until dawn, getting her apartment back into shape after the Crime Scene Unit finished up.

Except for the slashed furniture, everything else was salvageable. Even the couch and chair had been repaired with thick duct tape, though they'd be a constant reminder. At least she'd get by until she could save enough money for new furnishings from the consignment shop downtown.

Ray had called Dwayne Egan and explained what had happened and why Jordan wouldn't be at work that day, despite her protests. She couldn't afford to lose her job, even though it wasn't exactly what she'd envisioned after graduating top of her class. She and Brett had been the primary sportswriters for all the University of Texas athletic events, and here she was stuck in Ranchero, writing a fancy food column.

It was dawn before the gang finally left, and Jordan somehow managed to catch a few hours' sleep, waking around noon starving. After a quick shower and a bologna sandwich, she opened her laptop, wondering why the thief or thieves had left it behind. It wasn't worth much, but it would have at least guaranteed a quick fix for a junkie.

She hoped that was all this was all about—a crazy kid on drugs looking for his next high. Anything else was too scary to imagine.

She Googled Brittney Prescott, the girl Kenneth said might be J. T.'s girlfriend. The first entry that she clicked on was a story about McKinley High School with a picture of a young girl who looked barely fifteen.

J. T. was robbing the cradle?

She moved closer to the screen, staring at the pretty brunette in the black and red McKinley High cheerleading outfit. According to the article, Brittney Prescott was a senior and not fifteen like Jordan first thought. Since she knew J. T. had been a junior at the college, which only made him three or four years older, it wasn't officially robbing the cradle.

She clicked on another link and gasped as J. T.'s smiling face filled the screen, standing next to another guy wearing a similar red and black football uniform. Moving closer to the monitor, she grinned. She'd thought he was handsome as a waiter, but he was smoking hot in this picture. Something about a man in a football uniform always jacked her heart up to mach speed!

She scolded herself for being crass. A crushing sadness overwhelmed her as she thought about his death. J. T. had been too young to die.

Flipping back to her homepage, she Googled the McKinley white pages, hoping to find only one or two Prescotts listed. No such luck: there were six. Glancing at her watch, she decided it might be easier to catch Brittney at school to see if she would answer questions.

Grabbing her keys and her notebook, she left the apartment, making sure the door was locked behind her. Momentarily, she contemplated rigging a device to let her know if someone entered while she was gone. That was before she realized she had no idea how to do that and would probably scare herself silly when she returned home.

McKinley was a small town about forty miles south of Ranchero, and the high school was a sixty-minute drive from Empire Apartments. She stopped at Sonic for a cherry limeade, adding an order of fries to munch on until the high school let out for the day.

By the time she pulled into a visitor's space in front of the entrance, the mass of teenagers held too long behind closed doors streamed from the building toward the students' parking lot. Jordan knew if she missed catching Brittney on campus, she'd have to call all the Prescotts in the phone book trying to find her.

She turned off the ignition and stepped out of the car, and a boy running past nearly knocked her to the ground. Regaining her balance, she made her way to the principal's office without further incident.

"Excuse me," she said to the office assistant. "Do you know where I might find Brittney Prescott at this time of day?"

"At cheerleading practice," the young woman answered without turning away from a filing cabinet. "In the gym."

When Jordan cleared her throat, the receptionist twisted around to face her, pointing to her right. "Who did you say you were?"

Jordan pulled out her *Globe* ID and showed it to the woman. "I'm here to talk to her about a story I'm doing."

"Go that way down the hall and take the stairs to the lower level."

Jordan thanked her and headed in that direction, dodging at least four more kids who were too busy talking to notice her in their path. She spotted Brittney the minute she walked into the gym. That old saying about standing out like a blonde in a roomful of brunettes popped into Jordan's head. Only this time, Brittney was the only brunette in the crowd. Either there were a lot of natural blondes in McKinley or Miss Clairol was making a fortune in this town.

Jordan ambled up to the group and tapped the young girl on the shoulder. "Excuse me." When Brittney turned to face her, she said, "I'm Jordan McAllister from the *Globe*. I'd like to talk to you about J. T. Spencer."

Hearing his name, the young girl teared up. "I've already told the police everything I know."

The sadness in her eyes showed the girl cared a great deal about J. T. "I'm not writing a story, Brittney. I met J. T. a few nights ago at the Longhorn. He was on his way to my apartment to tell me something when he was killed. I'm trying to find out what—and why me."

When Jordan saw the surprise in the girl's eyes, she added, "We were only friends, nothing more."

Brittney stared for a few minutes before whispering

something to the girl beside her. "Let's go over there." She motioned toward the bleachers. "But like I said, I don't think I'll be much help."

Jordan followed her across the gymnasium and sat beside her on the shiny wooden bleachers.

"What do you want to know?"

Might as well be blunt. "A waiter at the restaurant said J. T. spoke to you several times on the phone that night. Is that right?"

Brittney lowered her head. "Yes."

"That friend also remembered seeing J. T. really upset over whatever you talked about."

Brittney kept her head down. "Yes," she repeated, her voice barely a whisper now.

Deciding this was like pulling teeth, Jordan jumped right to the point. "Kenneth mentioned J. T. talked to you a lot on the phone. Apparently, the night he was killed, some big guy in a Grayson County College jacket came to Longhorn Prime Rib shouting for him to leave you alone." Jordan paused. "Were you seeing two guys at the same time, Brittney?"

The young girl finally looked up, tears rolling down her cheeks. "It wasn't like that. I loved J. T. but not the way you think." She took the tissue Jordan offered and blew her nose. "He was more like a brother. Ever since Eric went off to A&M, J. T. took care of me, like he'd promised."

"Eric?"

"My brother. He and J. T. were best friends."

Jordan remembered the picture of J. T. and the other football player from the Internet, guessing that other guy was Eric Prescott.

"So, you weren't involved romantically with him?" Jordan knew she was crossing a line but pushed forward anyhow. "You weren't having a lovers' quarrel?"

"No," Brittney said emphatically. "I'm with someone else."

"A big guy who lettered at Grayson County College?"

The brunette nodded. "Derrick Young. He's the quarterback."

It was obvious this young girl was in a lot of pain over J. T.'s death, and Jordan had the sudden urge to take her into her arms. She held back. "Why would Derrick go after J. T. and tell him to back off if he knew the two of you weren't in a romantic relationship?"

Brittney sniffed and looked away. When she turned back to Jordan, a fresh set of tears had formed and were threatening to spill. "Derrick and I had been fighting. When I told J. T., he said if I didn't break it off with him, he'd be forced to tell my parents."

"Tell your parents what?" Jordan interrupted.

Brittney blew out a long breath. "You have to know, Ms. McAllister, Derrick is a sweetheart. He treats me like gold most of the time."

"What was J. T. going to tell your parents?" Jordan pressed for an answer.

Without changing expressions, Brittney pushed up the sleeve on her sweater to expose several large bruises on her upper arm in various shades of purple and yellow.

"Good heavens! Did Derrick do that to you?"

"It was my fault." Again Brittney lowered her head. "He caught me talking to one of his football buddies, laughing over something I can't even remember now. Derrick grabbed me and pulled me away. Called me a whore and said I had humiliated him." She sniffed back more tears. "I wasn't flirting, really, but I can see why he might think that."

This time, Jordan couldn't stop herself and took Brittney into her arms. "Of course, you weren't," she said, massaging the young girl's back, knowing nothing she did would stop the agony she was going through.

"Because of me, J. T.'s dead," Brittney managed between sobs, burrowing her head further into Jordan's chest.

"That isn't true," Jordan assured her. "His death had nothing to do with you. You have to believe that."

Jordan continued holding her until the sobs dissolved into an occasional hiccup.

Although Brittney might be right, Jordan couldn't let her carry the guilt that she was somehow responsible for J. T.'s death.

"Right now, I don't know why J. T. was killed, but I do know you weren't even remotely responsible, Brittney. I'm going to find out who did this, and I promise, when I do, you'll be the first person I call."

As Jordan continued to hold the young girl, her mind was already racing ahead to tomorrow after work. She intended to take a short ride into Connor to see an angry young man in a letterman jacket who might very well be more than a bully who manhandled innocent girls.

The next few days seemed to fly by as Jordan prepared for the second edition of her new gig—posting fancy recipes. Budin de Papitas Fritas con Pollo, otherwise known as

Potato Chip Chicken, was an instant hit with the readers, and she'd had to endure Dwayne Egan and his "told you so" attitude all day. He'd pranced around the copy room like a rooster who had just satisfied the hussy of the hen-house, as if he'd been the one to come up with the recipe idea.

Okay, maybe he deserved a little of the credit, but the Potato Chip Chicken casserole was Rosie's baby with Grandmother Rodriguez's so-called old-world touch.

It hadn't taken long for the reaction to hit, turning the newsroom into a madhouse. All day Friday, calls and e-mails poured in by the dozens. Seems the good people of Ranchero had no idea fancy food could taste so good.

Jordan didn't have the heart to tell them otherwise.

By the time she wrapped things up at the office late Friday night, she was already in a panic about the next week's offering, hoping whatever Rosie was cooking for tonight's potluck would be worthy of a fancy fictitious name.

This was her week to bring the salad, and after a quick trip to the grocery store, she headed home. The pent-up stress of the entire week began fading with each mile that brought her closer to friends and a relaxing night of cards.

Her visit with Derrick Young had gotten postponed, mostly because of time constraints. But that wasn't the only reason. The more Jordan thought about the bruises on Brittney's arm, the more she wondered if she shouldn't take Ray with her when she talked to the quarterback.

The problem was, if it looked like a cop and talked like a cop, it probably was one, and Ray definitely fit the bill on both counts. Derrick would no doubt clam up the minute he figured it out.

She'd have to go alone, bat her eyelashes a few times, and pretend to be a newbie reporter looking for a story. Still, the thought of facing Derrick without Ray made her heart pump. She decided the meeting would have to take place with a lot of witnesses around. Out in the open with the entire team watching, the football field qualified as the perfect place.

Besides, she'd wanted to check out the Grayson County Cougars ever since Michael had gushed about how good they were. She missed football—missed sports in general—and vowed to get back into it one day.

Rosie met her at the door and pulled her in, squeezing her shoulders. "See, kiddo, even before you called today, I knew people would like your recipe."

Jordan handed her the bag of salad with the bottle of dressing. "You mean your recipe, Rosie. And they didn't just like it, they loved it. People who haven't spoken to me once in the three months I've been at the *Globe* are now treating me like I'm the new Paula Deen."

"I love that woman!" Michael exclaimed, coming through the door with a loaf of bread. He eyed Jordan suspiciously. "Exactly how would you know about Paula Deen?"

"Egan mentioned her this morning. Said I ought to watch her show. I quickly fired back that if he paid me a decent salary, I could afford cable."

"What'd he say to that?" Victor asked, coming up behind Michael, suddenly drawn to the conversation.

Jordan grinned. "He decided I was doing so well, there was no need to watch Paula."

"Ha!" Rosie said. "Sooner or later that cheapskate is gonna have to pay you what you're worth."

Jordan sighed. "A girl can only dream." She turned to Victor and winked, planting a kiss on his cheek. "Ranchero apparently loved your grandmother's recipe." Rising on her tippy toes, she did the same to Michael.

"So, what's for dinner, Rosie?" Michael asked, picking the slightly plump woman up and whirling her around. "It smells divine."

"It's a surprise. Now put me down so I can take it out of the oven before it burns."

"Knock, knock." Lola pushed through the door and walked in, followed by Ray and a man Jordan didn't recognize.

"I tried a new dessert," Ray said when everyone stared at his contribution to tonight's dinner. "After an incredible amount of begging, Myrtle down at the coffee shop gave me her recipe for Mandarin Orange Cake. I finally had to give up the Pumpkin Pie Crunch recipe that's been in my family for years." He placed the cake on the counter and held up his hands. "I thought we needed a change. Hope it was worth making my dear old aunt Sally roll over in her grave. She guarded that recipe like it was for Neiman Marcus's famous cookie."

"It looks yummy," Victor said, reaching in to snag a fingerful of the fluffy icing before Lola slapped his hand.

"All good things are worth waiting on, Victor." She turned to the man who came with her and Ray. "That reminds me. I'd like to introduce y'all to my friend, Quincy Dozerly."

"The lawyer?" Michael asked, extending his hand.

"In the flesh," the man responded. "My friends call me Dozer."

After shaking Victor and Michael's hands, he stopped in front of Rosie. "My my, Lola dear. You never told me our hostess looked like an angel."

The older woman blushed before shaking her head. "And she forgot to tell me what a silver-tongued devil you were."

Everyone laughed, effectively erasing the awkward moment before Quincy moved to Jordan. "And here we have a younger version of an angel." He lifted her hand to his lips.

"Cut the crap, Dozer," Lola reprimanded, playfully punching his arm before her expression turned serious. "This is Jordan, the girl I told you about."

"Missing-knife Jordan?" He focused his attention back on her. "Sounds like you and I need to have a private conversation later."

Jordan eyed the man still holding her hand. Not much taller than her, Dozerly looked nothing like a lawyer. Dressed in jeans and a Cowboys T-shirt, he could have been any other good old boy in Ranchero.

"Any conversation I have with you will include my friends," she insisted. She stopped before adding that she had no intentions of being alone with this man.

His dark eyes held hers before he tilted his head and winked. "Smart girl. I like you already."

Jordan wished she felt the same about him.

CHAPTER 8

"When's the last time you saw the knife?" Quincy asked as Ray dished up the Mandarin Orange Cake.

Nothing like jumping right to the point. "I don't know." She glanced away, hating having to admit an utter lack of culinary expertise. "It's not one I used very often."

"Ha! Like never!"

Jordan shot Victor a don't-make-me-hurt-you look. "It's no fun cooking for one," she added, sending another glare Victor's way.

The lawyer rubbed his chin. "And the police have no idea it's missing?"

Jordan shook her head, positive he shouldn't know about Ray hiding it.

Dozerly leaned back in the chair, a slow grin snaking

across his face. "Well, okay then. Until they find out and actually charge you with something, there's really nothing else we need to do." His expression turned somber. "Tell me again how you knew the man who was killed."

"He waited on me at Longhorn Prime Rib."

"So, why was J. T. coming to see you?"

Jordan shrugged. "He never made it here, so I don't know. Whatever his reason, it was important enough to stop by after his shift at the restaurant."

No way she'd mention her initial reaction to the phone message. Nobody needed to know she'd assumed the guy was looking to trade sex for chocolate cake. "You knew him?" she asked, suddenly realizing the lawyer had called him J. T. when all the newspapers listed him as Jason.

Dozerly looked uncomfortable before smiling. "Not really. I've eaten at the Longhorn several times since it reopened, and he waited on me."

"Oh," Jordan said, suddenly sad because she would never have the opportunity to get to know J. T. better.

"And you never spoke to him at all?"

"No. I was here playing cards when he left a voice mail." Jordan reached for the plate Ray handed her and took a bite of the cake. "Aunt Sally would be proud, Ray. This is absolutely scrumptious."

For the moment, she put the real reason the lawyer was here out of her mind and finished her dessert. As they loaded the dishwasher and readied the table for the card game, Jordan sneaked a peak at Dozerly, wondering how a sweet woman like Lola knew a guy like him.

Then she remembered the tarot card readings. The man

was attractive enough, if you liked the cocky, suave type. She didn't. Apparently she was only attracted to the blond, sexy ones who broke her heart—or died.

"Hey, Rosie, my sweet, can you turn on the TV? I'd like to catch the scores on ESPN." Dozerly rested his hand intimately on the older woman's. He'd been flirting overtly with her since he'd walked through the door, and the weird thing was, Rosie seemed to be enjoying it.

Rosie, who'd been married three times before—four, if you counted the last time, when her third husband whisked her off to Vegas for a quickie wedding five days after the divorce became final. The woman who'd sworn off men more times than Jordan could remember now pinked up like a teenager each time the lawyer said something outrageous to her.

Jordan didn't get it and was glad Dozerly was only there the one night and not as a regular. With a little luck, the police wouldn't discover the knife rack, and she'd never have to sit across the table from him again. She couldn't put her finger on why he made the hairs on her arms bristle, but he did. Something nagged at the back of her mind, something that wasn't quite right. She chalked it up to an unexplained intense dislike for Quincy Dozerly.

"Yes!" the lawyer exclaimed when the Dallas Stars' score flashed on the screen. "What? I like hockey," he explained when everyone turned to look.

Who was he kidding? Everyone knew he'd probably just made a fortune from some poor schlub who'd bet his baby's college fund on the game.

Picking up the empty dessert plates from the table and carrying them to the kitchen, Jordan decided her intense dislike of the man was justified. Dozerly followed and once again flirted openly with Rosie. This time, they touched hips by the sink while Rosie loaded the dishwasher and laughed like he was as funny as Conan O'Brien.

Eew! Jordan looked away, hoping to get *that* visual out of her head forever.

She thought about the recipe she'd use for the week's column. Côte de Porc á la Cocotte. Compliments of the mouthwatering pork chop casserole Rosie had served and the brilliant French name Lola had given it. Pleased with the choice, Jordan breathed a sigh of relief. The recipe would give her at least one more week of seeing her name on a byline.

When the dishes were finished, the group gathered around the table to begin their game. As if she wasn't already uncomfortable enough around the lawyer, Jordan now found herself sitting next to the man.

How fitting. She reached for her first hand of Screw Your Neighbor. She didn't know which one would screw the other ones first, but she had the sinking feeling Dozerly had a lot more practice.

"Shazam, McAllister," Dwayne Egan said, giving her a thumbs-up. "The women of Ranchero absolutely love your new recipe. My old lady is even going to give it a whack, and she never cooks." He attempted to wiggle his bushy eyebrows Groucho Marx–style, but only his right ear managed to move.

Jordan turned her head so he wouldn't see her smile, then decided to find out if he had bionic ears or not. "Can you hear me, Mr. Egan?" she whispered.

"Speak up, Jordan," he bellowed.

Apparently, they were just for show, she decided. "I said I'm glad."

"Yep. You'd think these people had never tasted pork chops before." He motioned for her to sit. "By the way, Loretta called this morning from rehab. She's a little concerned about her job. Apparently, she's heard the buzz."

This was the perfect opportunity to tell him she wasn't interested in writing Loretta Mosley's column on a permanent basis. With Egan in a good mood, she should pounce on the opportunity.

"I hope you told her she had no worries." Jordan shook her head to strengthen her statement. "I'm more interested in the sports column."

Egan eyeballed her for a second before leaning in. "You do know Jim Westerville has been the top guy in that department for years, right?"

"And wasn't Loretta at her job for years?" Jordan fired back. "Yet here I am writing the Kitchen Kupboard column for her."

"You've got a point," he said, frowning. "I'll keep that in mind in case Jim ever decides to crash one of those personal watercraft deals." His eyes were unable to conceal his obvious amusement.

Jordan knew he was not taking her seriously. "I'm only saying that's where my passion is, and I'd like to be considered if something ever opens up in that department. I'd even be wiling to work under Mr. Westerville for the same money you're paying me now." She paused. "And I'd still do the personals, too."

The editor's brow furrowed. "Lemme see. You've been

at the new gig for two weeks now and you're already coming to me with demands?"

"No sir," Jordan answered quickly, realizing she'd better backpedal fast or she might find herself without her own byline. Or worse. "I meant I would jump at the chance. I'm perfectly happy doing Loretta's job while she's out."

"She'd prefer you weren't so good at it."

"Yeah, well, I would have preferred to be in the press box watching Ranchero High slaughter their rivals last night instead of writing about the Frito pie at the concession stand. But you know what that old Stones' song says: 'You can't always get what you want.' "

He laughed. "Get out of here, McAllister. You're lucky I've taken a shine to you." He paused, the pensive look on his face turning to a slow grin. "That and the fact that we're selling twice as many newspapers as we were two weeks ago." He walked around his desk and shooed her out the door.

On the stroll back to her cubicle, her step had a little more bounce. There. It was out in the open that she wanted the sports column, and Egan hadn't erupted like Mount Vesuvius over it. Maybe her life was changing for the better.

Sitting down at her desk, she noticed a yellow phone message propped against her computer. Scanning the newsroom for a clue as to who had left it there, she was disappointed when no one bothered to look up or acknowledge her. She'd thought she'd broken through the wall of invisibility at the *Ranchero Globe* since her culinary column had become a hit, but apparently she hadn't.

Yet!

Picking up the slip of paper, she bit her lip to hold back the grin. It was a phone message someone had taken from Alex that simply said, *He wants you to call him*, along with his number. Thinking he probably wanted to press her for more information before breaking into her apartment again, the fool-me-twice mantra her daddy always preached meandered into her mind. She crumpled the note and slam-dunked it into the trash can.

The rest of the day was uneventful if you disregarded the personal ad she rewrote for a certain woman who posted weekly, with an ever-changing profile. Loves to cuddle in front of the TV, loves to two-step, loves children, single and loving it.

Please. How desperate could someone get?

At five fifteen, she finally shut down her computer, grabbed her purse, and headed for the door. Halfway there, she turned back and scrambled to her desk, hoping no one noticed her retrieving the phone message from the trash.

Apparently that's how desperate one could get.

Jordan sat in the bleachers, her eye on the quarterback as the Grayson County Cougars worked out without pads. She missed this, thinking back to when she and Brett used to go to every athletic event on the Texas campus. Remembering how writing the inside stories together had always ended with beer and Cheetos and a raucous roll in the hay to see who could turn the other the most orange. She'd lost every time on purpose.

She turned her attention back to the young men on the field. Grayson County College, she'd learned, had a large percentage of out-of-state students and was considered one of the finest liberal arts schools in the area, with an equally lauded business program. The football team consisted of players recruited from all over the United States. Despite the fact that entry into the program required above-average SAT scores, the team consistently turned out winning seasons with postseason playoff runs.

She'd done her homework last night and had discovered that Derrick Young had been lured away from some big-name Division I schools offering more lucrative scholarships. This after he'd led his hometown school to three state titles with the best quarterback rating in San Antonio's history.

So why had he rebuffed the scholarship offers and settled on this Division II school? An article from the *San Antonio Gazette* noted the kid had offers from the University of Texas, A&M, and even from the University of Oklahoma, Texas's biggest rival.

She pulled out her notebook and jotted a reminder to double-check that fact. What could have coerced a talent like that to kiss off the big-name schools and head to Connor, Texas?

"Can I help you?"

Jordan nearly dropped her notepad, gasping as the voice caught her deep in thought. She glanced up to find the coach beside her in the bleachers.

"I'm just watching the team work out," she stammered. "I'm a fan."

He eyed her suspiciously. "I'm glad to hear that, but it's hard on the concentration with a woman who looks like you in the bleachers. I need my boys focusing on me when they're out there."

She resisted the urge to roll her eyes. *Spare me!*

"First off, if all it takes for you to lose control over your practice is a girl in the stands, I'd seriously think about changing the workout routines. And second, last time I checked, this was a free country."

She sized him up, guessing he was in his early thirties and had played some form of athletics before joining the establishment. When he reached down and rubbed his left knee absently, she mentally high-fived herself for being right. An old knee injury had probably sidelined him and was responsible for the extra forty pounds he carried, along with the large beer belly protruding over the waistband of his black soccer-style shorts.

That and one too many cheese fries.

His furrowed brow eased back into place, and he pointed at her notebook. "You a reporter?"

"You could say that."

"And what would you say?" He sat down beside her, giving her an up-close look at his tanned left hand with the white circle around his fourth finger. Either this guy was divorced—like yesterday—or he'd taken the ring off for practice. Or he was a sleaze.

She'd reserve judgment on that for later.

"I'm a reporter," she said, scooting over to put a little distance between them. He smelled of sweat and the outdoors, an odor that was normally an aphrodisiac to her. She scolded herself for even going there, especially because her evaluation of this guy was leaning toward scumbag.

He extended his hand. "Larry Trevelli. I've been coaching the Cougars going on five years now."

She reached for his hand, noticing it was as smooth as hers. "Jordan McAllister. I work at the *Globe*."

His eyes brightened. "You doing a story on us?"

"Kind of," she lied. The less he knew, the better. "I'd like to interview your quarterback."

Trevelli put two fingers in his mouth and whistled. "Young, get over here," he hollered, before turning back to Jordan. "You should have said that in the first place. I would have given you locker room access."

Jordan gritted her teeth, remembering how she'd had to get used to male nudity a long time ago when she'd covered the Texas Longhorns. What was it about men that gave them the green light to flaunt their junk to anyone passing by? Women, even women athletes, might let you see them in a bra and panties but not their birthday suits.

"Yeah, Coach?"

Jordan stared up at Derrick Young. He didn't look like a girl beater, although she had no idea what one actually looked like. The quarterback stood about six two with six-pack abs not entirely hidden under his half shirt. His thick brown hair curled on the ends and framed his hazel eyes, highlighted with eye black to stop the glare. No wonder Brittney was so enamored of him.

"Derrick, this is Jordan McAllister from the *Globe*. She's doing a story on the team and wants to have a few words with you."

The young quarterback squirted water into his mouth from his squeeze bottle before meeting Jordan's eyes. "What do you want to know?"

Jordan squirmed, figuring he weighed somewhere around

220 pounds without one ounce of fat anywhere on his body, which only infuriated her more. Brittney didn't stand a chance against him. She swallowed hard, thinking even someone as well built as J. T. would've been way out of his league by at least 30 pounds. Wondering if he'd put up a fight, she lowered her eyes to check out Derrick's hands for scratches or anything that might indicate he'd been involved.

There were none.

She needed to loosen Derrick up before she went in for the kill, a tactic she'd learned from Brett before he'd dumped her. Come to think of it, he'd used that same technique on her—loosened her up, then darn near killed her.

"You're quite a talent," she stated, knowing men of any age couldn't resist a compliment. When his smile verified he was no different, she continued, "I read about you last night. Found out you broke all the records at your high school in San Antonio."

She saw the first sign of a smile in his eyes. "Not just my high school," he said, his face now lighting up with excitement. "I shattered most of the records in the city. Even broke Joey Malone's long-standing one for touchdown passes in a single season." He paused as if to watch her reaction. She obliged and returned the smile.

"I even broke my own record—twice," he added.

Yeah, like you tried to break Brittney's bones.

Jordan forced herself to maintain the fake smile. "Fantastic! I'm guessing you had a lot of scholarship offers." She leaned closer. "Why'd you pick Grayson County College with all the Division I schools knocking on your door?"

Derrick's mouth dropped, and he turned to his coach.

"Because we offered him the best chance for breaking into the NFL," Trevelli answered for him. "At any of those other schools, he would have been just another really good player. Here in Connor, he's on the front page of the two newspapers every week. Even makes the *Dallas Tribune* at least twice a month."

What kind of idiot did they think she was? Who in their right mind believed going to a lower-division college would leapfrog you into the National Football League? She was tempted to tell them what a load of crap that was but guessed they already knew it.

"Interesting," she said instead, before focusing back on Derrick. "So, how did you feel last year when you nearly won the division championship?"

Again, Derrick shot a glance toward his coach before making eye contact with Jordan. "I'd give anything to get that last pass back."

Jordan remembered Michael's story of how the Cougars, down by four points with under a minute left in the game, were driving toward the end zone. With second and one from the twenty-five-yard line, normally a running play, Derrick had thrown a ten-yard pass. Unfortunately, he threw it in the middle of three players, none of whom was wearing a Cougar green and gold jersey. The cornerback for the opposing team had easily picked it off and ran it back for a touchdown, sealing the victory.

According to Michael, that play was still being debated by the old-timers at Myrtle's Diner at least once or twice a week. Texas was a football state, and the good old boys ranked the sport right up there with their beer, country music, and pride in their state, where the motto "Don't mess with Texas" needed no explanation.

"Yeah. Sometimes we all make bad decisions we can't undo," Jordan said, zeroing in on the quarterback for the first blow. "Like using Brittney Prescott's upper arm to show how strong you are?"

Both Trevelli and Derrick gasped, before the young quarterback's face colored like an overripe strawberry and his hazel eyes turned darker. Jordan leaned as far as she could until her lower back pressed against the next seat. She was convinced that if Trevelli hadn't been next to her, she would have seen Derrick's rage up close and personal, just as Brittney had.

"This interview's over," Trevelli said, jumping up and shoving Derrick toward the field with the rest of his teammates. "I thought you were a reputable reporter, Miss Jordan, not some paparazzi looking for dirt."

"I never meant to hurt her," Derrick growled through clenched teeth. Muscles twitched in his bulging neck, and he jerked away from his coach's grip.

"But you did hurt her, Derrick. I saw the bruises." Jordan fired back. "You should pick on guys your own size, not pretty young girls who can't fight back."

Larry Trevelli attempted once more to push Derrick toward the field, but even he didn't stand a chance against Derrick's strength.

"What goes on between Brittney and me is none of your business," Derrick growled, thrusting his face toward her and smashing a fist against the bleachers.

A cold knot formed in her stomach, imagining what he

was capable of. "Did you kill J. T. Spencer?" she asked, keeping her eyes directly on him.

She'd learned early on to watch for the initial reaction to a direct question. Everybody lied, some better than others, but that first reaction after the question was as telling as a lie detector. Most pathological liars recovered quickly, so it was important not to miss the way the eyes shifted or how the overall body language changed.

Derrick Young was no exception. He glared, breathing hard through a flared nose, his lips pressed together, his fists balled at his side. Jordan had no doubt the likelihood of her leaving with a shiner would have been quadrupled if the entire team hadn't been there as witnesses.

Before Derrick could answer, Coach Trevelli gave him a final push toward the field, then motioned with his hand to the team, who were all staring. "Y'all get back to practice. Now!"

When Derrick was out of hearing distance, Trevelli turned to Jordan, his eyes flashing the anger she knew she'd caused. "I'd appreciate it if you'd get off my practice field, Ms. McAllister. I have a game to get ready for Saturday night, and none of us have time for your insane accusations."

He started toward the team, then stopped and whirled around to face her. "Oh, and you can expect a call to Dwayne Egan," he said, a smirk replacing the scowl. "I give the *Globe* unlimited access when it comes to my team, and I'm guessing your editor isn't going to be too happy to hear about all this."

Great!

She had to pick on a guy who was tight with her boss. "Suit yourself, Mr. Trevelli." Jordan stood and walked down the steps to the landing. "And, Coach, with a running back as fast as number twenty-two out there—" She pointed to the team who had resumed practice. "What's he run? A four-three-forty?"

When Trevelli's mouth dropped, she smiled. "I would have put him in the Wildcat Formation and let him scramble for those twenty-some yards you needed to win that trophy last year."

With that, she turned and walked away, still a little shaken by how quickly she'd seen Derrick Young transform into someone she seriously suspected could kill in the heat of the moment.

CHAPTER 9

Friday night rolled around quickly as Jordan shut down her computer and headed home, excited about a night out with her friends at their favorite hangout. After a week that could only be described as hairy, she needed to be around friendly faces where her main objective was to eat, drink, and . . . drink some more.

Her interview with Derrick Young still unnerved her every time she thought about it, which was often. Up that close, the anger radiating from him had been almost palpable, and she had no doubt he might have erupted into uncontrolled rage if the coach hadn't been there.

A wave of apprehension coursed through her. Derrick was definitely a possibility on her short list of who killed J. T. Much bigger than J. T., Derrick might as well have worn a sign proclaiming his physical superiority. Brittney wouldn't have stood a chance against his brute strength. Mix that with his short fuse, and she was certain the boy could be lethal. Mentally, she put a star by his name on her list of suspects.

Jordan debated whether to tell Ray about the interview, not looking forward to the tongue-lashing she knew she'd get for confronting Derrick on her own. Even if she reassured him that Coach Trevelli had been right there, she was positive her ex-cop neighbor would not be happy when he heard. Eventually she'd have to confess, but the longer she put it off, the better.

And thinking back on the interview, how much help would Coach Trevelli have been if Derrick had decided to give her some of what Brittney probably got on a regular basis? Larry Trevelli was a big guy, but even he was a good four or five inches shorter than his quarterback. He would have gone down faster than the *Titanic* if the younger man had suddenly gone Rambo on her.

As expected, Larry Trevelli called Dwayne Egan to complain, which meant Jordan had to sit through a grueling lecture on how long it had taken the *Globe* to get unlimited access to the Cougars. Even Jim Westerville, the sports editor, received a call and joined in the what-the-hell-did-you-think-you-were-doing reprimands.

In the end, Jordan agreed to apologize to both Trevelli and Derrick Young, although she was still convinced the quarterback was somehow involved in J. T.'s murder.

"And I have your absolute word there will be no more shenanigans involving the football team, McAllister?" Egan had demanded.

"I won't make any more accusations," she'd promised,

pleased she had managed to appease her editor without actually agreeing not to question the two men once more. She had no intentions of apologizing to them, at least not sincerely, but promising to do so would give her another excuse to revisit the practice field.

She needed one more shot at the quarterback.

Alex spotted Jordan McAllister leaving the building and walking to her car, noticing she didn't interact with any of the other employees filing out. He hadn't pegged her as antisocial and wondered if her co-workers still labeled her an outsider. He'd been lucky when he arrived at the bank several weeks ago and everyone had been helpful and friendly.

Of course, most of the people there were women and he'd always been able to warm up the female gender, as far back as junior high. The loan officer had even invited him to dinner, but he'd come to Ranchero for one reason, and it wasn't female companionship.

Watching Jordan McAllister swing her legs into her car made him reconsider that decision, maybe throw in a little pleasure with work. But if he'd learned anything from his last job, it was that the two didn't mix. Moving from city to city, wherever he was sent, left no time for building friendships, let alone a relationship. His past experiences proved the consequences were too steep.

He pulled into traffic, far enough behind her to avoid being noticed. He still hadn't figured this woman out. If she was involved, she was being very careful about flaunting it. Empire Apartments wasn't the worst housing complex in

Ranchero, but it was among the cheapest. And cheap didn't come with great views or jetted bathtubs. If she had extra cash coming in, she was hiding it well.

Sliding into a parking slot several spaces down from where Jordan parked, he pretended to read the newspaper in case she glanced his way. Even if she did, he was far enough away she shouldn't recognize him. He opened the glove compartment and pulled out his binoculars, zooming in on the sign in the window of the building she entered.

LOLA'S SPIRITUAL READINGS.

What in heaven's name was she doing visiting a psychic? He definitely didn't picture her as someone who believed in that garbage.

But then, he'd never suspected she might be a killer, either.

Settling back in the seat to get as comfortable as his six-two frame allowed, he wished Ranchero wasn't such a small town. He'd kill for a Starbucks right now.

He jerked up, fully alert when Jordan exited the psychic's shop and got back into her car. Watching her pull away, he reached down to turn on the ignition and froze in mid-act when a sudden idea hit him.

Since he'd been following Jordan the last three days and she'd always gone straight home after work, he decided to play a hunch and check out the psychic. After making the possible connection between Jordan and the dead waiter, as weak as it was with Ray hiding the knife rack, it was time to dig deeper into her life for more clues.

Or perhaps one solid motive.

He waited until her Camry was out of sight before exiting his car and walking down the street to the cornball psychic place.

As he grabbed the doorknob, a sudden chill coursed through his body, and his fingers automatically touched the Glock tucked into the shoulder holster. Unsure what he would find inside, he needed to be prepared for anything. His boss always said, "A surprised man is usually a dead one."

He pushed through the door. The jingling bells announcing his arrival reminded him of Joan Crawford's charm bracelet in the horror movie *Strait-Jacket,* and he hesitated. In the movie, every time you heard the bracelet jangling, you knew someone was about to lose a head. It had been his mother's favorite spooky story, and he'd watched it once with her, wanting to prove he wasn't a sissy. He'd had nightmares for weeks after that, and sissy or not, he'd climbed into bed with his older sister many nights after she'd fallen asleep.

Pushing the unexpected memory out of his mind, he glanced around the small, dimly lit room. He breathed in the unmistakable scent of flowers, noticing the dozen or so candles of varying sizes and colors, all lit in strategic places around the room.

A sudden rattle caught his attention, restarting the Joan Crawford movie in his brain again. His eyes darted to an entryway where a rotund elderly woman wearing a long flowing caftan was coming through the doorway, which was covered by a hippielike cascade of vertical beads.

Again, his hand slid under his jacket to the holster.

"May I help you?"

She didn't look like a killer, but then again neither did Jordan.

"Alex Montgomery," he said, crossing the room with his hand extended. Up close, he noticed her perfectly shaped, ruby red lips that seemed a little large for her face.

The woman accepted his hand with a firm grip of her own. Alex made a mental note not to make the mistake of treating her like a helpless old lady.

"Are you interested in a reading, Mr. Montgomery?"

"What? No . . ." he started, before catching himself. It would serve no purpose if he made this woman suspicious of why he was there and have her call the cops. "It's probably too late today, right?"

She glanced at the clock above the door. "I have time for one more." She pointed to a small table in the middle of the room. "Have a seat."

"I can come back tomorrow," Alex protested, suddenly wishing he had stayed in the car.

The woman smiled. "No need to. If you walked into my place, there must be a reason. Something is troubling you. Let's find out what it is."

She walked around the table and sat in the chair opposite the one she indicated for him.

Alex hesitated briefly before easing into the seat. The table was covered with a dark purple scarf embellished with a variety of gold squiggles bordering the material and forming an intricate design in the middle. A shiver slid up his spine as the woman reached behind her and picked up a white candle, which she placed in the center of the linen, facing him.

He debated whether to get up and run like hell or stay and tough it out.

Something about this stuff had always freaked him out. His sister, Janie, used to make him play the Ouija board with her. He still remembered some of the responses, particularly the one that said he would die before he ever fathered a child.

He knew it was bunk, that it was just Janie guiding the Ouija piece across the letters on the board to scare him, but still . . .

"Have you ever had a reading before, Mr. Montgomery?" the woman asked, striking a match and lighting the white candle.

"Call me Alex."

"I'm Lola." She reached for his hand before closing her eyes. "We need to get in touch with your spiritual guides." She spoke almost in a whisper.

"I light the white candle to entice the spirits around me," she began. "Mr. Montgom—Alex—close your eyes and feel the energy in the room."

He pressed his eyes shut, wondering how she knew they'd been open in the first place.

"Come, Divine Spirits, and form a protective circle around this man who is looking for answers in his life. Stave off evil spirits, keep them out of this space and burn off any obstacle that might interfere with his journey."

Alex could have sworn the room grew suddenly colder. It took him a moment to realize Lola had stopped speaking and was humming some sort of chant. Visions of the Ouija board, coupled with the swirling vanilla-smelling smoke from the candle supposedly circling him with good spirits dueling with evil ones, fueled his desire to bolt without looking back.

Sheesh! Who believes this stuff? He tensed when another chill skittered down his spine.

"You can open your eyes now, Alex."

When he looked up, the woman was smiling. "Let yourself believe," she said, making him think she'd read his mind.

She reached under the table again and produced a potted lily, a windmill, and a purple candle that matched the silk scarf spread on the table. She placed each one in a corner of the cloth and pushed the white candle to the fourth corner.

"These signify earth, wind, and fire," she explained, reaching under the table for a deck of cards which reminded him of the large Old Maid ones he used with his nieces.

After placing them facedown in the center, she fanned the deck before glancing toward Alex. "Take your time and pick the one that seems to be drawing you to it."

This is getting a little ridiculous.

But unless he played along, he probably wouldn't find out why Jordan had stopped by. Slowly, he reached in, prepared to grab the card at the far end, when an impulse sent him to the middle of the pile for a card concealed at the bottom. After retrieving it, he handed it to the psychic.

"This is your Relationship card," she explained, placing it directly in the center of the cloth, facing him.

After several more picks, there was a total of six cards which Lola placed in a circle around the first one. Then she moved the white candle back to the center, vacated when she picked up the card there.

"We'll start with the Relationship Guidance." She turned the card over to reveal a picture of a man staring sadly at three cups of spilled wine without seeing the other two still upright. "You've chosen the Five of Cups."

Alex smirked, not sure he wanted to know what that

meant. He glanced nervously at his watch, wondering how he could extricate himself from this séance before she went any further. He'd had a long day and hadn't stopped for lunch. Any hope of getting her to discuss Jordan was dwindling by the second, and a nice quiet night at home with a tray of pizza and cable TV sounded inviting.

Not to mention, this whole spirit thing was freaking him out.

"You've waited a long time for that special person to come into your life. You've had several 'almost' opportunities that haven't panned out, and you've given up hope of ever finding that one woman to complete you." She paused and met his gaze. "You obsess over what is lost rather than looking forward to what might be right in front of you."

Alex thought of Jordan. How ironic that he'd finally met a girl who looked like she did and made him laugh, about the same time an old woman told him he would meet a special person in his life. More ironic was it looked like his dream girl probably knew her way around a knife.

"Open your eyes and quit looking for what is wrong in the world. Get past your own blindness and see the good in your life."

He opened his mouth to respond but couldn't find the words. The woman had to be reading his mail.

"Your next card is the Moon." Lola closed her eyes again. "There are important facts hidden from your view right now. When you discover them, you'll have choices to make about your career and other personal matters in your life. By the next full moon, it will all be clear to you."

"Hey, Lola, it's after five. Why are you still here? Did you forget about tonight?"

Both Lola and Alex looked up as a man rattled the beaded door.

"Oh, sorry," the guy said. "I didn't know you had a client." A sheepish grin covered his face. "There are no cars parked out front."

Alex sized up the newcomer, trying to decide if he'd need his weapon. The guy was Hispanic, about five eight with dark hair, wearing a red vest over a red and gray plaid shirt that matched his gray Dockers. Either he had just left an Ivy League frat party or he'd walked away from the nineteenth hole at a country club somewhere.

Alex relaxed. No way this guy was a threat. "It's getting late, Lola." He reached for his wallet. "How much do I owe you for the session?"

"I never charge unless I do a full reading. Do you want to continue?"

Not in this lifetime!

She was hitting too close to home, and although he didn't know how she did it, he still wasn't buying into this mumbo-jumbo. "He said you have plans tonight, and I don't want to hold you up. Besides, I need to head home, anyway."

"I'm Victor Rodriguez," the Ivy Leaguer said. "I own the antiques store next door, and I'm a friend of Lola's."

Alex squirmed, sure the guy was checking him out. "Alex Montgomery," he responded, accepting Victor's handshake. "I'm new to Ranchero and saw Lola's place. Decided to give it a whirl."

"Lola's a master at giving you a new perspective on life." Victor paused. "You said you were new in town?"

Alex nodded, again feeing uncomfortable under Victor's gaze.

"Married?"

"No, why?"

"Attached?"

When Alex shook his head, Victor smiled. "Can you carry a tune?"

"I've been known to hold my own with my sisters and an Everly Brothers song or two. Why do you ask?"

"A bunch of us are heading to Connor tonight to a little bar on the corner of Ames and Loy Lake Road. It's karaoke night."

"I couldn't barge in on your party," Alex protested.

"Nonsense!" Lola exclaimed. "It's just a small group of friends getting together to blow off steam. We'd love for you to join us." She turned to Victor. "Before I forget, Jordan stopped by. Said she had something to do and would meet up with us later at Cowboys."

At the mention of Jordan's name, Alex perked up. So, these were Jordan's friends. Suddenly the prospect of drinking margaritas and getting an up-close and personal view of Jordan when her guard was down escalated on his checklist of things to do.

"Sounds good," Victor said, before turning back to Alex. "So, are you coming?"

"If you're sure it will be okay with the others." He felt the heat spread across his face. This man was definitely checking him out.

"Of course it will. See you at seven."

Back in his car, Alex let the smile he'd held back finally

spread across his face. This might be the break he needed. He'd be able to observe Jordan in her own backyard as he tried to figure out what was going on.

Pulling into traffic on Main Street, he drove toward the Pizza Palace to grab a slice or two before heading home. A niggling thought found its way into his head as he remembered Lola's words when she'd held the Relationship card.

You won't have long to wait for that special person.

He hoped she was wrong.

•

CHAPTER 10

Jordan pulled into the parking lot at Cowboys Bar and Grill, grumbling silently for being so late. Karaoke night always packed them in, and tonight was no exception. She drove around the lot twice before finally parking down the street.

She hoped the others had arrived early enough to snag a good table. She was so in the mood to sit down with her friends and forget about her week with a pitcher of margaritas and a microphone. While her singing ability was something best left for the shower, the same could be said for most of the people who showed up on karaoke night, especially after they'd consumed a few beers.

What sounded like Carrie Underwood to her own ears came out more like Willie Nelson on estrogen to everyone else. But tonight she didn't care. Although the gang didn't come here often, they always had a blast when they did, and she definitely needed to get her mind off J. T. and his killer.

Usually everyone crammed into Ray's vehicle for the excursion. He'd given up drinking in his early twenties, the summer before he went off to the police academy, and was the official designated driver. After hearing stories of his pre–Alcoholics Anonymous days, Jordan understood why. His forty-year clean and sober record, along with his nine-passenger Suburban, made him the perfect chauffeur.

That was no help tonight. Her spur-of-the-moment trip to Grayson County College after work meant she'd have to go easy on the margaritas or leave her car in Connor, which was something she'd prefer not to do.

And the kicker? It had been a totally wasted trip. She'd gone there hoping to talk with Derrick Young again, praying he'd blurt out something in the heat of anger. Although he made her blood run cold, she'd looked forward to getting him off to the side without the coach hovering when she had another go at him.

None of which happened. Because of an away game on Saturday night, the coach had cut practice short, and according to the groundskeeper, she'd missed them by about thirty minutes.

Quickening her step when she heard the sounds of a good time a half block away from the bar, Jordan wondered if the people who lived nearby ever complained. If they did, it had obviously fallen on deaf ears.

After pushing through the door, she spotted the gang immediately. They'd commandeered a huge table two rows back from the stage where a girl resembling Dolly Parton held the mic. Unfortunately, that's where the resemblance ended. Her rendition of "I Will Always Love You," reminded Jordan of a cat in heat on the high notes.

Weaving her way through the standing-room-only crowd hugging the bar, Jordan waved when Rosie noticed her, swinging her arms like a cheerleader. Jordan's exuberance quickly faded when she recognized Quincy Dozerly sitting beside Rosie. Spending more time with that man was not her idea of a good time and letting her hair down.

And what was up with his hat that read WOOF ARTED?

This was the guy who was supposed to keep her out of jail if the police discovered the missing knife and dragged her down to the station for more questions?

Trying to re-create the happy face, Jordan changed directions and moved to the other end of the table where the rest of the gang sat, facing the stage as they watched the wannabe Dolly slaughtering the song.

Who is that next to Victor? she wondered, staring at the back of an unfamiliar head.

"There you are, Jordan!" Victor exclaimed, his face lighting up when he saw her.

She relaxed and gave him a hug when he jumped up to greet her. "Darn! You guys started without me," she said, pointing to the two empty margarita pitchers.

"Victor's already wowed us with his version of 'Bad to the Bone,'" Michael said, obviously as proud as if his partner were the next American Idol. "Take a load off. Sit next to Alex." He gestured toward the empty chair next to the stranger.

Alex?

When the man turned to face her and flashed his pearly whites, Jordan's heart began to beat like a drummer on speed.

"Jordan, meet Alex Montgomery."

She narrowed her eyes. "We've already met."

Michael turned to the newcomer. "You didn't mention you already knew our Jordan."

Alex shrugged, his eyes holding her captive. "I didn't connect the name," he said. "We shared lunch one day last week."

"Great," Michael said. "Sit, Jordan. We've got to get you juiced so we can hear that Shania Twain you did the last time we were here."

"Not!" Victor joked, pouring a margarita from one of the three full pitchers the waitress had just placed on the table. "Here, sweetie, drink up."

No way Jordan wanted to sit next to Alex, but other than the one next to Quincy Dozerly, it was the only empty chair. Plopping down as gracefully as she could with his intense stare unnerving her, she decided things could be worse. She could be forced to make small talk with Dozerly while he played "touchy-feely" with Rosie.

Gag me!

She reached for the glass, scolding herself for not absolutely hating being stuck next to Alex.

"Why didn't you return my calls?" Alex asked, his eyes twinkling with mischief.

She so wanted to fire back, *Why'd you ransack my apartment?* "Busy, I guess," she said, squirming in her seat. Up close, his Paul Newman eyes were burning a hole in her brain. She looked away, pretending to be interested in the guy on the stage singing and dancing in a hard-to-watch James Brown imitation.

When the guy spun around, Jordan nearly spit her drink across the table. His T-shirt had pulled out of the back of his waistband, worn low because of his beer belly, and the whole world got an up-close-and-personal look at his "line of demarcation."

"Think of it as rear cleavage," Alex said, handing her a cocktail napkin to mop up the spill.

Despite her best efforts, Jordan laughed, blotting the margarita from her chin. "Please God, keep him facing us, or I'll never get through this drink without making an even bigger fool of myself," she quipped. The liquor, already warming her insides, had begun to erase the day's tension and make it easier to talk to her unexpected companion.

"This is becoming an everyday thing."

"What is?"

"Watching liquids shoot from your nose." He reached up and wiped a droplet from her cheek.

Trying unsuccessfully to recover some of her dignity, Jordan did the one thing she shouldn't. She stuck her tongue out at him, a carry-over from growing up with brothers. "A gentleman doesn't remind a girl about things like that."

"Who says I'm a gentleman?"

He leaned close enough for Jordan to get a whiff of aftershave, and for a second, she thought he was about to kiss her.

Like a dork, she closed her eyes.

After what seemed like an eternity with no kiss, she glanced up to see him smiling down at her.

"I will if you want me to," he teased playfully.

Feeling the blush shimmy up her cheeks, Jordan reached for the pitcher. If she had to tolerate this man all night, she'd need help. She glared when he took the pitcher from her and refilled the glass.

"The cat seems to get your tongue a lot, Jordan. Do you want me to kiss you or not?"

The heat consumed her face and she bit down hard on her lower lip. "Look, Montgomery," she started, searching for some way to come out of this without looking totally lame. "You obviously think there's some chemistry going on between us. I assure you, it's wishful thinking."

Okay, maybe that wasn't entirely true, but Jordan wasn't about to admit she visualized rose petals and silk sheets every time she looked his way.

"I'd suggest you have another drink, too." She paused briefly before adding, "Or take a cold shower."

Alex threw back his head and laughed out loud, causing the others to stop talking and look their way. "Jordan wants to sing with me," Alex lied.

Lola raised her arm in the air. "Yes! But she needs at least one more margarita."

"That can be arranged," Jordan said, grateful Alex hadn't outed her for the idiot kissing thing. She chugged the last half of her current drink and slammed the empty glass in front of him. "Let's do it!"

"Yes, ma'am," he said, before his facial expression turned somber. "Sure you can handle it?"

"You trying to back out of singing with me?" She prayed that was exactly what he was doing. Letting him hear what could never be described as one of her talents was not particularly enticing, especially after she'd already made a complete fool of herself in front of him.

But she didn't want to be the one to back out of a challenge. She'd like to be able to walk out of this place with at least some of her dignity intact.

"Alex knows the Everly Brothers, Jordan. How about

you two get up there and impress us with 'Dream'?" Victor hollered to be heard above the current karaoke singer.

"I don't know that one," Jordan said, adding a dig Alex's way. "That's a little before my time."

Instead of commenting, he grabbed her arm and lifted her off the chair. "Come on. Who doesn't know 'Dream'? The words will come up on the screen." His eyes narrowed. "Unless this is a pathetic copout."

Jordan whirled around toward the stage, surprised by how dizzy she felt. Three margaritas usually didn't affect her like this. Then she remembered she'd missed dinner to hurry to the college. She should have stopped at the 7-Eleven for a burrito.

"Well?"

"Bring it on," she challenged, heading for the stage.

"That's what I wanted to hear." Alex reached over to give her a push up onto the stage. "I'll take the harmony."

Jordan's eyes widened, realizing his hands were on her hips. She prayed he'd be able to boost her up there. How much more embarrassment could she take?

"You're on," she said, after he lifted her in a single swoop.

Thank you, Jesus.

She watched as Alex hashed out the details with the disc jockey, silently praying the song was not in the catalog.

"Ready?" Alex handed her a microphone. "Don't forget. You have the high part."

Crap!

When the record began, Jordan surprised herself and held her own. Before long, everyone in the bar was hooting and hollering. There were even a few whistles. As much as she hated to admit it, Alex had a nice voice and canceled out her not-so-nice one.

When the song ended, he picked her off her feet and swung her around. "You did the Everlys proud."

"I did, didn't I?" She laughed, taking his hand when he helped her off the stage over shouts from the loosened-up crowd for an encore.

The night turned out to be the best stress reliever Jordan could imagine and a nice ending to a horrendous week. Everyone took turns belting out a song or two. Jordan eventually did her Shania Twain imitation of "Man! I Feel Like a Woman!" complete with a black boa the DJ handed her for effect.

Closing time came way too soon, and everyone began to pile out. After two more margaritas, Jordan was feeling really relaxed and looking at Alex in a whole different light. Brett had always joked she went through three stages when she drank. Giggly, then frisky, but you had to get her home quickly because sleepy soon followed.

"Where are your keys?" Alex asked, helping her weave toward the exit.

"I'll take her," Lola said. "We're all going to the Burger Hut for a late-night snack."

Jordan groaned. Her empty stomach couldn't handle a greasy burger right now.

"You go on," Alex said. "I'll get her home safely. You guys can check on her when you get back."

"Jordan?" Lola asked, stepping closer.

"It's okay, Lola. I just want to climb into bed." She gasped, hearing her own comment. "I didn't mean . . ."

"I know what you meant," Alex responded. "I'm pooped, too. We'll leave my car in the parking lot and I'll drive yours home. Tomorrow I'll pick you up and you can drive me back over here to get it."

"Okay," she said, getting another whiff of his aftershave. Calvin Klein's Obsession. He was wearing the cologne her first real boyfriend had worn, a nice manly fragrance that made her nostalgic. The roses and silk sheets idea snapped back into her brain, and she forced it away once more.

Outside, Jordan said good night to her friends and walked with Alex to her car. After holding the passenger door open for her, he walked around to the other side and slid into the driver's seat.

Chivalry is not dead!

Maybe Alex wouldn't have to drive home tonight, she thought, before scolding herself. She'd never been a one-night stand, and she didn't intend to start now.

The ride to her apartment was long enough for the sleepy stage to set in, and Jordan fought to keep her eyes open and stay semi-alert.

After Alex parked in her spot behind the building, he helped her out of the car. Walking to the entrance, Jordan stumbled and fell into him.

"Whoa! You really did overdo it tonight."

"I'm fine," she fired back. "You try walking in heels."

Alex laughed. "You don't have heels on, Jordan."

Again, her cheeks grew hot from yet another idiot remark. Or was it alcohol flaming the fire? "Oh," she muttered.

As soon as they entered the building, Jordan pointed down the hall. "This way."

Halfway there a man jumped from the shadows and charged at them. Jordan screamed. Alex let go of her and shoved the stranger, knocking him backward. The man recovered and pushed back before racing past them. In a flash, he opened the door and disappeared.

"Who was that?"

"I have no idea," she said, her stomach in her throat. Too many weird things were happening to her to pretend it was coincidence, but she wasn't about to share her suspicions with Alex.

"Let's get inside your apartment, and I'll call the police."

"No," she answered quickly.

Alex's brow furrowed. "Why not?"

"I'm too tired to deal with them right now. Besides, the more I think about it, the more I'm sure it was someone more afraid of us than we were of him." She sighed, wondering if this had anything to do with her visit to the college. Had Derrick sent someone to scare her? "Please, Alex, just open the door. I'm exhausted."

He held her stare for a few seconds before doing as she'd requested. Safely inside, Jordan stumbled again and Alex caught her. Lifting up on tippy toes, she touched her lips to his. When he didn't respond, she snaked her arms around his neck and pressed her body into him.

This time he did react, groaning as he kissed her back. Jordan couldn't remember ever falling so deeply into a kiss, wanting so badly to continue doing it for hours.

But Alex apparently had other plans.

He pulled away and walked to the door, turning to face her one more time. "I have to get home, Jordan. Get some sleep, and I'll be back in the morning around ten with coffee. Lock the door behind me."

Then he was gone, and Jordan once again felt the sting of rejection. Even though she barely knew the guy, this rebuff hurt almost as much as when Brett tossed her out like dirty dishwater.

She'd literally thrown herself at him, and he'd passed. What red-blooded man turned down sex? She'd felt his body respond to hers. Why then was she standing alone feeling so unloved in her apartment?

"Screw him!" she said aloud. He would probably have gotten her into bed then robbed her on the way out.

She walked to the door and slid the chain over, her mind wandering back to the man who had confronted them in the hallway. She hadn't been able to see his face clearly with the hoodie, but for an instant, he'd made eye contact with her. There was no denying the man was tall and strong enough to be a match for Alex.

What was it about those eyes?

They should have called the police as Alex had suggested, but then, she would've had to tell them things she'd rather not just yet.

Specifically, her encounter with Derrick Young.

She wasn't even sure there was something to tell except that the quarterback was abusing his girlfriend. She made a mental note to talk with Brittney again and convince her to tell her parents. If that failed, she'd find a way to tell them herself.

She stripped off her clothes and threw on an old T-shirt and gym shorts before slipping under the covers. As relaxed as she was from the alcohol, something kept her from falling asleep.

Something about the guy in the hallway.

What was it?

She was sure she'd seen him before, but where?

CHAPTER 11

Alex exited Empire Apartments and walked to Jordan's car, his senses on high alert. Instinctively, his hand moved to his shoulder before he remembered he'd left his weapon back at his own apartment. It wouldn't have been cool if someone had discovered he'd brought a gun to karaoke night, even with the right-to-carry credentials in his wallet.

At the thought of Cowboys Bar and Grill, a slight grin crossed his face. Although he hated to admit it, he'd had more fun tonight than he'd had since arriving in Ranchero—hell, since he could remember. It seemed he'd forgotten how to let go and just be in the moment. Tonight Jordan's friends had made him feel like he'd known them for years.

And Jordan . . .

He sighed, thinking how she'd awakened emotions that hadn't stirred in a long time. Having grown up with three sisters in Houston, he knew exactly how to get her to do what he wanted. He'd challenged her. No self-respecting, twenty-first-century female wanted the world to think she wasn't up for anything a man could do.

What was the old saying about Ginger Rogers—she did everything Fred Astaire did, except she did it backward and in heels?

Alex chuckled at Jordan trying to blame her wooziness on high heels when she was wearing flats. He hadn't minded one bit when she'd fallen into him in the parking lot and definitely not when it happened later in her apartment. He'd tried to ignore her lips on his but had lost that battle with himself when she'd pressed into him, awakening every nerve in his body.

Especially those south of his belt buckle.

A sudden rustling of leaves catapulted him out of his daydream. He turned in the direction of the sound, ready to confront the stranger again. Cursing his lack of a weapon, an audible sigh of relief escaped his lips when he saw a squirrel scampering up a tree.

After the incident in the hallway, he'd better get his head out of his ass and stay alert if he wanted to make it home in one piece. Confrontation without a weapon was something he'd prefer not to experience, especially if he was surprised.

Despite Jordan's protests, he should have insisted on calling the police. The man had been hiding in the shadows, and who knew what would have happened if he hadn't been there. He would feel better once Ray returned home.

But why had she been so determined to keep the police out of it?

In all his professional life, he had only come across one reason for that—she wanted to avoid the cops asking a lot of questions.

Why? He shook his head, knowing the obvious reason.

He reached Jordan's car, taking his time to open the door. If the intruder was watching, and he felt certain he was, he wanted to give him every opportunity to make a move. He hadn't noticed a gun, and although the guy had him beat in height and weight, Alex had taken on bigger men in his career and lived to tell about it.

He slid behind the wheel, taking a deep breath of Jordan's perfume lingering in the air in the closed space. Lola's words about meeting that special someone sprung into his mind. He shook it off and started the car, driving out of the parking lot with a final look in the rearview mirror.

If things were different.

But he was here for only one thing, and so far, he wasn't having much luck. His idea of getting closer to her to find out how deeply she was involved had nearly backfired when her warm body had snuggled into his. Everything he'd ever learned warned that getting too close meant dropping his guard.

If he'd stayed in her apartment one more minute, he was positive, training or not, he would still be there now—under the sheets doing what he'd wanted to do from the first time he'd looked into her eyes.

That couldn't happen, and he'd damn well better get it into his head. Besides, he'd never taken advantage of a female who had consumed enough alcohol to wipe away her inhibitions, so why start now?

He pulled under a tree a few houses down and killed the

motor, knowing Ray and the others would enter the street from the opposite end. He was confident Jordan's car wouldn't be noticed, and even if it was, he'd say he was waiting on them. Once he saw them pull around back, he'd head home, but there was no way he was leaving until then.

Not while the guy who had jumped them still lurked out there.

Not while the sensation of her lips on his still burned his entire mouth.

Jordan swallowed three ibuprofen tablets and stumbled back to bed, thinking it was those last two margaritas that did her in. She wasn't much of a drinker, usually only having one or two, but for some reason, she'd felt she needed the alcohol to wipe away a particularly stressful week.

Who was she kidding? She'd had bad weeks before and never felt the urge to drink until she turned stupid.

She groaned, leaning her head back on the pillow. Stupid was putting it mildly. What on God's green earth made her think she could handle that many margaritas? She'd be sucking down pain meds all day for the headache.

Swearing off liquor forever, she closed her eyes and willed herself back to sleep. It was Saturday and she had nothing planned except cleaning the apartment, something she'd neglected for two weeks. Maybe she'd even catch up on her reading. She had a stack of to-be-read *Sports Illustrated* magazines on her nightstand, begging for attention.

But all that would have to wait. Right now she had some serious z's to catch up on.

When the doorbell rang, she sprang up, causing the

annoying man behind her forehead with the sledgehammer to kick it up a notch. She decided whoever was at her door would have to come back later to peddle magazines or to try to convince her that his or her God was better than hers. Leaning back, she lowered herself down to the mattress, relieved the medicine had finally started to work.

When the doorbell rang again and then a third time, she slid out from under the covers, intending to give someone a piece of her mind.

Opening the door, she gasped. "Alex!" Suddenly she remembered she had to drive him to Connor to pick up his car at the bar.

The smile on his face spread as his eyes wandered down her body. Self-consciously, she brought her hands up to her chest as she realized she was still braless, in a paper-thin T-shirt.

She was grateful she wasn't cold!

The gesture didn't go unnoticed as Alex laughed. "Unless you want to miss this great breakfast I picked up, you probably should change into something less sexy."

Her skin tingled. "It didn't seem to affect you last night," she blurted before her brain could filter her words, making her want to slap herself.

He laughed again. "About that . . ."

"Come on in," she interrupted, not wanting to go down that road with him. "Kitchen's to your left. I'll be right back." She turned and scampered to the bedroom, wondering if he was watching, wishing she'd worn her cute little sleep shorts to bed instead of her old gym shorts.

Hurrying, she slipped into jeans and a lightweight sweater, stopping to brush her teeth and run a comb through her hair before returning. She really needed another five minutes to put on some makeup but knew he'd probably make some wisecrack about her getting all dolled up for him if she did.

No, she'd have to face him au naturel.

When she walked out of her bedroom, she saw him in her kitchen, and she bit back a grin. He looked like he knew his way around, a tidbit she filed away in her mental folder on the guy.

He glanced up as she crossed the living room. "What do you want in your coffee?" he asked, again checking out her body.

"I'm up here, Alex," she quipped, pointing to her face when his eyes finally traveled up from her chest.

He had the decency to look embarrassed. "Sorry. With that wild red hair and those jeans, I lost my head. Who can blame me?"

She turned away so he wouldn't see her reaction. After she sat down at the dinette table, he carried over the coffee, then went back to the kitchen and emptied the grocery bag he'd brought. "Hope you like bagels and cream cheese," he said opening the package.

"I don't usually eat breakfast."

Unless it's chocolate.

As if he read her mind, he pulled out a box from the doughnut shop around the corner. "Éclairs for dessert but first the healthy stuff." Reaching over, he pulled the toaster from under the counter. "Aha! I was just going to ask where you kept the knives."

Jordan jumped out of her chair. "What did you say?"

"I wondered where I should look to find a knife, but there was one behind the toaster."

Jordan crossed over to where he stood. "Let me see that."

With a confused look on his face, Alex held up the knife.

Jordan smiled, realizing it was the one missing from the knife rack. "It was behind the toaster?"

"Yeah," he replied, still eyeing her suspiciously.

"I've been looking for that," she explained. "I must have accidentally dropped it back there the other day. I use it to pull out Pop-Tarts without burning my fingers." Blowing out a breath, she settled back in the chair and sipped the coffee. She couldn't wait to tell Ray about the discovery.

"This looks like part of a set. Where are the others?"

This time Jordan was the one with a confused look on her face. "Why?"

Alex studied her. "No reason. It's just that sometimes a knife like this comes in a set with a rack."

Jordan nearly choked on the hot coffee. When her coughing jag was over, she purposely kept her eyes glued to the cup in her hand, sure that Alex knew about the hidden knife rack.

But how?

"Oh well, it's not a big deal." He sliced the bagel in half and popped it into the toaster.

As she felt her shoulders relax, she knew she'd overreacted. No way Alex could know about the rack since Ray had hidden it a few hours after the cops left. She smiled up at him when he set the bagel in front of her, trying to read his expression for any assurance that her knife secret was still safe. His return smile satisfied her that it was.

They finished breakfast and drove to Connor to pick up his car. By the time she returned to her apartment, it was afternoon. Although her head begged for more ibuprofen, she raced to Ray's apartment and pounded on the door.

When Lola answered, Jordan rushed in, planting a kiss on the older woman's cheek. "Hey, Lola. Where's Ray? I have something I need to tell him."

"Here I am, doll," Ray said, emerging from the bathroom in only his jeans and a towel wrapped around his head.

For an old guy, he's still buff, she thought. No wonder Lola transformed into a giggling teenager when they were together.

"I found the knife," she said. "Well, actually, Alex found it."

Ray's eyes widened and he stopped drying his hair, letting the towel drop to the floor. He sat on the couch and patted the cushion next to him. "Where?"

"Behind the toaster."

"That's good news. I meant to run over to the storage unit a few days ago to pick up the rack. I'll do it this afternoon." He let out a breath. "That's one less thing we have to worry about. Now all I have to do is install the security camera I borrowed."

"You got it?" Jordan paused, wondering if she should tell him about the stranger they'd encountered last night.

"Yeah. The guy I know in Dallas loaned it to me for a few weeks, but I've been too busy to install it."

Jordan sat down beside him on the sofa. "I think it might be a good idea to get it up today."

When both Lola and Ray stared at her, she blurted, "Last night a man jumped out of the shadows when Alex and I got home."

"Ohmygod!" Lola exclaimed. "You're okay, right?"

"Alex shoved the guy, and he ran past us and took off out the door."

"Did you call the cops?" Ray asked.

Jordan lowered her head and mumbled, "No," half hoping he didn't hear.

"Sweet Jesus! Why not, Jordan? Did you know the guy?" Ray's voice rose an octave.

"Something about him seemed familiar, but no, I didn't recognize him."

"So, why didn't you call, honey?" Lola asked.

How could she tell them the real reason without confessing to all the other things she knew would cause Ray to throw a fit? "I figured he was just lost, and we scared him into running."

"A lost person doesn't hide in the shadows and jump out at you," Ray said, his eyes burning her with that you-should-know-better look.

"In retrospect, I agree we should have called, but I was so tired."

"And tipsy," Lola added with a smile. "Good thing Alex was with you. Did he stay for coffee?"

Jordan smiled. "You are a nosy one, Lola. Yes, I did have coffee with him, but before you go jumping to conclusions, let me put them to rest. Alex stopped by this morning with breakfast and afterward I drove him back to Connor to get his car."

"Darn," she said, playfully.

"Jordan, are you sure you didn't recognize the guy?" Ray asked, his tone demanding they get back to business. "What was familiar about him?"

"I don't know, Ray. His eyes, maybe."

"I'll definitely get those cameras mounted today. There are too many things going on to pretend it's nothing."

"Are you going to see Alex again?" Lola asked, apparently tired of the more serious conversation.

"I don't know. I can't quite figure him out."

"What's to figure out?" Ray piped in. "A good-looking guy who's new in town and who's obviously attracted to you . . . I don't see the problem." He had that look on his face that all men get when things seem black-and-white and they don't understand why everyone else can't see it, too.

Jordan laughed. "What makes you think he's attracted to me?" she asked, remembering the sting of his rejection all over again.

"Sugar, no man looks at a woman the way he was looking at you without fantasizing about a motel room and breakfast in bed," Ray joked, before putting on his serious face again. "Enough of this. I've got to get busy so we can catch the next SOB who thinks he can wander in here and spook us." He walked to the kitchen and poured a cup of coffee. "After I get some caffeine in my blood, I'll get the rack and bring it over this afternoon. By tonight, the cameras will be operational."

"Do you think we'll catch someone on tape?" Lola asked.

"They have no idea who they're playing with," Ray said, more to himself than to the women.

Jordan stood and made her way to the door. An uneasy feeling about the guy lurking in the hallway still nagged at her, and she wasn't sure they would ever find out who he was.

Truth be told, she wasn't even sure she wanted to know.

CHAPTER 12

Jordan stared at the empty computer screen, willing her fingers to fly over the keys and come up with the perfect recipe for the week. The Kitchen Kupboard had taken off with the good citizens of Ranchero, especially since the pork chop casserole, effectively called Côte de Porc á la Cocotte, had boosted the print runs at the *Globe* for a second time. Needless to say, Dwayne Egan pranced around like a proud papa, taking all the credit for the column's amazing success.

In three fast weeks, Jordan had gone from low reporter on the totem pole in the newsroom to hearing her name mentioned simultaneously with "culinary goddess" on the local morning radio program. Even though it was only her friend Michael plugging her on his show, it was way more than she'd dreamed could happen after moving to this sleepy little town just three months before.

She sighed, thinking back to the way Michael and her other neighbors had instantly taken to her. It was as if an entire building of misfits had found yet another person who "got" them. With her new friends, she never felt the need to pretend she was someone other than the quirky girl who preferred curling up watching *Saturday Night Live* with them than going to a club with people her own age.

The phone on her desk suddenly blared, jarring her from her thoughts. "Jordan McAllister."

She smiled, thinking she no longer had to say "Personals" when she picked up the phone. She still had to write them, but Egan had insisted she answer with only her name now. Okay, so he only did that because he was cheap and didn't want to spring for a separate line for culinary fans who wanted to chat about recipes. Still, it was a step up in her book.

"McAllister," she repeated when there was no response on the other end.

"Jordan."

She gasped, nearly dropping the receiver. She'd never forget that sensual tone. "Hello, Brett."

She heard him take a deep breath. "I've been thinking a lot about you lately. I wondered how you were."

Really? Was this while you were boinking your thunder-and-lightning girl?

"I'm fine," she replied, trying to keep the anger out of her voice. She'd thought she was over him, and it ticked her off that just the sound of his voice blew that theory all to pieces.

"I called your mother this morning to find out where you were. She filled me in on your new job."

Jordan opened the notebook in her head and added "Kill Mom" to her mental to-do list. Sylvia McAllister had adored Brett Wilson from the day Jordan had brought him home over the Thanksgiving holidays her junior year at Texas. Like every other red-blooded female on the planet, Sylvia had been taken in by his rugged good looks and sweet-talking line of bull.

"What do you want, Brett?" Jumping right to the point would get her off the phone faster. She hated that the man who had broken her heart so easily could now speed it up simply by saying her name.

He laughed, one of those fake attempts he'd always used when he was bored with an interview. They'd called it his that's-a-wrap giggle.

"I've missed you."

"I've moved on," she lied, squirming in her chair. She hadn't realized it wasn't true until this very moment. She had no idea why her ex-boyfriend was calling out of the blue, but a warning bell pealed in her head.

In the seven years she and Brett had been together, he'd used this same technique many times when he'd screwed up and wanted her back. God help her weakness, it had worked every time. You couldn't blame the guy for sticking with a winning plan.

"What happened to your weather girl?" she blurted out, wishing the filter in her brain worked. The last thing she wanted to hear about was Brett's love life with the woman who had marched up to him his first day on the job and rubbed her store-boughts all over his chest.

"Christy and I decided we're better colleagues than we ever were as a couple. She never understood me the way you always did."

Jordan held the phone away from her mouth so he

wouldn't hear her gag. The arrogant assumption that he could dump her so easily, then try to pick up where they'd left off like nothing had happened infuriated her—as if humiliating her three weeks after she'd packed up and followed him to Dallas like a loyal roadie wasn't enough.

She strummed her fingers on her desk then noticed the girl three cubicles over watching her intently. She'd spoken to her a few times at the coffee machine and knew her name was Sandy and that she was a fact-checker for the Business section. When Sandy mouthed, *Do you want me to call you?* and made the classical phone signal with her hand to her ear, Jordan nodded gratefully.

She brought the phone back up in time to hear Brett ask, "So, what do you think?"

"About what?"

"I'd like to come up this weekend and talk."

"Not a good idea, Brett. I told you, I've moved on. I'm seeing another man." Maybe making a complete idiot out of herself by trying to seduce a guy when she was drunk didn't exactly constitute "seeing" him, but it was all she had right now.

Maybe it was even a little wishful thinking.

"I only want to talk, Jordan. Surely I deserve that much."

Deserve that much? She huffed into the phone. "You don't *even* want to get me started, Brett," she said, before the beep came across indicating another call coming in. "Sorry, it's my other line. I have to run." She quickly disconnected, then gave a thumbs-up to Sandy, thinking she should make an effort to get to know her better.

The rest of the day zoomed by without Jordan replaying Brett's phone call in her head more than once every five minutes. No doubt a part of her was excited he wanted to get back together, but her smarter self warned her to cut and run without thinking twice.

Blowing out a breath, she tried to concentrate on her work. Since they'd gone to the karaoke bar instead of having potluck last Friday, she had nothing for this week's column.

She wondered if she could talk Ray into giving up the Mandarin Orange Cake recipe he'd snagged from the owner of the diner but decided it wasn't his to give. If she wanted Myrtle's recipe, she'd have to ask her permission. She wasn't about to do that since it would be admitting she had none of her own. That wouldn't bode well with her newfound popularity as a kitchen diva.

No, she'd have to come up with one by herself or as a last resort, beg Rosie for yet another one of hers. Not that Rosie would mind, but she'd been preoccupied lately, entertaining Quincy Dozerly. Jordan scrunched her nose at the thought of the man, and her lips puckered as if she had just put something sour into her mouth.

She packed up her things and headed toward the exit, wishing her mother had taken the time to teach her how to cook instead of leaving her life's training to her dad and four brothers whose curriculum didn't include home economics. Needing her outside to even up the teams when they played football in the afternoons, her brothers left her no time to develop baking skills. Although she had no clue how to cook a roast, she could throw a mean touchdown pass from forty yards out. Because of that, she was usually the first one chosen for the teams.

A lot of good that did for writing a food column!

Hence, her current dilemma with the weekly recipe

since her only expertise was frying bologna and toasting Pop-Tarts.

Walking down the hallway at her building, Jordan spied two policemen outside her apartment who snapped to attention when they spotted her. Her anxiety escalated, fearing she had been burglarized again. Getting closer, she recognized both Sergeant Calhoun and Officer Rutherford.

The short, stocky sergeant held out a legal-looking paper when she approached. "I have a warrant, ma'am," he said, almost apologetically. "We need to have a look around your apartment."

"Why?" Jordan took the paper and skimmed it. It looked legit enough, signed by a judge from the Fifth District Court in Connor. "What are you looking for?"

"We have reason to believe you might have a knife missing." He motioned to the door. "Could you open it for us, please? We'll get out of your hair as quickly as possible if you cooperate."

Jordan fumbled with the lock, trying hard to stop her hands from shaking. How could they possibly know about the knife?

Once inside, Calhoun immediately went to the kitchen and pointed at the knife rack. Fortunately, Ray had remembered to bring it back on Saturday, and all the knives were safely in their slots.

The officer pulled one out and examined it. "Do you have any other knives, Miss McAllister?"

She shook her head. "Surely you don't think I had anything to do with J. T.'s death?" she asked, half hoping she had mistakenly jumped to conclusions.

"Too soon to say," Rutherford replied, although the look

in his eyes confirmed her suspicions. "Are you absolutely positive you're not missing one?"

"We found a knife in the grass across the street earlier today," Calhoun added, pulling out the drawers and emptying the contents on the counter.

Jordan pointed to the rack as a wave of nausea washed over her. "They're all I have." She stopped short of confessing that most of them didn't get much of a workout. "Are you asking everyone in the apartment building if they're missing a knife?"

Both Calhoun and Rutherford lowered their heads, giving her the answer she needed.

"So why me?" She was feeling harassed and let her play-nice attitude slip a little. "Why would I break into my own apartment and shred my furniture when I clearly have no money to replace it? Tell me that."

Calhoun responded first. "Sometimes people who commit crimes do things to throw suspicion away from themselves." He paused. "Would you be willing to take a lie-detector test?"

"Absolutely not."

They all turned toward the sound of the voice just as Quincy Dozerly walked into the apartment.

"I'm representing Miss McAllister now, and I would appreciate it if you gentlemen directed any further questions to me."

For the first time since Jordan had met Dozerly, she was genuinely glad to see him.

He took the warrant from her and studied it. "Unless you have the evidence to charge my client with something, there will be no more questions and definitely no interrogations at the police station without me present."

"You found a knife across the street?" Jordan asked, unable to stop thinking about it. "And you think it's the one that killed J. T.?"

Rutherford crossed the room and stood in front of her. "It was positive for dried blood, and they're testing it for DNA. The ME says the serrated pattern is similar to the victim's entry wound. We should have positive identification in the next few days."

"You're sure there are no other knives here besides the ones in the rack?" Calhoun asked, again pointing to the counter behind him.

Dozerly shot up from the couch and walked to the kitchen, staring at the rack for a few minutes before speaking. "As you can see, clearly they are all here. The warrant only covers the kitchen, so if there are no other questions, I'd say we're done here."

Both Calhoun and Rutherford stared at the rack as if they half expected blood to ooze out of one of the slots.

"We'll be in touch," the shorter one said on his way to the door.

"Sergeant?"

He turned back to face her. "Yes, ma'am?"

"May I ask why you specifically thought I might have a knife missing in my kitchen and why you aren't questioning the other residents about it?"

Calhoun glanced toward his partner, who nodded. "We received a tip that mentioned the knife we found might have come from your apartment. We had to check it out."

"That's it, boys. Let us know if we can be of further assistance," Quincy said, placing himself between Jordan and the cops. "Miss McAllister has had a busy day, and you've taken enough of her time, not to mention the hours she'll have to spend putting her kitchen back together."

He held the door open and waited as the two police officers exited.

"Who would have called about the knife?" Jordan asked when she was alone with Dozerly. "Only my friends knew about it."

"Where was it?" he asked, ignoring her question.

"Alex found it behind the toaster." As soon as the words left her mouth, she gasped. She'd forgotten the way Alex had questioned her about the knife rack Saturday morning. He must have been the one who called the police.

But why?

Did he think she might be a killer? Or worse, was he covering his own tracks and trying to mislead the investigators?

Dozerly studied her face. "Do you think one of your friends called them?"

She shook her head.

"Then who else knew about it?"

"Alex," she said, almost in a whisper.

Quincy's eyes widened. "You think Alex may have been the one who tipped off the cops?"

Hating that it was the only plausible explanation, Jordan nodded. "Who else?"

"I don't know, but for now, Jordan, I'd keep my distance from him." Quincy patted her shoulder.

Shrugging out of his reach, she tried to return his smile but only managed a smirk. Knowing she should be thanking him for protecting her, she tried to ignore the uncomfortable feeling she got when he was around.

Jerking her body toward the door when there was a sudden knock, Jordan quickly turned back and made eye contact with Quincy. In that split second the man became her guardian angel when he pushed past her and walked to the door. She moved up behind him, hoping it wasn't the police back for another go-round about the knife.

She was surprised to see Roger Mason standing in the hallway when Quincy opened the door. She couldn't help but notice the look that passed between the two men. At the potluck dinner last week Quincy had said he didn't know Mason personally, but that look said otherwise. She wondered if the Longhorn Prime Rib owner had an appetite for gambling.

"Miss McAllister," Mason started. "May I come in and talk with you for a minute?"

Jordan hesitated, wondering why he was here. The last critique she'd written of his restaurant had been a good one. She'd raved about the Rattlesnake Pasta and the phenomenal service she'd received.

"Call me Jordan," she said, swooping her hand in a come-on-in gesture. "Sorry, my couch is not in the best of condition." She motioned to the duct-taped cushions.

The man had the good grace not to flinch when he glanced that way. Instead, he moved closer to her, checking his watch. "I only have a few minutes. There's something I want to discuss with you."

Suddenly, Jordan remembered her manners. "Mr. Mason, do you know Quincy Dozerly? He's my lawyer." She had almost bitten her tongue to keep from saying it.

Mason shook hands with Dozerly before turning back to Jordan. For an instant, she was mesmerized by the restaurant owner's dark, smoky eyes and the faint whiff of a citrus aftershave.

"Call me Roger, Quincy."

"I'll leave you two alone to discuss whatever it is Roger came by to talk about," Dozerly said, again making direct eye contact with the man. Something about the way the lawyer said his first name indicated they knew each other better than they pretended. "Jordan, don't answer any questions without me if the police come back." He opened the door with a final glance at the newcomer.

Then he was gone, leaving her with Roger and with a more then nervous feeling about being alone with the well-dressed man, who even now had on a navy blue suit and tie in the middle of the afternoon. For once, she wished Dozerly had stuck around a little longer.

"What do you want to talk to me about?"

Mason took a minute to scan her apartment, probably thinking it was a closet compared to his own. "I think it's time we talked about your first visit to the restaurant."

Jordan gave him a confused look. "My first visit?"

"I know about the foie gras that ended up in your purse."

She gasped, realizing J. T. must have sold her out. "I'm sorry, Mr. Mason. I thought I was ordering chicken."

His eyes seemed to bore a hole into her before he spoke once again. "Did you and J. T. have a thing going on?"

Again she inhaled noisily. "Why in the world would you ask that? I only met him that night, not that it's any of your business." She knew her green eyes must be tipping him off to her anger. Where did he get off coming into her house and asking personal questions?

He stared for a full minute before a smile tipped the corners of his lips. "So you only met him that night?"

"Yes." She walked to the door. "I think it might be a

good idea if you left. I've just had a grueling interrogation by the police. I don't need another one."

"I'm sorry," Mason said, his voice hinting he wasn't just blowing smoke. "I didn't mean to get off on the wrong foot with you. Actually, I came over to ask you something, and before I get your answer, I had to know if anything was going on between you and my waiter."

"There wasn't," she reassured him. "Look, Mr. Mason, I'm exhausted. I would appreciate it if you'd ask me whatever it is you came for, then go."

"Roger," he reminded her.

"Okay, Roger, can you get to the point?"

He scanned her apartment once again before his eyes settled back on hers. "Looks like you could use some new furniture around here," he said. "Money a bit tight?"

She sighed, exasperated. How many different ways could she tell this man he was out of line and no longer welcome in her apartment?

"I'll take that as a yes." He picked at an imaginary speck on his sleeve with a perfectly manicured finger before glancing back up. "You did a great job on the article about the restaurant in this week's *Globe.* I like your style, Jordan, very much."

"Thank you." She inched closer to the door. "Is that what you came by to tell me?"

For the first time, a smile covered his entire face, and he shook his head. "I came by to offer you a job."

CHAPTER 13

"A job?" Jordan repeated. "What could I possibly do for you?"

Mason pointed to the small kitchen table. "Do you mind if we sit and discuss this?"

Shaking her head, she led him to the table. When they were both seated, Mason reached into his suit jacket and pulled out a folded piece of paper.

"I pay an advertising firm in Dallas to write ads for my restaurant." He shoved the paper toward her. "Nothing fancy, just basic ad copy."

Jordan skimmed the papers before shrugging. "Looks like they do a good job."

"They do," he agreed. "But after reading your exposé about the ducks, which by the way, I'm still investigating, and your second critique of the restaurant, I had this brilliant idea. Think how much better it would be if I had the ad copy done closer to home." He paused, studying her face. "Who better to write it than the one person who seems to have created a fan base overnight? Rumor has it the newspaper's circulation has nearly doubled since you took over the Kitchen Kupboard."

"Doubled is a gross exaggeration, Mr. M—Roger," Jordan said, secretly wishing it was true.

"Nonetheless, you can't argue with your increased popularity since you started writing the column."

"I'm really not interested in changing jobs," Jordan blurted, fighting to hold back a yawn. She'd been up since the yappy dog next door had decided to serenade the world at five in the morning. She'd hoped to catch a power nap before *Castle* came on at eight.

"No one's asking you to. You could write the copy from your apartment and e-mail it to me once a week. You'd earn enough money to lighten your financial responsibilities."

Jordan's first instinct was to chastise him for butting into her business, but then she reconsidered his offer. A little extra money would be a welcome addition to her bankroll or lack thereof. Plus, it would give her something to occupy her free time and keep her mind off other problems, mainly J. T.'s murder and more recently, the phone call from Brett.

But could she work for a man who imported foie gras knowing the history behind it?

"Do you still serve foie gras at Longhorn?"

She watched his eyes harden.

"There's no way I could do that after your report, Jordan. I've taken it off the menu temporarily until we can verify your story with our supplier in Canada."

Score one for the good guys!

"I'll have to think about this, Roger. I'd need to talk to my editor."

"Why would he discourage you from making extra money doing a few hours of work in your spare time? You won't be reviewing my restaurant again now that we've been open for a few weeks." Mason stood and walked out of the kitchen, turning a complete circle to take in the entire living room.

Jordan followed, letting her eyes stray in the same path as his.

Why is he so interested in my walls? An uncomfortable feeling swirled in her stomach.

She walked to the door and opened it. "I've had a hard day, Roger. Give me some time to mull this over, and I'll get back with you in a few days."

He stared for a few seconds as if trying to figure out why she wasn't all over his offer. "Don't take too long, Jordan." He walked past her out the door. "I'd hate to see you get hurt because you waited too long to come to me," he added over his shoulder as he walked down the hall toward the front of the building.

With the door closed behind her, Jordan leaned into it and blew out a breath.

He'd hate to see her get hurt? That sounded more like a thinly veiled threat than a business offer.

She shook her head, scolding herself for being so paranoid. It must be all those cop shows she watched. Settling in front of the TV, she turned the channel and smiled when Castle's adorable face covered the screen.

A writer solving murders. Now, that was a novel idea.

Alex finished off the taco and threw the wrapper on the passenger's-side floorboard. Picking up his binoculars, he scanned the front entrance of Empire Apartments. Ever since Dumb and Dumber, the names he'd chosen for the two local cops, had entered the building, his mind had been in overdrive wondering why.

He'd stopped at Mi Quesadilla on his way home, hoping to catch a quick bite before curling up in front of the television. After an earlier phone call to his boss admitting he'd made no progress so far, all he wanted to do was chill. He'd agreed to step up the game if only to appease his boss.

When he saw the police cars racing down Main Street toward Empire Apartments, he'd followed, parking far enough away to observe what was going on without being made. Usually cops charging into a building with a piece of paper in their hands meant a warrant. He didn't know if Jordan's apartment was the one being searched, but after the weird incident with the knife he'd found behind her toaster the other day, he wouldn't be all that surprised if it was.

He remembered the way her facial expression had turned to panic when he'd questioned her about the knife rack. Things would go south in a hurry if the cops found out Ray had hidden it. The last thing he needed was having Jordan hauled off to jail before he could find out how involved she really was in all this.

A maroon Cadillac Seville caught his attention when it pulled up to the curb in front of the apartment. Slumping forward for a better look, he saw a man run from the car and head up the steps. Though he didn't get a good look, Alex was pretty sure it was the lawyer he'd met at the bar Friday night. Instinct told him this wasn't a social visit. Someone inside needed his services.

He hoped it wasn't Jordan.

Settling back in the seat, anticipating a long wait, Alex thought of ways he could up the pace on all this. With nothing solid to give him, he knew his boss wouldn't wait patiently much longer.

After the police left, he decided to hang around and see if Dozerly left, too. That would tell him if the lawyer was there for business or pleasure, remembering the way his hands were all over Rosie at the bar. He straightened up and focused the binoculars on a black Audi A8 that pulled in behind the Caddy. The curb outside the apartment was getting crowded in a hurry.

Holy crap! he mouthed, recognizing Roger Mason walking up to the brownstone.

What is he doing here in a hundred-grand car like that?

His sudden move closer to the windshield had his stomach rumbling, and he wished he hadn't inhaled that last taco. Relief would have to wait until he got home and could take some antacids because things had suddenly gotten very interesting here. His mind raced, considering all the possible explanations why the owner of Longhorn Prime Rib would pay a visit to Jordan only minutes after the police had served a warrant.

That's if Mason was actually here to see her and if it really was her apartment the police had searched.

Whatever it was, something was definitely going down.

His hope that Jordan wasn't involved was fading as fast as his initial impression that she was your average girl next door. There was nothing average about her. He'd have to find some way to break her shell to pick out the information he needed. There was no doubt he would eventually, no matter what he had to do, but time was getting critical.

He trained his binoculars on the window to the left side of the main entrance, knowing that was her apartment. Wishing he were a fly on her wall, he sighed, resigning himself to the fact he'd have to wait for the police report to satisfy his curiosity.

By Thursday, Jordan was getting desperate. She had to come up with a good recipe for Tuesday's edition. After scanning the Internet, she decided to try a taco bake. How hard could that be? You fry up ground beef, throw in a little RO*TEL and veggies, and voilà!

Then she remembered her last attempt at cooking. She'd tried a simple grilled cheese sandwich, a staple from her childhood. After calling her mother to get the recipe, she'd hopped in her car and rushed to the grocery store for the ingredients.

Who doesn't keep bread and cheese around?

And who burns a simple grilled cheese sandwich? According to Rosie, her patient instructor who tried to make her feel less incompetent, it probably hadn't been a good idea to cook it on high.

It was all too depressing, she thought, reaching into the desk drawer for her secret stash of Ho Hos. They never failed to lift her spirits. Savoring the gooey chocolate and white cream filling, she leaned back in her chair and closed her eyes, repeating her new mantra to herself. "I can cook if I put my mind to it. I can. I know I can."

"Jordan?"

Her eyes opened wide, and she nearly choked on the last bit of the chocolate treat. "Victor, what are you doing here at this time of day?"

"Hostess should pay you for advertising," he said, pointing to the three empty wrappers in her trash can before looking around. "I can't believe you don't have your own office, girl. How can you think in here?"

"It's not like I'm saving the world researching a cure for cancer." She smiled. "I write personals, Victor. Remember? On my busiest day, it doesn't take much concentration."

"You have your own column, too. Which, by the way, has everybody in town talking. How much longer do you get to do this gig?"

"Loretta is scheduled back in four weeks. I can't say I'll be that upset when she returns," Jordan said, remembering her no-recipe dilemma this week. But even as the words left her mouth, she knew it wasn't entirely true.

Despite the constant stressing before deadline, having name recognition was addictive. Just the other day, the clerk in the grocery store had made a fuss when she saw her name on the debit card.

Okay, so the lady was in her seventies, but so what?

Nobody said her fan base had to be teenyboppers. And how many people her own age picked up the newspaper and zoomed to the Food section?

"What brings you to the other side of town, Victor? You've never set foot in this place before."

He scrunched his face. "And I probably won't again. How can you stand all this"—he waved his hand around the room—"energy?"

"You get used to it. So, why aren't you at the shop?"

He flopped down on the edge of her desk. "Michael's filling in for one of the guys at the station tonight, and I'm starving since he does all the cooking. I know you're not the kitchen goddess he made you out to be, so I thought we could hang out and grab a bite." He giggled. "The kitchen goddess? What was he smoking?"

"Who's covering Yesterday's Treasures?"

"Not many people antiques-shop on a Thursday afternoon around here. And I'm the boss. I can close whenever I want." He sighed. "So, are you game for chowing down with me tonight or what?"

Jordan pretended to think about it, loving the way her friend's face turned into a pout. "Give me five minutes to close down here, and you're on," she said, figuring she'd teased him long enough.

She clicked off her computer and grabbed her purse. "Come on. Let's blow this honky-tonk."

"This really is a dungeon," Victor commented, entwining his arm in hers. "Tell your boss to spring for fluorescent lighting to brighten things up. It's a great stress reliever."

"Why do I think you just made that up to impress me?"

"I did no such thing!" He stopped to face her. "You've

seen the way my orchids thrive under it. It's got to be good for humans, and admit it, weren't you just a little impressed?"

"Sheesh! Call me gullible, but I'm impressed you're such a talented liar and can come up with anything off the top of your head and make it seem believable." She led him toward her car. "I'll drive. We can pick up your car afterward."

"That's not gonna happen, my dear. I've seen you drive. You're like Jeff Gordon on a Red Bull high." He nudged her to the other end of the lot and opened the passenger door on his T-Bird for her. "I said I was starving, not crazy."

"You got someplace in mind?" she asked, ignoring the slam on her driving skills. She did like to drive fast.

"Someplace yummy."

"And cheap?" she asked. "I'm low on funds until payday tomorrow."

"I heard that," Victor said with a laugh. "There's this hole-in-the-wall Italian joint off the beaten track in Connor that Michael and I go to every now and then. You can get really good spaghetti and meatballs with a salad and garlic bread for under eight dollars."

"Sounds excellent," she responded, thankful she'd been too busy for lunch and still had ten bucks in her wallet.

On the way to Connor, Jordan remembered she'd planned to drive to Grayson County College after work to apologize to Larry Trevelli and get her boss off her back. "What time does Michael get home tonight?"

"After ten. Why?"

Jordan hesitated. She definitely didn't want Ray to know about her amateur attempt to find J. T.'s killer but decided

Victor was a whole other story. Everything was an adventure to him. She could even bribe him into keeping her secret by volunteering to work in the antiques store for a few hours on Saturday. It wasn't like her social calendar was crammed, and she loved all the old stuff there even if she couldn't afford any of it.

"I need to run by the college to talk to the football coach for a few minutes before we eat. I can do it tomorrow after work if you don't feel up to it."

"Seriously, Jordan. Do you really think I would pass up an opportunity to check out fine young studs, all hot and sweaty in those skintight uniforms?" He glanced her way. "You couldn't tell Michael, though."

"I won't tell him if you promise not to mention this to Ray."

"Ray?"

"Don't even ask. Do we have a deal?"

Victor lifted his fist and bumped her outstretched one. "Deal. Now tell me why you need to talk to the coach. Is it about last week's game?"

Jordan straightened in her seat, her interest suddenly escalating. She could use any tidbit that might make eating crow and the fake mea culpa to Coach Trevelli a little more believable. "What about the game?"

"The Cougars played in Tyler last week against a team they were supposed to slaughter. Not only was there no bloodshed, but they were lucky to make it out of there with a win. The Dallas papers were all over it at the beginning of the week, some even saying it was doubtful the team would make the Division II championship game if they continued to play like that." He stopped at the red light and faced her. "Heard the quarterback threw three interceptions and fumbled twice. It wasn't pretty."

He had her full attention now. If she thought the coach was grumpy the first time she talked to him, she was sure he would be a bear today after all that negative publicity. She would have to turn on the charm.

"It sure made the old guy upstairs in 3A happy, though."

"What did?" Jordan asked.

"The game. Apparently he had a lot of money on the other team. I saw him Sunday morning, and he was still celebrating. Guess he made a killing when the Cougars didn't cover."

"What was the spread?" Jordan asked.

"Grayson County spotted the other team thirteen points, which was supposed to be a walk in the park for them. I guess the odds on the other team were off the charts because of it. The final score was twenty-four to twenty-one."

"Sounds like a good game," Jordan commented, wishing she could have been there to write about it and wondering if Brett had been. Was that why he'd called this week? Did he think she might have the inside scoop about what was going on at the college? It would be just like him, the lying jerk.

"Ramsey—he's the guy upstairs—drove all the way down to Tyler to watch the game. Said the Cougars smelled up the place and only scored the winning field goal in the last few seconds."

"Interesting," Jordan mused, thinking Coach Trevelli was really going to be sensitive about it.

They pulled into the parking lot at the practice field and got out of the car. A sudden feeling of dread surged through

Jordan's body at the thought of facing Derrick Young again. She'd have to take extra precautions about ticking him off, after the game he'd just had. She knew what he was capable of. And if J. T. wasn't strong enough to fight him off, Victor at five eight would be a pushover.

As soon as they were settled on the bleachers, Jordan scanned the field for Trevelli. Just when she decided he wasn't there, she saw him move out of the center of the huddle, and she gasped. He was on crutches. Deciding to go easy on him since it looked like he'd given up and had that bum knee scoped, she would simply apologize and get out of his hair. When he looked her way, she waved. Much to her surprise, he started toward them instead of dispatching security to ask her to leave.

As he hobbled to the edge of the bleachers, Jordan stole a glance at the team. When her eyes connected with those of Derrick, who was facing them, she didn't need to be any closer to feel his anger. Pasting a smile on her face, she shrugged. If she was going to play nice, she might as well go all the way. He turned back to the huddle.

"Egan mentioned you'd be stopping by," Trevelli said.

"I owe you an apology."

"Holy cow, man. What happened to you?" Victor exclaimed.

Up close, Jordan got a better look at Trevelli. This guy didn't have surgery on his knee. It looked like he'd run into a brick wall at full speed. Both eyes were black and he had a cut above his left eye with Steri-Strips holding it together. It was obvious he had some kind of rib injury by the way he splinted his right side as he lowered his body to the bleachers.

"I got mugged a few days ago," he replied, avoiding eye contact.

"Mugged?" Victor blurted. "You look like you went a few rounds with a heavyweight, bro."

Jordan glanced toward the field, where Derrick Young was again standing away from the huddle, his hands on his hips as he glared at the bleachers. The tiny hairs on her arms stood at attention at the horrible probability she was staring at a cold-blooded murderer.

CHAPTER 14

Larry Trevelli followed Jordan's eyes to the middle of the field. "Around midnight a few weeks ago I was walking to the car. I'd been studying film from our next opponent, and my mind was on the game this week. I didn't notice the guys in the shadows until they jumped out and wrestled me to the ground. Between the two of them, they roughed me up pretty good."

"You're lucky you're still around to talk about it," Victor said. "Nowadays the thugs leave no witnesses."

"My guess is they knew I wouldn't recognize them. They probably blew into Ranchero for a couple of quick scores, then disappeared. Unfortunately, the only description I could give the cops was generic—medium build, dark hair—nothing specific." He shifted his body as if sitting had suddenly become painful. Then he turned his attention to Jordan. "I take it you've thought a lot about how you disrupted my practice the other day, Ms. McAllister, and how you upset my quarterback."

Jordan hoped her eyes didn't give her away. "I have, Coach, and I'm sorry that happened. I only wanted to know if Derrick knew why his friend was coming to see me the night he was killed."

"J. T. and Derrick weren't friends. They didn't even know each other."

Jordan tried to hide the surprise she knew must be all over her face. "According to Derrick's girlfriend, they'd talked a few times."

"Are you referring to Brittney Prescott?" Trevelli snorted. "That little lady would say anything to get more of Derrick's attention. He's told me how manipulative she is."

It's hard to be manipulative when you're being used as a punching bag!

Jordan bit her tongue to keep that thought from spilling out. Her goal today was not to rile this man up again. God only knew how her boss would react if she did. "I didn't know that," she said, swallowing down the sarcastic remark she wanted to spit at him. "Brittney showed me the bruises on her arm, and apparently J. T. saw them, too. It was my understanding that's why there was a confrontation between J. T. and Derrick at the Longhorn Prime Rib the night he was killed."

Trevelli's eyes narrowed. "If there was a confrontation, Ms. McAllister, it was over and done with when Derrick explained his relationship with Brittney to J. T."

"Thought you said Derrick didn't know J. T.?" Victor chimed in.

Trevelli swung around to face him, his eyes flashing anger for a split second. "I meant the two weren't good friends."

"What happened to the team last week?"

Cringing at Victor's sudden question, Jordan focused on Trevelli's reaction. As red blotches of anger left over from the last remark crept back up his cheeks, the coach visibly struggled to maintain his cool. She'd bet those last ten bucks in her wallet his blood pressure was off the charts.

"That's what happens to a team when everybody fills their heads with how good they are and how they're gonna whup up on someone. They start believing their own rhetoric," he said, recovering quickly from his initial shock. "That and the fact that our quarterback was still shook up over Ms. McAllister's implications." He shot Jordan a look that clearly said he had neither forgotten nor forgiven her last visit to the field.

"Again, I'm sorry about that. I've been so upset since the murder I'm not myself." She realized she was laying it on pretty thick, but she was anxious to get the apology over with so they could leave. It was obvious she wasn't going to get an opportunity to talk with Derrick this time around, and her stomach was growling like a mama bear protecting her cubs.

Not to mention there was a plate of spaghetti and meatballs with her name on it waiting in some cheap dive across town.

To her surprise, Trevelli's face softened. After he struggled to an upright position, he put his hand on her shoulder. "That's understandable. If you want, you and I can continue this conversation over a cup of coffee or a drink.

Right now I have to get back on the field unless I want a repeat of the debacle last Saturday."

"The bookmakers are calling you the underdogs this week for the first time in two years," Victor said, standing up before reaching for Jordan's hand to help her.

Trevelli smiled. "If you have any extra money lying around, you might want to bet it on the Cougars. No way we're coming out losers this week." He turned and headed toward the team. "I'll call you about that drink, Jordan," he said over his shoulder.

Jordan? When did she say he could call her by her first name? "That would be great, Coach." The phony smile strained her muscles.

Back in the car, Victor turned to her. "So, are you going to have that drinkie-poo with him?"

She huffed. "Didn't you notice that white circle around his tanned ring finger?"

"Oh, yeah. Not much I miss with these eagle eyes. I just wondered if you had."

"The first time we talked."

"I'll get the skinny on him from Michael. He went to college here and knows everything about everybody." Victor drove several blocks before turning into the parking lot at the Italian restaurant. "Come on, honey. All those tight ends made me ravenous."

Jordan made it through the rest of the week without another summons to Egan's office. Figuring Larry Trevelli must have bought her pseudo-apology, she applauded her own self restraint. She'd wanted to take him to task when he'd tried to make Brittney out to be the bad guy, but that wasn't the time or the place to set him straight.

At the thought of the young girl, she remembered intending to have another talk with her to convince her to go to her parents about what Derrick had done to her.

Lounging in her pajamas and sipping coffee, she took her time reading the *Ranchero Globe*. That only made her anxiety level rise, thinking about Tuesday's deadline for a new recipe. She'd have to waste the weekend surfing the Internet or, worst case scenario, come up with Plan B.

She'd meant to use whatever Rosie served last night at potluck, but her friend had spent the day at the racetrack with Quincy Dozerly and didn't have time to cook. Dinner had been an extra-cheese pizza from Guido's and a tray of peach cobbler from Myrtle's Diner.

Much to Jordan's dismay, the lawyer was fast becoming a regular at their Friday night get-togethers. Although she was now less annoyed when he was around, she still wished it was just the old gang getting together like it used to be. But even she couldn't deny that Rosie was bubblier than ever when she was with Quincy, both acting like teenagers laughing at each other's jokes. As Rosie's friend, Jordan would tolerate the guy and hope she didn't need to count on him to keep her out of Grayson County Jail.

She walked to the kitchen and poured her second cup of coffee from the four-cup machine she'd invested in her first day as a Ranchero resident. Her dad may not have taught her how to make eggs Benedict, but he'd passed on his talent for brewing the best cup of joe in all of Texas.

Curling up on the couch, Jordan knew she couldn't put off calling Brittney any longer and picked up the phone book. As luck would have it, Eric Prescott was listed. Since she remembered that was Brittney's brother's name, she took a chance. After dialing the number, she waited, and when an older voice answered, she asked for Brittney.

"She's at school setting up for tonight's dance," the woman said.

"Are you her mother?"

"Yes, why?"

Jordan debated only a minute before making her decision. "Mrs. Prescott, I'm Jordan McAllister from the *Globe*. I spoke with Brittney last week about J. T. Spencer." She paused, wondering how to say it. "Did you know Brittney is being abused?"

Jordan heard the sharp intake of breath on the other end. "What do you mean abused?"

"Talk to your daughter about Derrick Young. If she won't open up to you, call me back. I'd like to give her the opportunity to tell you first."

There was a long silence before the woman thanked her and hung up.

Hopefully, she'd opened up a dialogue between Brittney and her parents, who would know what to do next. After seeing Larry Trevelli's injuries, she knew it couldn't wait any longer despite the coach's insistence he'd been mugged.

She settled back on the couch, not quite ready to get up and face the world. Saturday had always been her favorite day of the week. Still was. It was the only day she allowed herself to be lazy, sometimes staying in pj's all day, catching up on reading, television, or just taking cat naps.

When the doorbell rang, she jumped, annoyed with whoever had the nerve to disturb her at ten in the morning on *her* day. The front door of Empire Apartments was clearly posted with NO SOLICITATION, but every now and then a zealous salesperson or religious advocate braved the wrath of the residents and ignored the sign.

"What are you doing here?" she asked when she opened the door.

"That's a warm welcome, for sure." Alex responded, a glint of mischief in his eyes. "Nice jammies," he said over his shoulder as he walked past her into the kitchen carrying a glass dish.

Jordan's hands automatically crossed over her chest, this time out of actual apprehension rather than modesty. "Why are you here?" she repeated.

"Let's face it, Jordan. You are no Emeril in the kitchen. I thought it was about time I showed you how living in a houseful of women paid off."

Her eyes drifted to the dish he'd placed on the counter as he lifted the lid. Whatever it was, it smelled delicious. "I can cook," she said, defensively.

He laughed out loud. "I don't think Pop-Tarts count as cooking."

She opened her mouth to protest, then thought better of it. "I'm sure in some cultures, they do," she said, defiantly, moving closer to the counter. "What'd you bring?"

"My mother's favorite recipe—Tex-Mex Breakfast Casserole. She fixed it every holiday when we were all together. I called last night for the recipe and whipped it up this morning. Impressed?"

Despite herself, she smiled. "How can I be impressed when I haven't even tasted it yet?"

His eyes trailed down her body, making her suddenly

wish for a blanket. She had on a pair of baby-doll pajamas Brett had given her for Christmas last year and was sure the color of her cheeks now matched the hot pink of the sheer fabric. With her whirlwind week, she hadn't done the laundry yet, and the pajamas had been a last resort.

"Like what you see?" she asked boldly, determined not to give him the satisfaction of knowing she was embarrassed.

"Oh yeah!" he said, his eyes rising to her face.

Crap!

She didn't have to look to know her face had changed from pink to red in record time, and she sprinted to the bedroom. Hurriedly, she threw on a pair of jeans and a lightweight sweater. When she returned to the kitchen, he handed her a plate before rooting around in a drawer and coming up with a fork to go with it.

"Sit down and eat while it's still hot. Mom always said there was nothing worse than cold eggs." He opened the cabinet above the sink. "Got any glasses?"

"Of course I do," she fired back with as much indignation as she could. In truth, the only ones she had were the plastic cups from Pizza Palace. "Let me put on a fresh pot of coffee," she offered.

"Already done. Sit down and eat, Jordan. I'll bring your juice."

She sighed, knowing he was about to discover the extent of her incompetence in the kitchen. "Sorry. No juice."

Pulling a container from the bag he'd brought with him, he poured the orange juice into the Pizza Palace cups. He brought them to the table and set one in front of her before bending over and kissing her cheek. "Who doesn't have juice in the fridge?"

"I usually run to Mickey D's for a breakfast burrito."

"Why doesn't that surprise me?" He sat down opposite her and attacked the food on his plate. "Remember about those cold eggs," he cautioned in between bites.

Jordan picked up the fork and took a small taste under his watchful eyes. Then she scooped a larger bite and started cleaning her plate. Whatever this dish was, it was excellent, and she finished off her serving.

"You made this?"

"Just this morning. Looks like you approve," he said, obviously pleased.

"I hate it," she deadpanned, handing him the empty plate. "This time, don't be so stingy."

After he refilled her plate and set it in front of her again, she thought of a brilliant idea. "What's in this dish, Alex?"

"If I told you, I'd have to kill you."

She felt her face fall. For a minute, she'd hoped his Tex-Mex dish might be the answer to her prayers.

"Just kidding. It's got eggs, sausage, bread, a little milk, and lots of hot-pepper cheese. Why?"

She licked her lips after swallowing the last bite. "I think this would make a great recipe for my column this week."

"Really?" His eyes lit up with excitement. "I thought you only printed fancy recipes."

She tried not to look desperate. "I'll have Victor come up with a Spanish name for it. For some reason people think it's gourmet food if it has a foreign name." She paused. "It would be a big hit."

He wrinkled his eyes in thought. "Tejano Casserole Desayuno."

"Excuse me?"

"That's my very own translation for Tex-Mex Breakfast Casserole." He puffed his chest out. "I took Spanish in college," he explained when she stared at him.

"Can you get this recipe to me by Monday morning?"

"I will if you tell me why the cops were here the other day."

She gasped. The only way he could have known that was if he'd sent them. "You tell me."

"How would I know? I only heard it on the police scanner in . . ." He paused, as if he had just said something he wished he could take back. "I got a scanner for my car when I moved here so I wouldn't die of boredom. It's a hoot hearing the calls for stranded cats and drunken rednecks. One time a girl called to report the clerk at the pharmacy wouldn't sell her condoms. Seems her mother had paid the worker. Guess it was her idea of birth control for her daughter." His smile faded. "So, what about the cops?"

Jordan wanted to believe he wasn't the one who tipped off the cops, but she couldn't. The only people besides Alex who'd known she had a knife missing from the set were her friends and Quincy Dozerly.

Her friends would never sell her out, and Dozerly was her lawyer, for Pete's sake.

Suddenly, she remembered how quickly Quincy had appeared like a bloody savior the day the police showed up with the warrant. Since none of her neighbors even knew the cops had been there until after they'd gone, how did he get the word she might need legal help?

Her thoughts were interrupted by a sudden knock at her door.

Geez! Doesn't anybody know this is a Saturday?

She opened the door, prepared to give whoever it was a piece of her mind. Saturday morning interruptions were worse than telemarketers calling at dinnertime.

Instead, her mouth gaped open and she was speechless for one of the few times in her life.

"You look great, Jordan. You gonna invite me in or what?"

Still unable to find her voice, she motioned for him to come in. He walked past into the living room just as Alex sauntered out of the kitchen, a dish towel over his shoulder and soapsuds up both arms.

For a few seconds, the two men glared at each other, and a flash of guilt coursed through Jordan's body as if she'd been caught cheating.

"Alex, this is Brett Wilson, my ex-fiancé."

CHAPTER 15

"Is this the guy you're seeing now?"

Jordan stiffened, mentally kicking herself for lying about that the other day on the phone.

"Yeah, I'm the guy." Alex squeezed between them, extending his hand. "Alex Montgomery." He gripped Brett's hand hard enough to make him wince. "Funny, she never mentioned you."

Brett turned beet red. Pulling his hand out of Alex's death grip, he turned back to Jordan. "Can we talk somewhere"—he glanced over his shoulder before icing her with his gaze—"private?"

"There's nothing to talk about, Brett. I'm afraid you drove all the way out here for nothing."

She avoided looking directly into his eyes. Although time had eased most of the pain of his rejection, he still had that boy-next-door appeal, though his appearance had changed since she'd seen him last. His hair was longer, his blond locks touching his earlobes with a hint of a curl, and his face, too pretty to be a man's, sported a five-o'clock shadow.

Dang! The *Miami Vice* look was hot on him!

When she finally met his stare, his eyes were squinted like he couldn't believe she was brushing him off.

And why did that surprise her? He'd always been able to flash that big-man-on-campus smile and soften her up, even when she was so mad at him she'd sworn hell would freeze over before she gave him another chance.

Hell had become an ice-skating rink in the last two years.

"I didn't come all this way just to talk to you," he said, obviously soothing his injured ego. "I have a one o'clock interview with Derrick Young, the quarterback . . ."

"I know who he is, Brett. This is my neck of the woods, remember?"

"Last I heard, you were writing personals, Jordan. I figured you were out of touch with the local sports." Brett touched her upper arm, massaging the soft flesh with his fingertip. "I talked to my boss, and he mentioned there might be a position available for you on his team. Of course, it would only be entry level—for a while—but it would definitely be a step up from this place."

Ouch! If he'd intended to knock her down a few notches with that remark, it had worked. No way did she have a comeback after that.

Alex moved to her side in a few strides. "You must really be good at your job, Brett, if you've been sent way out here to interview someone at a no-name school like Grayson County College."

Brett recoiled, and Jordan realized Alex's barb had hit a little too close to home. When she and Brett had arrived in Dallas, he was hailed as the heir apparent to Jason Wimberley, NBC's hottest sports anchor. Apparently, he'd fallen out of someone's good graces as Alex had implied. She wondered if it had anything to do with little Suzie Sunshine, his weather girl. As curious as Jordan was, she wasn't about to give him the satisfaction of thinking she cared enough to ask.

"The kid's the topic of the day on all the sports talk shows in Dallas," Brett said defensively. "They're even discussing his sudden decline this past season on a few national programs."

At the mention of Derrick again, Jordan's interest was piqued, and she decided finding out if Brett could shed some light on the quarterback was worth indulging him. "What do you mean decline?" For whatever reason, some men responded better if they thought they were dealing with a dumb female. Brett was one of those guys.

She'd play that role if she had to.

"Ever since the team's big loss at the Division II championship last year, it seems like his head isn't in the game." The grin had returned to his face as he was suddenly center stage.

Hiding the smile of victory for knowing him so well, Jordan plunged ahead. "Did you know he signed with Grayson County because of some scandal back home in San Antonio?" She was fishing, but if he thought she knew more than she really did, maybe he'd blurt out something she could use as leverage the next time she faced Derrick.

She glanced Alex's way to find him staring at her, his eyebrows meeting in a perfect V at the top of his nose.

"That's what I heard," Brett responded. "It's one of the things I plan to ask him about."

"I've been told he has anger management issues." Jordan stopped short of adding, *And he just might be a killer.* As mad as she still was at Brett for dumping her, she couldn't let him go into the interview without knowing he might not leave in one piece if he said something Derrick didn't like.

Alex eyed her suspiciously. "How do you know so much about him?"

"Michael told me," she lied, before turning back to Brett. "He's my landlord and Grayson County College is his alma mater. Since he's privy to insider information, he found out the only reason the team was lucky enough to nail Derrick down with a letter of intent on signing day was because none of the bigger schools would touch him." She'd pulled that lie out of nowhere and now waited for the surprise to show up on Brett's face.

"That's because something happened two months before he graduated," Brett fired back.

"What?" Jordan gasped, unable to hide her shock. She knew the kid had a problem with anger and wondered if that something that happened with Derrick had anything to do with his short fuse.

"It was hush-hush," Brett continued. "Even my boss hasn't been able to find out the details."

There was little doubt in Jordan's mind Derrick had killed J. T. and even less that his anger was the reason he had been scratched from the recruit lists of most of the bigger universities.

"So, Jordan, will you at least consider what we talked about on the phone?" Brett moved closer, his voice barely a whisper now.

"You speak English, Wilson? The lady said she's moved on." Alex stood beside Brett, legs apart, hands on hips in the all-too-familiar testosterone-challenge stance.

If growing up with brothers had taught her anything about men, it was recognizing the warning signs that fists were about to fly. She edged her body between the two of them and gently pushed Alex back. "Give us a few minutes, please. I'll walk Brett to the door."

Alex released a long sigh, his eyes darting back and forth between Jordan and Brett. Finally, he reached for the dish towel draped over his shoulder and turned toward the kitchen. "I'll finish up in here."

Jordan peeked up at the clock. "You've got just enough time to grab a quick home-cooked lunch at Myrtle's Diner on Main Street, Brett."

"What about—"

She put her fingers to his lips. "Sometimes things work out the way they're supposed to." She nudged him toward the door before lifting up on tiptoes to brush her lips across his cheek. "Take care of yourself, Brett, and be careful with Derrick."

As if he finally grasped that she'd made up her mind, he nodded. "You know where to find me if you ever need anything." Without another word, he turned and left.

Jordan stood facing the door for several seconds after he was gone. Although she was sad, she knew she'd done the right thing by letting him go. It would have been so easy to fall into his arms and go back to what they'd had.

But it wouldn't have lasted. The troubling signs had been there even before they'd graduated, but she'd chosen to ignore them. They were different people now. When she'd first wandered into Ranchero with no friends, no family to support her, and no one to cuddle up with at night, she'd thought she would be miserable.

But she wasn't. She loved the small town, loved her new friends who were so different from any others she'd had. For the first time, she understood the meaning of unconditional love, knowing these people had her back no matter what. Although her dreams of writing a sports column would never die, she'd even begun to like her new job.

Yes, Ranchero had turned out to be a blessing.

"Thought you could use one of these."

She turned and smiled as Alex handed her an éclair and a fresh cup of coffee.

"I was saving them for a rainy day," he joked, grinning like a teenager who'd just heard the most popular girl in school say yes to his invitation to the homecoming dance. "Looks like today might be wet."

So, he'd been eavesdropping.

Jordan reached for the pastry, her eyes never leaving his. She hadn't quite figured him out yet, but there was no way she'd turn down chocolate. "Why'd you say you were the new guy I'm seeing?"

He laughed. "Your old boyfriend looked like the kind who would be hard to convince. What's your story with him, anyway?"

It was her turn to laugh. If she didn't know better, she

might have interpreted his facial expression as jealousy. "College sweetheart," she started. "Things didn't work out after we moved to Dallas together."

"Is that how you ended up in Ranchero?"

She was surprised that talking about it no longer upset her like it used to. "Yes. Now enough with all the questions. I need sugar." She settled on the couch, careful not to spill the coffee.

Alex reached for the remote and clicked on the TV, settling in the chair opposite her. "I've been invited to play a round of golf this afternoon in McKinley. Mind if I check to see if rain is still in the forecast?" He flipped through the channels, searching the four Dallas stations to see if anybody was talking about the weather.

"Stop!" she shouted. "Go back to that last one."

With a question in his eyes, he clicked back as a man's photo flashed on the screen.

"Oh no!" she said in a half whisper as she leaned forward on the couch. "That's him."

"Who?"

She focused on the picture to be absolutely sure she wasn't mistaken. "Ducky."

Alex got up from the chair and plopped down on the couch beside her. "Who's Ducky?"

"Shh," she admonished. "I want to hear." After grabbing the remote out of his hand, she turned up the volume just as the camera switched to the reporter.

"Joseph Parker, an Oklahoma City businessman, was found dead this morning in a remote area of Rochester Ranch, fifteen miles east of Ranchero near Lake Texoma, by a group of men in a helicopter. According to the coro-

ner, Parker had been dead for several days, his body ravaged by what looks to be feral hogs. Police say he was shot at close range and apparently dumped in the area, well known to hunters across the state. Positive identification was made by his sister, who was unable to offer any clues about the murder. Local police will work with officers from Oklahoma City, where the man is being investigated on an unrelated assault charge."

Jordan stared at the close-up of Joseph Parker, her mind racing. Although she'd only spoken to him a few minutes the first night she visited Longhorn Prime Rib, there was something about seeing his picture that nagged at her. She racked her brain but came up empty.

"How do you know this man, Jordan?"

"I talked to him about foie gras the night I reviewed the restaurant. He was angry with the bartender about something and—" Her hand flew to her mouth.

"What?" Alex moved closer.

"The eyes! How could I forget them?" She turned away from the screen to face Alex. "He's the man who was hiding in the shadows the night you brought me home from the karaoke bar."

The minute Alex slid into the front seat, he reached for his phone.

"Ranchero Police Department," a cheery voice answered.

"Sheriff Delaney, please."

"He's in a meeting. Can I have him call you back?"

Dammit! Alex needed information now. He blew out a frustrated breath, knowing there was nothing more he could do but wait. "No, I'll call later. What time do you expect him to be available?"

"Hard to tell. He's with the mayor."

I'm sure he is!

Alex thanked her and hung up, then started the car. In the past three weeks Ranchero had seen two murders. That number equaled the total from the last fifteen years combined if you counted the restaurant co-owner several months before. Add that to the homicide ten years ago when an old rancher shot and killed his neighbor over a property line dispute and that was pretty much it.

He'd done his homework before coming to Ranchero. The good country folks in this small town were probably more than a little spooked about the killings right in their own backyard and no doubt had deluged the mayor's office with frantic calls. Alex imagined that was the reason Delaney was locked in a room with the mayor right now, probably debating whether it was time to call in the big dogs.

That would definitely complicate his life.

He pulled away from the curb, glancing one last time at the window to the left of the building's entrance.

Jordan's window.

He smiled, remembering the way she'd scarfed down the breakfast casserole. For someone who liked to eat as much as she did, she seemed totally out of her comfort zone in the kitchen. He wondered how she managed to pull off the gig as a culinary expert before he remembered how good she was at deceiving people.

Him in particular.

If what he suspected was true, why had Joseph Parker hidden under the stairwell that night when they'd come home from the bar? Was he looking to get rid of her, and if so, why? Had she double-crossed him?

As he turned into the lot at his own apartment building, he realized he'd have to wait on those answers but hopefully not for long. If results weren't forthcoming, he'd be pulled from the assignment. He wasn't ready to give up just yet. He still hadn't figured out exactly what game Jordan McAllister was playing, but if his hunch was right, she just might get that sexy little caboose of hers in a heap of trouble—or worse.

Something about that woman made him gravitate toward her like a bear to a honeycomb. He needed more time to investigate those feelings even though the probability of things not ending well loomed high.

When it was all said and done, he suspected Jordan McAllister would not come away unscathed.

CHAPTER 16

"Hello."

This was the third time today Jordan had picked up the phone and heard heavy breathing. "Okay, the joke's over. When I hang up, I'm calling the police. Not only do I have your number, but I also have your picture flashing across my computer, you little creep. Call up one of your idiot buddies and bother them."

She clicked the phone off, hoping the kid bought the lie about the computer image. She wasn't even sure it was possible, but unless he was computer-savvy, he wouldn't know, either.

Sheesh! It would be just my luck to get a heavy breather in geek's clothing.

She slumped on the couch and grabbed another slice of the pizza she'd picked up at Guido's on the way home. Saturday nights you got a large three-topping thick crust with a liter of soda for under seven bucks. As much as she loved pizza when it was hot, eating it right out of the refrigerator was her all-time favorite. This under-seven-dollar investment would feed her all weekend.

When the phone rang, she leaned over to check caller ID. The same number as the last three times! She picked it up and powered it off, slamming it down with such force the end table shook. Apparently, the little nerd did know computers and figured out she was bluffing about calling the cops.

She eased back into the cushion, determined not to let a pimply-faced prankster ruin her night. Grabbing the remote, she clicked on the television, about the same time her lights went out.

Crap!

Swallowing the mouthful of pizza, she placed what was left of the slice back in the box and headed to the bedroom for the flashlight in her nightstand, feeling her way around the couch.

Halfway there, she heard a faint noise outside her door and stopped to listen. Turning in that direction, she couldn't stop the chill that started at the base of her spine and traveled north.

What if her caller wasn't a preadolescent kid having a laugh with his friends at her expense? What if someone was scoping out the place to ransack it again?

She shook her head to clear those thoughts, scolding herself for freaking out. Ranchero had power outages all the time, lasting anywhere from a few seconds to several minutes. And although the blackouts were hell on electrical appliances, they usually didn't cause the suffocating fear gripping her now.

She told herself this was just another blackout, glancing toward the clock above the archway separating the living room and the kitchen. Unable to see, she waited, expecting the lights to come back on any second now. She jumped when she heard a knock at the door.

Her imagination in overdrive, she ran to the kitchen to get the iron skillet her mother had given her to make corn bread. Anyone who knew her saw the absurdity in that gift, but apparently her mother had a guilty conscience for turning her over to the males in the family. Maybe she'd thought having the skillet would inspire her to suddenly become culinary.

But corn bread? Why would she go to all the trouble to make it when she could get it at Popeyes anytime she needed a reminder of home?

When there was another knock at the door, Jordan ran over and stood behind it, the skillet above her head. The pitch black house was silent, exaggerating the sound of a scraping noise on the other side.

Someone was trying to pick the lock. She sucked in a breath and held it as her heart pounded out of her chest.

When she heard the telltale click that said the intruder had succeeded, she bit her lower lip to stifle the scream. Pushing her body as close to the wall as she could, she waited. The figure of a man, outlined by the flashlight he carried, eased into her apartment. With all the strength she could muster, she brought the skillet down on his head, moving out of the way when he crumpled to the floor, facedown. A trickle of light from the flashlight he'd carried outlined the back of his head.

She had just knocked Alex unconscious.

Her senses warned her to get help, but first she had to get out of there before he woke up and finished what he'd come to do.

She inched her way around his sprawled-out body and was almost out the door when a hand on her shoulder pushed her back into the apartment.

"Going somewhere, Jordan?"

Although she couldn't see his face, she recognized the voice and the citrus-smelling cologne, could even picture the dark blue tailor-made suit he was probably wearing. "Roger! What are you doing here?"

She heard him slam the door, then lock it. Instinctively, she backed up toward the kitchen, trying to put space between them.

"You shouldn't have hit your boyfriend so hard. He'll have one nasty headache in the morning."

"What do you want?" she repeated.

He laughed, low and dirty, and for a split second Jordan wondered if she was alone in her apartment with a pervert.

"I have herpes," she blurted. She'd heard a cop talk about saying that on some show giving pointers on how to ward off a potential sexual offender.

This time his laugh was really slimy and made her skin crawl. "You think I came here to rape you?"

Her mind raced. If not that, then what? She took another step backward, hoping he wouldn't notice.

If only she could make it to the kitchen and the knife rack . . .

"As inviting as that sounds, Jordan, you and I have another matter to discuss."

"What other matter?"

"Don't play coy with me. I'm a patient man, but even I have my limits."

She was almost to the kitchen now. Just a few more steps and she'd be close enough to the sink and the knives. She had to keep him distracted. "Help me understand what you want."

When her back touched the edge of the counter, she turned and fumbled for the rack, for the biggest blade. Her scream echoed through the darkened apartment when he grabbed her from behind and jerked her away from the counter. Her five-eight frame was no match for him.

"I thought you were smarter than that." He huffed. "You don't think I'd turn out the lights without wearing night goggles now, do you?"

She twisted in his arms, but he was much stronger than she gave him credit for. Pulling her leg up to back-kick him in the groin, she lunged just as he released her. When she fell forward, her hip caught the corner of the counter and she groaned in pain. Frantically, she swept her arms across the top, searching for the knife rack.

"Looking for these?" he asked before throwing them into the living room.

Glass splintered when the heavy wooden rack connected with the lamp on the end table. Jordan opened her mouth, but the scream settled in her throat, choking off the air to her lungs.

As Mason's bone-chilling laugh vibrated in the room, someone pounded on her door.

"Jordan, are you okay?"

"Ray, help me," she hollered before Mason grabbed her again, covering her mouth with his hand.

The sound of Ray's foot connecting with the door startled Mason, and he pushed Jordan toward the window that opened on the side of the apartment. After karate-kicking the pane out, he shoved her through, still keeping her close, so close she felt his heart beating.

Once outside, he shoved her across the side lawn, through the neighbor's yard, and around the corner. When he came to a black Audi, he freed one hand and clicked the key to open the trunk.

With one swoop he picked her up and swung her in, slamming the door before she could catch her breath. When she heard the engine start, she screamed as loud as she could, knowing if Mason got away with her, there was no way anybody could help. As she kicked frantically at the trunk door, tears gushed down her cheeks. She was in the hands of a madman who wanted something from her she couldn't give because she had no clue what that something was.

Silently, she said the Lord's Prayer.

Alex awoke with a start when cold water hit him in the face. "What the—"

"Where's Jordan?"

He pulled himself into a sitting position as a throbbing pain seared across his forehead. Reaching up, he felt a goose egg and suddenly remembered how he'd gotten it.

"Call 911. Tell them Jordan's missing." He tried to stand but fell backward as his vision blurred. "He's got her."

"Who's got her?" Lola asked, coming up behind Ray, her eyes scanning the room. "Oh God, Ray, what's happened here?"

He patted her shoulder. "That's what I intend to find out." He turned back to Alex. "Start talking, Montgomery, and fast."

Alex closed his eyes, willing the room to stop spinning. In the background, he heard Lola on the phone with the 911 operator, her voice frantic.

"We don't know where she is. No, we didn't see who took her, but she called for help before she disappeared."

"One last time, Montgomery. Where's Jordan?" Ray demanded, poking Alex with the flashlight.

Alex took a deep breath and opened his eyes. "I don't know. I thought she might be in trouble and knocked on the door. When it opened, someone clobbered me." He turned away as Ray directed the flashlight on him.

"What made you think Jordan needed help in the first place?"

Alex sighed. He should weigh his words carefully and not blow the whole operation, but Jordan was in trouble. "Tell the cops Mason's in a black Audi A8."

"Mason? What's he got to do with this?"

"I think he's got Jordan." Alex made another attempt to stand and this time managed a sitting position. "Help me up. I have to go after her."

Ray reached down and pushed his shoulder, sending him back to the floor. "You're not going anywhere until you tell us what happened to Jordan." He slapped what was left of the door with his fist. "Dammit, man. Focus!"

As if by magic, the lights came on, causing Alex to squint in the brightness. One glance around the apartment was enough for him to know his worst fears were true. Jordan was in danger, and whether she was involved or not, he had to find her. He couldn't do that without at least telling these people some of what he knew.

"When the lights went off, I panicked and ran in here."

Ray eyed him suspiciously. "Jordan never leaves her door unlocked."

Busted!

The truth was he'd been following Roger Mason since he'd left his house near the Connor–Ranchero border, hoping to trip him up. Since he'd made his presence more obvious the other day in an attempt to step things up, he'd felt sure the man would slip up under the pressure.

He should have known better. Mason was a professional. It would take more that a little intimidation to crack him.

When the restaurant owner parked his car a block from Jordan's apartment, Alex had assumed his first impression of her innocent involvement had been right on the money. Then he wondered if he'd been fooled by her naive persona. Wondered if perhaps she could be the one actually calling the shots.

It wouldn't be the first time he'd been fooled by a woman.

After Mason exited the car and snaked through the backyard of the house on the corner, Alex had lost him and trained his binoculars instead on the light in Jordan's window. From that angle, he'd known he would probably only see shadows, but at least he'd finally have a connection between the two.

For some reason, he brushed off the earlier notion that Jordan was a pro. Usually sidekicks like her were easy to flip. He was convinced he would have her spilling everything from those full, pouty lips in no time, an hour tops.

At the thought of her lips and how they'd felt on his when she'd kissed him, he shook his head. For a moment he wondered if Lola's prediction of finding someone special might come true. She said that would happen soon in his life.

Part of him wanted that to be Jordan. She was definitely special, and he hated that he would have to be the one to bring her down.

"Sweet Jesus! What happened here? Where's Jordan?" Rosie screamed, running into the apartment with Quincy Dozerly on her heels.

Lola wrapped her arm around Rosie's shoulder. "We don't know, but she's in trouble. Ray walked out into the hallway when the lights went out to see if it was just us or if everyone else lost power. When he heard a loud crash from her apartment, he knocked, and she cried out. That's when he kicked in the door."

"Oh dear! Are the police on the way?" When Lola nodded, Rosie spotted Alex. "Why's he on the floor?"

Before anyone could answer, Victor ran into the apartment. "The fuse box was a mess and—" He scanned the room, taking in the shattered lamp and the block of wood that had dented the wall. "Geez, Louise!" He turned to Ray and held out something pink and furry. "Do we need these?"

"What the hell are they?" Ray asked.

"Handcuffs, darling." Victor turned to Alex. "Put your hands behind your head."

"Not in this lifetime!" Alex glared, daring him to try to put those things on him. "I've got to go after Mason."

All eyes turned on him.

"The owner of Longhorn Prime Rib?" Victor asked. "How's he involved in all this? He offered Jordan a job last week."

This was news to Alex. She hadn't mentioned it the other night. "Did she take it?"

"No," Rosie chimed in. "For some reason she doesn't trust the guy. I never could figurc out why. Quincy and I had drinks with him at the racetrack the other day. He seems like a really nice man."

Alex tried to stand and this time made it with help from Victor and Michael. He rubbed the bump on his head, knowing he should put an ice pack on it. But he was beginning to get a really bad feeling about this. "Call the police station and ask for Sheriff Delaney. Tell him Mason has Jordan. I'll call him in the car with details."

He took a deep breath and leaned against the wall. When he was sure he was steady on his feet, he made his way toward the door.

"Where are you going, Alex?"

"To find Jordan before—" As soon as the words left his mouth, it hit him.

It might already be too late.

CHAPTER 17

Curled in a ball in the small trunk, Jordan shifted her weight to knead the cramp knotted in her calf. Without a watch, she could only guess they'd been traveling for about thirty minutes. Realizing no one could hear her, she'd stopped screaming soon after the car pulled away from the curb. She had no idea where Mason was taking her or why he wanted her in the first place.

Reaching up to stabilize her body when the car suddenly turned onto what she thought must be the bumpiest road in Texas, she pondered her dilemma. She racked her brain, but the only thing she could come up with was the initial lousy review she'd given his restaurant and the fact that she'd turned down his job offer.

Neither was enough for him to assault and kidnap her. She'd since written a glowing report on the Rattlesnake Pasta, and he hadn't seemed bent out of shape when she'd declined his freelance writing opportunity. She'd used a phony excuse about the newspaper frowning on extracurricular stuff. But even though he'd smiled, he'd mentioned again that his patience was wearing thin. She had no idea what that meant.

The man gave her the creeps, but she hadn't realized it soon enough. He'd already said he wasn't interested in sex, so why kidnap her and drive to God-only-knew where?

What if he was simply a psychopath who enjoyed killing for the thrill of it? She swallowed hard, trying not to cry. She had to keep her senses about her and find a way to get out of this alive.

Her stomach caught in her throat when she realized the car was no longer moving. In the overwhelming silence, she was positive she heard her own heart pounding. When the car door opened and slammed, a fresh set of tears erupted while she waited for Mason to open the trunk.

When he did, her eyes locked on his hand. He had a gun and it was pointed directly at her head.

Our Father, who art . . .

"Get out, Jordan," he barked. "You and I are finally going to have that chat."

As she tried to unfold her body enough to lift herself up, he reached in and grabbed her arm.

Yanking her out of the trunk with one pull, he chuckled. "The dealer told me this trunk would hold two large duffel bags comfortably. Guess he lied."

When her head banged the lid of the trunk, she bit her lip so he wouldn't have the satisfaction of seeing how much it hurt. Mason appeared to have a sadistic streak, but she had no intentions of adding to his pleasure.

Blinking to refocus her eyes after being in the dark trunk for so long, she glanced around. With night fast approaching, the moon gave off enough light that she made out a row of trees and underbrush edging the boundaries of a field. Probably out in the boonies. "Where are we?"

When he shoved her toward the trees with the butt of the gun, she stumbled, catching herself before falling to the ground.

"Ever hear of Rochester Ranch?"

Oh God!

Rochester Ranch was a place where men from all over the country came to hunt feral hogs for sport and also where they'd found Ducky's body. Because it was so isolated, it seemed like the perfect place to leave a body, but apparently the hogs had dragged what was left of the man out into the clearing for the helicopter "warriors" to discover from the air. At the thought of Ducky's demise, Jordan's hopes of seeing another day took a dramatic nosedive.

"Are we hunting hogs tonight?" she asked sarcastically, praying he didn't hear the fear in her voice.

He laughed. "Not quite, my dear, although the pigs may have other ideas about that."

She tried not to react, instead wrapping her arms around her chest. With the sun down, the temperature had dropped, and all she was wearing was a short-sleeved T-shirt with her jeans. When they reached the line of trees, Mason grabbed both arms and spun her around to face him. For the first time, she noticed the thick rope slung over his shoulder.

"Sit down against that tree and reach backward behind it." He pointed to the biggest tree, sitting in the middle of the grove.

"What do you want, Roger?"

His dark eyebrows slanted in a frown. "It's just you and me and several hundred hungry pigs out here, Jordan. Save your little innocent act for someone else."

At the mention of the pigs, she froze, picturing front teeth sharp enough to slice a big dog in half.

Mason tightened the rope behind her back.

She cried out. Rough bark dug into her skin, and the muscles in her arms were stretched beyond their limit.

Apparently satisfied the rope would hold, he walked around and stood over her. "Now's the time to tell me where you hid them."

"Hid what?"

His eyes narrowed. Like a snake striking its prey, he pounced, slapping her sideways across the face. "Please. Don't insult my intelligence. If you think for one minute I bought your little 'I hate red meat' excuse, you're sadly mistaken. I know you went home that night with the foie gras in your purse."

Still feeling the sting of his hand, Jordan cringed as her mind raced. Surely he wasn't this angry because she didn't like a strange French dish. "What does that have to do with anything?"

He moved close enough to her face for her to detect a slight odor of garlic on his breath. "Playing dumb will only get you killed, Jordan. Is the money worth your life?" He paused. "Money you'll never see, I might add."

"Roger, I don't have a clue what you're talking about, I swear." She tried not to panic, but she was totally confused. The realization that this ranch might be the last thing she ever saw hit her like an F-5 tornado.

Roger Mason was a madman who had tied her to a tree in a pasture. No further evidence was necessary. Her chances of making it out alive were not good.

He straightened up and stared for a few seconds. "I'm willing to make a deal. Tell me what you did with them, and I'll let you live. Maybe even give you a small cut."

"What I did with what?" she shouted, unable to hide her frustration.

"The diamonds, Jordan. Where are my bloody diamonds?"

This was getting too weird. The man was totally crazed. She prayed her friends had called the cops, hoping somehow they had picked up the trail and were on their way. "Why would you think I had your diamonds?" she asked again.

"Like I said, I never believed red meat was the reason you ordered duck that night," Mason said. "J. T. said he recommended it, but I don't buy that. Was he cutting you in on the deal?"

The more he talked, the more confused she became. Why was he talking about J. T.? A horrible thought crossed her mind. "You killed him, didn't you?"

He glared. "He wanted a bigger cut. Started making threats, and I couldn't take a chance on him blowing the whole operation. We had finally found the perfect way to bring in the diamonds."

"So, why kill him in my apartment building?"

Mason shook his head, the confusion showing in his eyes. "I'm talking about Joseph Parker, the guy they found out here last week. The guy who ended up as hog food? He's the one who decided to put the squeeze on me. Who are you talking about?"

"J. T."

"Why would I kill J. T.?"

"Because he was coming to my apartment that night to warn me about you." Okay, that was a long shot, but as soon as she said it, she noticed the change in Mason's face.

"I should have known he was on to me. He asked too many questions when I approached him about you."

He turned and fired a shot into the underbrush. Three huge pigs ran out, squealing loud enough to be heard in the next county.

Jordan closed her eyes, imagining how it would feel to be ripped apart by the animals. When she opened them again, the pigs were gone and Mason was smiling.

"One last time. Where are my diamonds?"

Jordan was quickly losing hope that somehow she could talk her way out of this. Why would this man think she stole his diamonds? "Roger, you have to believe me. I don't have anything of yours."

He snorted, before his eyes hardened. "So, this is how you want to play it? Need I remind you of the description of Parker's body your newspaper printed after the pigs were done with him?"

She gasped, recalling the gruesome account.

The twinkle in Mason's eyes told her he took pleasure in her reaction.

"Did you notice the container in the trunk with you? That's hog food. When I leave I'll be sure to scatter it all around you—maybe even on you, like I did with Parker."

He turned and fired in the air again. This time four pigs ran from the brush, squealing past Jordan before they disappeared into the line of trees.

Although terrified, Jordan still didn't know why he thought she had his gems. She had to figure out a way to stall him and pray that help was on the way. "How did I get your diamonds?"

He stared, obviously trying to decide what she was up to before a hint of a smile tipped the corners of his lips. "Okay, I'll play along. Do you think for one minute I believe it was a coincidence you ordered foie gras that night?"

"Foie gras?"

He huffed. "As if you didn't know that's how we move the diamonds. I spent the better part of a year working the deal with my Canadian counterpart in the meatpacking plant up there. Every few days we served Parker the duck from specially marked cans. It was the perfect setup until you ordered it, too." He jerked his body around when another hog ran from the brush and startled him.

"How could I have known I was eating diamonds?" She had to keep him talking. The more time they wasted, the better chance of help arriving.

"I'm guessing J. T. told you after he switched the regular foie gras with the one intended for Parker. He was tight with my old partner before he was tragically killed in the robbery at the restaurant several months ago. Maybe he told J. T. about the diamonds just like he planned to tell the Feds." Mason snorted. "That's before I discovered he was getting cold feet and wanted out." He raised his eyebrows in a pleased-with-himself sort of way. "He got out, all right, just not the way he expected."

A flashback of Egan on the day she agreed to be the temporary culinary reporter came to her. He mentioned one of the owners had been killed in an after-hours robbery. "You killed your own partner?"

Mason leaned in and whispered. "He wasn't the first, nor will he be the last." He pressed the gun to her forehead. "I hope you don't wait too long to come to your senses, Jordan."

With her eyes tightly closed, expecting the shot any second, Jordan's mind raced, trying to connect the dots. "I swear I don't . . ."

An image of Maggie swimming around in her fishbowl with rhinestones flashed across Jordan's mind. They'd fallen out of the purse she'd borrowed from Rosie when she'd cleaned out the squishy duck.

Holy crap! Could they be Mason's diamonds?

Apparently reading her reaction, Mason pulled the gun away from her forehead, a smirk covering his face. "Suddenly remember something?"

Jordan fought off panic. Should she tell him about Maggie, or would that almost assure Jordan a sudden death? Why would he need to keep her around if he got his precious diamonds?

"I might be, but I'd be a fool to hand them over to you with the expectation you'd be grateful and let me go." She shook her head. "You want your diamonds, Roger? You'll have to untie me. I'll take you to them."

He reached down and slapped her again, this time with more force than the last one. "Maybe you haven't noticed, but I'm the one holding the gun."

He tapped the barrel against her forehead. "Here's how it's gonna work. You tell me where you hid the diamonds, and I'll drive back into town. After I'm sure you're not lying, I'll call the cops and tell them where they can find you."

After that, I'll bet you'll sell me some oceanfront property in Nevada!

"Sorry, no can do. If you want your precious jewels again, you'll have to take me with you." She was glad her hands were behind her back because they were shaking like the apartment washer when she overloaded it. "How much are they worth to you?"

"Like you don't already know they'll bring in a half million on the black market. Even though that's small change to me, I stand to lose more than just the money. If my Canadian investors think I'm losing control over the shipments, I might not be in business much longer." He glared. "You see my dilemma? That's why I'm giving you one more chance before I leave your fate in the hands, or should I say jaws, of the hogs."

As terrifying as that was, Jordan knew if there was even the slightest chance of living through the night, her only option was to somehow buy more time. The only thing in her favor was that Mason wanted the diamonds back and couldn't risk killing her until he found out where they were.

"You can stew out here all night thinking about my offer. I'll be back in a few hours to see if you've changed your mind."

Her gamble paid off—at least temporarily.

Satisfied she'd outsmarted him if only for a while, Jordan concentrated on slowing her breathing. This maneuver had bought her time. Surely someone would be looking for her.

She watched him slide into the front seat of the Audi and drive back through the opening in the trees. As tears threatened to spill over, she wondered how something as innocent as trying a gourmet food item on a menu had ended up so terribly wrong.

And what if the sparkly things at the bottom of Maggie's fishbowl really were Rosie's outdated crystals? Without leverage, there was no reason for Mason to keep her alive. When he came back, would he finish her off or leave her for the hogs?

Those thoughts were quickly dispelled when she caught a movement out of the corner of her eyes and watched a large pig, followed by two smaller ones, emerge from the underbrush and head directly toward her. When she screamed, the porkers turned and hightailed it back into the bushes, squealing like they were the ones tied to a tree and she was the pig with the big-ass front teeth.

Sure they weren't coming back, she relaxed her shoulders. But she feared the worst-case scenario was true—her friends had no clue where to even start looking for her. Mason had her in the trunk and out of sight before anyone knew what had happened. Taking deep breaths, she willed herself to stay positive. Struggling to break free, she twisted her hands trying to get out of the rope, but the effort only dug the twine into her flesh causing more pain.

Out of options, she hunkered down, believing there would be a miracle and somehow they would find her.

Leaning her head back, she glanced up at the sky. Without the city lights, the stars twinkled overhead like thousands of cell phones at a rock concert. An image of the Christmas manger scene where the brightest star had lit the way for the three wise men flashed across her mind. As ridiculous as that was now, it gave her a little hope.

She blew out a breath, anticipating a long night and wishing she had a sweater. But things could be worse.

Mason could have scattered the hog food around her.

CHAPTER 18

Jordan shifted, trying to get more comfortable, but it was a wasted effort. Mason had tied the ropes too tightly, which came as no surprise since she'd already decided the man was definitely a sadist walking around in custom-made Italian silk suits.

She wiggled her fingers to get the blood circulating, but the tips still tingled when she could feel them. Despairing, she gave up and pressed her back into the tree to wait for the cavalry or a knight on a white horse to show up. Shivering slightly, she guessed the temperature had dropped into the low fifties. Considering numb fingers and the fear of being attacked by monster hogs, cold was the least of her worries.

So far the pigs had stayed out of sight, but she could hear them rooting around in the bushes and occasionally got a glimpse of a brave one who ventured out of the hideout. Fortunately, they acted as if they were more afraid of her than she was of them. Her high-pitched scream would send them scurrying for cover every time one made a move to approach her. With that discovery, she reasoned Ducky must have already been dead when the animals went after the hog food Mason had piled on his body. At least she hoped that was true for his sake.

She moved her head in a circular motion, trying anything to keep from getting stiff in the cool night air. Glancing up, she said a quick thank-you for the blessing of an almost-full moon that kept the pitch black terror of the night partially at bay. She might be hallucinating, but the big melon-colored circle in the sky surrounded by the dazzling display of twinkling stars reminded her of the giant disco ball hanging in the center of the school gym at her senior prom.

An image of Joey Montero, the star wide receiver who made her dreams come true when he'd asked her to be his date, played in her head. She remembered feeling like a princess in his arms on the dance floor, the envy of just about every girl in her class. The night had been perfect.

Until he demanded she put out or get out when they were in his car on the way home.

Sheesh! Didn't guys know you can catch more bees with honey, like her mother always reminded her? That a little romance scored more points than demands?

She'd ended up walking home that night, knowing full well she'd extract her ounce of revenge after she told her brothers what happened. She didn't know what they said to him, but stud-muffin Joey had ended up apologizing to her in front of the entire student body. Thinking back to those days with her overprotective brothers, it was no wonder most of the boys in the small West Texas town had been afraid to ask her out.

She hoped it wasn't a bad omen comparing the moon overhead to that night long ago that had not ended well.

In the distance, she heard an automobile, and her entire body jerked suddenly, sending a pain rocketing up her arm to her shoulder. It was coming her way! Holding her breath, she listened as it grew louder, then nothing, only silence.

Sweet Jesus! Mason is back to kill me.

Clenching her teeth to keep the tears in check, she thought about all the things in her life she hadn't accomplished yet. Hadn't even made a "bucket list" like Jack Nicholson and Morgan Freeman in that movie. It was weird that learning how to cook stood out in her mind as something she really should have done.

She was too young to die.

As she lost the battle with her emotions, tears blurred her vision, and she said the only prayer she could remember from her Catholic school days, about forgiveness. "Oh my God, I am heartily sorry for having—"

Her scream shattered the silence of the night as a gun went off way too close for comfort. Squeezing her eyes closed, she waited.

"Jordan?"

Startled, she looked up. Someone was calling her name and it didn't sound like Mason. A flash of hope pulsed through her body. She wasn't going to die.

"Over here," she screamed, laughing and crying at the same time.

Thank you, God. You answered my prayers. My knight on a white horse has arrived.

The euphoria was short-lived, however, when she saw a man emerge from the other side of the trees.

It was Alex Montgomery, but he wasn't on a horse and he had a huge gun in his hand.

Alex cursed as he dodged another rattler. Before he could kill it, like the gigantic one he'd nearly stepped on when he'd jumped out of his car, the smaller snake slithered away into the underbrush.

He wished he'd had time to pick up the three-watt flashlight from his apartment, but he'd lost valuable time dealing with Jordan's friends. He had to make do with the small one he'd found in the glove compartment. By the time he'd finally gotten away from everyone at Empire Apartments, Mason already had a decent head start.

Thinking about Jordan's friends and Victor's fuzzy pink handcuffs brought a smile to his face. He couldn't even imagine the razzing he would have taken from his colleagues if they'd seen him with those around his wrists.

Slicing his way through the branches and the thick brush, he wished he had on hiking boots in case another rattler was curled up in his path. As long as he was wishing, having his own off-road-capable SUV would have made things a lot easier, too. He could have driven closer in and wouldn't have had to be hoofing it right now. He glanced down at Mason's tire tracks, cursing the fact that the Audi had all-wheel drive and could have been driven pretty far into the brush.

As soon as he cleared the thick line of trees and found

an opening, he scanned the pasture in the moonlight. The unmistakable snorts of hogs in the underbrush surrounding him upped the fear that he might be too late. When he'd placed the tracking device under Mason's car, he had no idea it might become key in saving someone's life. Not in his wildest dreams did he think that someone might be a woman he considered a friend.

Who am I kidding?

Although he wasn't sure exactly what it was he felt for Jordan McAllister, she was way past just-a-friend status. Against his better judgment, he'd broken his own rule about mixing business with his personal life. At least emotionally so far and maybe even physically, he thought, remembering the kiss.

When his GPS directed him almost to the Oklahoma border, he worried Mason had taken her across the state line, and he might never see her again. He'd almost missed the Audi pulling away from an out-of-sight road off Highway 82 and heading south right past him.

Unless Mason had her in the trunk or on the floorboard, Jordan was not in his car. Since he knew Mason hadn't driven all the way out here for the scenery, Alex followed his instincts and turned down the dirt road. He could flush out the restaurant owner back in town later.

A rush of apprehension washed over him as he'd passed through the gate with a sign swinging above it that read ROCHESTER RANCH. This was the same place they'd discovered Joseph Parker's body last week ravaged by wild boars. Alex quickened his step praying Jordan hadn't met the same fate as the man he suspected had been Mason's partner in crime.

When he heard her, he burst through the grove of trees into a clearing. A slight movement drew his attention to the large tree centered among several smaller ones on the back edge of the clearing. Jordan was on the ground with her hands behind her and her head slumped.

"No," he screamed, running toward her, covering the distance in only a few strides. Just as he got close, her head shot up, the terror in her eyes unmistakable.

She thinks I came to kill her.

Quickly, he shoved the gun back into the shoulder holster and bent down beside her. "Are you okay?" he whispered, noticing the dark bruise across her cheek.

She nodded as tears ran down her cheeks.

Dammit!

The sight of a woman in tears always turned his knees to jelly. It brought out every protective instinct his mother and three sisters had instilled in him. And made him do things that went against everything he'd ever learned on the job.

God help him, he was about to blow his own cover!

Pulling out his badge, he offered it to her to inspect, shining the light directly over it. "I'm a federal agent," he said simply.

Instead of screaming with delight as he'd anticipated, Jordan once again lowered her head and began to cry in silence, sniffing every few seconds in perfect synchronicity with the spasms of her shoulders.

Quickly he untied her hands and took her into his arms, cradling her in a rocking motion until the sobs, no longer silent, finally subsided. "I won't let him hurt you again," he promised, stroking her hair as she whimpered.

After a few minutes, she pulled away and looked into his eyes, the skepticism not entirely gone from her face. "Why did you break into my apartment?"

That brought back memories of the large bump on the top of his head. "I've been watching Mason for six months. I had a tracer on his car. When I saw him park down the street and head for your apartment, I panicked."

"Someone knocked, but I was afraid to open the door. I'd been getting hang-up calls and my imagination was running wild. When I heard the sound of someone picking the lock, I ran for anything to protect myself." She lowered her eyes and added softly, "I'm sorry I hit you with my iron skillet."

He chuckled. "Wouldn't you know I'd get hit with a virgin skillet? Have you ever even used that thing, Jordan?" he asked trying to inject a little humor into the situation.

"I have now," she deadpanned, her face unchanging. "So, tell me again why you broke in."

"When you didn't answer the door, I thought the worst." He clamped his mouth shut before he told her more. The less she knew about Mason, the better off she'd be when she was questioned about him.

As for Mason, slapping a kidnapping charge on him wouldn't close Alex's own investigation or solve his problems at hand. He still had nothing on the man that would hold up in court.

"You know about the diamonds?"

His heart sank. Hoping she wasn't involved was no longer an option. "We knew diamonds were being smuggled in from Sierra Leone, and all our sources seemed to think the delivery site was right here in Ranchero." He held her at arm's length. "I'll do whatever I can to make sure the judge is lenient on you for your part in it."

"My part in it? What are you talking about, Alex?"

"We'll tell him you had no idea the diamonds were illegal," he said before adding, "You can say you were an innocent bystander who got caught up in the crime."

"Are you crazy? I *am* an innocent bystander. That man was about to kill me over the dopey things. No way I was in on it with him."

He eyed her suspiciously. "Then how'd you know about the diamonds?"

"A little ducky told me."

He thought he detected a touch of sarcasm in her tone, but before he could call her on it, a sudden rustling in the underbrush caused her to scream. He reached for his weapon before realizing it was only the animals and not Mason returning to finish what he started. Still, they were getting too close.

"Let's get out of here before the pigs start checking us out." He led her to the path. "You hang on and watch your step. I've already run into a few pissed-off diamondbacks."

Jordan grabbed his shirttail and followed as instructed, her mind racing. Alex was an FBI guy? It was hard to wrap her brain around that one.

When they reached the opening on the other side of the path, she searched for Mason's Audi, half expecting the man to jump out and confront them.

"He's gone," Alex assured her, opening the door on the

passenger's side of his car. "You can tell me all about him on the ride into town."

Neither spoke as Alex wheeled the car in a 180-degree turn in the tiny area and headed back down the dirt road. Jordan still wasn't convinced she was out of danger. There were too many unanswered questions. Like why Alex thought she was in on the diamond smuggling.

Or was that just a trick to get her to tell him where the jewels were? Was he in bed with Mason and simply being the good cop to Mason's bad one? She had to keep her head on straight and stay smart about this, especially since she wasn't even sure those were diamonds in the fishbowl.

One thing she was sure of was that as long as they thought she could lead them to the diamonds, they had a reason to keep her alive.

"So, what should I call you?" Keeping the conversation away from the gems was the way to go, she decided, now that she'd had her girlie cry and shifted back into survival mode.

"What do you mean?"

"You said you were undercover. I'm guessing Alex Montgomery isn't the name your mother gave you after the doctor slapped you on the butt and handed you to her."

Okay, she was trying to be flippant but was failing miserably. When she recognized a few landmarks outside the city limits, she felt a little less worried. The closer she was to town, the more the odds of making it home safely increased. If Alex was working with Mason, at least her chances of being recognized were better with all the lights from the businesses lining Highway 82. Surely, by now, her friends had alerted the cops.

"Alex Moreland," he responded, his eyes leaving the road long enough to glance her way. "Obviously, I'm not a banker."

"Tell me about your investigation," she demanded, wanting so badly to trust him.

She watched his hands tighten on the steering wheel as if he was conflicted about telling her. Her skepticism slid into overdrive.

"They pulled me from Houston after another agent thought he had Mason's partner ready to turn and—"

"Mason is the one who killed his partner," Jordan shouted excitedly, interrupting Alex. "He also killed the guy the other night and left him with the hogs."

He gave her a sideways glance. "How do you know that? Did he tell you?" He swiveled back just in time to avoid crossing the center line.

"He knew the guy was about to blow the whistle on the operation. I thought he was talking about J. T., but he wasn't."

"Did he kill J. T., too?"

"My gut says he probably did, but he denied it. Even acted surprised I would consider it. Apparently he had a talk with J. T. the night they found him under my staircase." She stopped before she told him about the duck pâté going home in her purse.

"Did he say what the conversation was about?"

"Me."

"You?"

She heard the accusations in his voice. "Apparently he lost some of the diamonds and thought I might have them."

"Why would he think that?"

Jordan licked her lips, stalling to come up with a plausible reason without telling him about Maggie and the crystals decorating her fishbowl. She had to keep that information to herself or she would be throwing all her leverage out the window.

"I have no idea except that he mentioned the diamonds were being smuggled into the country in cans of duck liver from Canada."

Alex slapped the steering wheel so hard Jordan saw him flinch in pain.

"I knew it!" he exclaimed, the excitement in his voice evident. "That's how they made the transfer. Parker would order foie gras, slip the diamonds into his napkin when he was sure no one was looking, then enjoy the rest of his meal. Maybe even have a cocktail or two. Son of a . . ." He paused. "That's freakin' brilliant, you know."

Until someone else orders the duck and suddenly you're out a half million.

"Why would anyone go to all that trouble to bring in diamonds across the border? It's not like they're contraband or anything," Jordan said.

She heard him blow out a breath. "In some African countries, the corrupt politicians and rebels have forcibly taken over the diamond mines, using the proceeds to fund their terror campaigns. It's not unusual for the rebels to cut off a hand if they catch someone stealing one of the rocks. These conflict diamonds, or blood diamonds, as some like to call them, are sold to mercenaries who make millions on the black market."

She leaned closer to hear more.

"Several years ago, the United Nations introduced the

Kimberley Process in an attempt to make sure these conflict diamonds didn't get mixed in with the legal diamonds that aren't controlled by rebel groups. It required diamond-producing countries to provide proof the money made from the sale of the gems wasn't used to fund criminal or revolutionary activities."

Jordan shook her head. "And you're thinking these diamonds coming from Canada are blood diamonds?"

"No doubt about it," Alex said. "Obviously Mason is in cahoots with a diamond dealer up there who cuts and polishes the raw stones. That's the only way they could smuggle them in the small cans of duck liver." He sighed. "Although Canada has set up a system to better authenticate their diamonds, smuggling still remains a problem since it's still fairly easy to slip conflict diamonds out of Africa. Plus, no one suspects Canada because they're allies."

"How did you trace the diamonds to Ranchero?"

"We knew there was a Texas connection, and we'd narrowed it down to the North Texas area. Then a few months ago, we got a tip someone was willing to talk for full immunity. My partner was sent here to meet with the guy who only identified himself as Travis. One night Rocco, that's my partner, arranged to meet the man after midnight, but the guy never showed up."

"How do you know Travis was Mason's partner?" Jordan asked. This story suddenly had her full interest.

"We traced the calls to a phone inside the restaurant. After one of the owners was found dead in a suspicious robbery where very little was taken, we put two and two together, but we still had nothing solid to connect the restaurant or Mason to the smuggling. I was sent in when my boss suspected Rocco had been made. Since I have an accounting degree, it was only logical I work at the bank."

"They know you're a cop there?"

He laughed. "Only the president, and he was sworn to secrecy, although I have to tell you, he thinks I'm doing such a bang-up job, he's trying to persuade me to go legit."

Jordon pondered the information. It all made sense and explained a lot to her. She still had no idea how it was connected to J. T.'s murder except that he was the one who told Mason about how she shoved the foie gras into her purse that night.

At the thought of the duck, she made a split-second decision. "When we get to my apartment, I want to show you something."

She prayed she hadn't just signed her own death warrant.

CHAPTER 19

Propped against the window, Jordan stared at the passing landscape. Alex radioed ahead for the local police to swing by Longhorn Prime Rib and see if Mason's Audi A8 was there. When she wrapped her arms around herself, he reached and aimed the vents her way before turning on the heater.

She smiled. "I didn't realize how cold I was."

"Do you want to stop by the emergency room to check out those bruises on your face? You might have a broken bone."

Her hand shot up to touch her cheek, flinching when she made contact. "I'm okay. I'm in a hurry to get home." The thought of being surrounded by friends started her eyes watering. Sniffing, she squeezed them tightly to stop the flow before she completely lost it.

Alex pulled up to the curb in front of Empire Apartments, and both Victor and Michael rushed out the door and ran to the car.

"Geez, girl, we've been so worried," Victor said, opening her door and leaning down to hug her.

For the first time since the ordeal with Mason began, Jordan allowed herself to believe she wasn't going to die. Victor held her at arm's length and swiped the lone tear escaping down her cheek.

"I'll kill that bastard," Michael said, moving up behind her and wrapping his arms to complete the circle of love around her with Victor.

"Get in line." Alex hopped out and walked around the car to join them.

Jordan met his gaze, hoping she wasn't making a mistake. "Come on. I have something I want to show you."

Following her lead, they walked into the building, stopping in front of her apartment. She cried out, seeing into her apartment through the splintered door.

Michael squeezed her shoulder. "I've got someone coming tomorrow to fix it." He walked through then reached back for her hand like the gentleman he was.

"Are you able to talk about what happened?" Victor asked gently.

"It was Mason," Jordan replied, heading for the kitchen counter. A smile tipped her lips watching Maggie swim at full speed, oblivious to the fact her watery castle might well be decorated with five hundred thousand dollars' worth of smuggled diamonds. "Alex, come a little closer." She pointed to the fishbowl.

All three men leaned down to see.

"What are we looking for?" Michael asked, nearly falling over Victor to see.

She huffed. "You don't see those sparklers?"

"Unbelievable!" Alex exclaimed. "They've been right here all along?"

"What?" Victor shouted. "Help me out here. What's so exciting about Maggie and Rosie's rhinestones?"

Alex lifted the glass bowl for a better view then dipped his hand into the water to retrieve one of the stones. "If my hunch is right, you're looking at a diamond, Victor, not a rhinestone."

Just then, Ray barged into the apartment with Lola and Rosie close behind. "A diamond?"

Startled, Alex jumped, dropping the gem back into the fishbowl before quickly shoving his hand back in the water to get it.

Rosie ran over and grabbed Jordan, laughing and crying at the same time. "I can't tell you how hard I prayed, sweetie. I cursed God, then begged Him to bring you back to us. I ended up bargaining, promising a lot of things. Guess I'll be in church on Sundays now." She stroked Jordan's hair.

"Okay, someone enlighten me." Ray glanced at the stone in Alex's hand. "I was a cop for a lot of years, and I can tell you that a diamond in a fishbowl is usually not a good thing." He stared at Victor, waiting for an explanation.

"Don't look at me." Victor shrugged, turning to point to Alex.

Alex held up the diamond for all to see. "This little baby's why Mason has been coming around lately and why he nearly killed Jordan tonight."

Lola gasped and Rosie tightened her grip on Jordan.

"How'd they end up in Maggie's fishbowl?" Michael asked, his face expressing his utter disbelief.

Jordan pulled away and looked into Rosie's eyes. "Remember when I borrowed your purse the night I reviewed Longhorn Prime Rib?" When Rosie nodded, Jordan continued, making eye contact with each of them now. "Mason was smuggling diamonds from Canada in the duck pâté."

"Holy Lord! You found them when you cleaned out my purse that night?"

"I thought they were leftovers from your jewelry collection. Even mentioned it to you, and you said to let Maggie have them." Jordan paused, watching their faces change from unbelieving to serious captivation, as the puzzle pieces finally began to fit together.

"Oh, good grief! Is that why your apartment was ransacked?" Lola asked.

"Probably," Ray answered before turning back to Alex. "Does Mason know Jordan has these?"

"He knows," Alex said. "But he has no idea where they are. That's the only reason he kept her alive."

Again Lola gasped. "Where'd he take you, honey?" she asked, touching the bruise on Jordan's cheek. "I have some homemade salve that will help reabsorb the blood and make this less noticeable."

Jordan smiled at her friend. Leave it to Lola to worry about skin care at a time like this. "He tied me to a tree at Rochester Ranch."

A deafening silence filled the room at the mention of the site where they'd found Ducky's body.

"He left me there when I wouldn't tell him about the diamonds."

"So, you knew these were the real thing?" Rosie asked, tilting her head as if she was trying to understand.

"Not at first. When it finally dawned on me that the stones from your purse might actually be his diamonds, I was afraid to tell him. He probably would have killed me right then and there."

"Good thinking." Ray turned to Alex. "So, how did you find her? Mason got a pretty good jump on you." His eyes left no doubt he had reverted to cop mode, and he wasn't entirely convinced Alex wasn't somehow involved.

All eyes turned to Alex, who had just fished the other five gems out of the bowl and cradled them in his hand. Without a word, he tore off a paper towel sheet from the roll on the counter, wrapped the diamonds, and placed them beside the fishbowl. Pulling his wallet out of his back pocket, he flipped it open to display his badge.

"Jesus, Mary, and Joseph!" Victor exclaimed. "He's a Fed."

"Anybody can buy one of those on the Internet," Ray said, his body language verifying he wasn't entirely buying into Alex's story. "That still doesn't explain how he found Jordan so quickly."

"I've been undercover for over two months," Alex said. "Two weeks ago I put a GPS tracker on Mason's car. I've suspected—" He paused when his cell phone rang. Digging it out of his pocket, he checked caller ID before answering. "Is the Audi A8 there?"

Jordan listened to Alex instruct the caller to sit tight until he got there.

"Gotta run. No way they're picking up that slimeball without me."

Suddenly Jordan remembered something Mason had said. "Alex, I forgot to mention that Roger said the chef was part of the smuggling ring, too."

"Figures." Alex shook his head. "How else could they be sure the duck with the diamonds didn't end up going to the wrong person?"

"Like me?"

He gave her a fleeting smile. "Exactly. I'd say someone screwed up royally."

"Do you think that's why they killed the waiter?" Ray asked.

"Mason denies killing him," Jordan said. "But it stands to reason someone had to take the blame."

"They traced the knife that killed him to Longhorn Prime Rib."

She whirled around to confront Alex. "And you were going to tell me this when exactly?"

"That was Calhoun on the phone a few minutes ago. They just got the report back tonight." He headed toward the door. "I'll call when I know something. In the meantime, stay with Ray, Jordan. At least until we have Mason in custody." He held her stare for a second then he was gone.

"Who would have believed Alex was a cop?" Victor said, flopping down on the couch.

"Don't get comfortable, Vic. It's after midnight and we have a long day ahead of us." Michael pointed to the door.

"It's Sunday, for goodness' sake. Even God rested on the Sabbath."

Michael laughed. "God didn't own a rundown apartment

complex with the entire second floor desperately in need of an update."

Reluctantly, Victor got up and walked to the door with his partner. Rosie left next but not until she was reassured Jordan would spend the night with Ray. Grabbing a T-shirt, a pair of old shorts, and fuzzy socks, Jordan followed Ray and Lola to his apartment.

"You sleep in the bed, honey. I'll stay in my own apartment tonight," Lola said.

"No way. I'll take the couch. Besides, I kinda wish you'd stay with me tonight, too."

Lola was one of the kindest women Jordan had ever met. A bit eccentric but with a heart of gold. As sweet as Ray was, he didn't have that mothering touch Jordan desperately needed tonight.

Lola smiled. "You've been through more than anyone should ever have to experience. We won't let anything happen to you on our watch. Right, Ray?"

"That's right. You can stay here as long as you want. You're definitely not leaving until Alex gives us the all-clear signal and it's safe for you to go home."

Jordan took the blanket and pillow and set them on the couch before heading to the bathroom to clean up and get ready for sleep. Walking across the living room, she noticed the large modular piece of equipment on the TV.

She stopped and pointed. "What's that big thing?"

"The receiver for the security camera in the hallway. I probably should think about getting that back to my friend in Dallas when Alex tells us J. T.'s killer is behind bars. I told him we'd only need it for a few weeks."

Jordan hoped Ray was right—that the police had already

picked Mason up. "Was it recording tonight when everything started happening?" For some reason she felt the need to verify Alex's story.

"Of course it was. It's on every night and records for forty-eight hours before I have to change the tape." He stopped. "Actually I only have one tape, so I tape over it when it's full." He went to the machine and switched it on. "It's pretty boring most of the time."

"Can you fast-forward to when Alex and Mason knocked on my door?"

"Sure, honey, but are you absolutely sure you're ready to watch that?"

"I'm curious, that's all." She settled back on the couch and focused on the screen as Ray pushed another button.

"There," she said when she saw the outline of Alex holding a flashlight and bending down to pick her lock.

Watching him walk into her apartment, Jordan winced, thankful she couldn't see when she hit him on the head and knocked him out cold. Although it was too dark to see much, she made out a tall man walking in shortly after Alex and knew that must be Mason.

"Okay, you're right, I'm not ready to relive this again, but I'm curious if Mason came back to my apartment to search for the diamonds while I was tied to the tree."

Ray fast-forwarded again and she saw Alex rush out; then there was no activity for a few minutes.

"The speed is two hundred times normal, Jordan. We're almost up to the point when you came back."

"Stop!" She pointed at the screen. "Is that him?"

Ray leaned closer, squinting at the screen. "No. I've never seen this guy before."

They watched as the man knocked on Jordan's apartment door several times. When he turned to leave, Jordan gasped.

Ray was by her side in an instant. "Who is that, honey?"

She took a calming breath before speaking. Even knowing Mason was probably J. T.'s killer, the sight of Derrick Young at her residence sent a wave of panic through her body. Her address was public knowledge to anyone with a phone book, but still it was a shock seeing him literally on her doorstep.

Why had he been there?

"Jordan, do you know him?" Ray asked.

She felt regret holding back on filling Ray in, but now wasn't the time to hear another one of his lectures. For sure he'd blow a gasket if she told him she'd been bird-dogging the kid, knowing he had a thing about hurting women.

"I thought I did at first, but now that I look at him, I don't. He must be some kind of delivery guy."

"At ten at night?"

"I don't know, Ray. Maybe he was at the wrong apartment. All I know is that I've never seen him before." She crossed her fingers behind her back and hoped the Big Man upstairs wasn't listening.

With Ray staring at her, his eyes begging her to tell the truth, she nearly spilled her guts about the whole Derrick thing. She hated lying to her friend and promised herself she'd tell him the truth eventually. Maybe after things were back to normal and Friday night card games were as much fun as they used to be, they'd all have a big laugh over her lame attempt at sleuthing.

"Okay, then. Come on, honey. Let's let our girl get some

sleep. She must be exhausted." He nudged Lola toward the bedroom after he clicked off the television. "Good night, Jordan. Tomorrow, I'll run down to Myrtle's and pick up some of her Chocolate-Chip Coffee Cake."

Jordan smiled. She loved this man. She lay down on the couch and pulled the blanket up to her chin, her mind still on the video of Derrick at her front door.

She wondered if Brittney's mom had intervened and forced her daughter to break it off with him. If so, he would be one mad hombre, looking to blame everyone but himself.

Is that why he was here tonight?

She decided she didn't want to find out. Tomorrow she'd confess everything to Ray and face his anger for keeping it from him in the first place.

Right after he brought her the Chocolate-Chip Coffee Cake.

CHAPTER 20

The scent of freshly brewed coffee tickled Jordan's nose, and she slowly roused, but it took several minutes to acclimate herself to her surroundings. Along with the realization she was not in her own apartment came memories of the night before. She shot up from the couch, nearly colliding with a smiling Ray, standing in front of her with a plate of Myrtle's Chocolate-Chip Coffee Cake in one hand and a cup of java in the other.

"We were worried you might never wake up," Ray teased, handing her first the cup, then the cake. "You must have been exhausted."

Taking a sip before leaning back into the cushions, Jordan smiled up at him. "Mmm. You should think about making coffee for a living, Ray." She set the cup on the end table then sampled the cake. "Oh wow, I've died and gone to the big newsroom in the sky."

Inhaling sharply at her own words, she looked from Ray to Lola, a war of emotions raging in her stomach. It was too soon to be making jokes about something that had come so close to being reality.

"I still can't talk Myrtle into giving up this recipe," Ray said, changing the subject. "She says I'd have no reason to come by and flirt with her if I could make this baby myself." He winked at Lola. "She was just kidding about the flirting part, sweet pea."

"You old coot," Lola said with a twinkle in her eyes. "Never forget I have an authentic voodoo doll down at the shop. I'd hate to see your name on it along with several long pins attached."

"Ouch!" He feigned fright. "You know I only have eyes for you." He turned to Jordan, who had just shoved the last bite of cake into her mouth. "Want seconds?"

When she nodded, he made a beeline for the kitchen.

"I'm not helpless, Ray. I can get it myself."

"Oh, let him wait on you, sweetie. It makes him feel useful," Lola said, smacking his bottom when he passed by.

Jordan smiled, thinking she should be so lucky to find someone that devoted to her. Gratefully, she accepted the plate upon Ray's return. Before she had a chance to dig in, the doorbell rang, and she nearly dropped the cake.

"Chill out, honey. I'm sure that's just Victor or Michael," Ray said, heading for the door.

A surge of excitement coursed through her body when Ray opened the door and she recognized the voice. Quickly, she smoothed her bed-head hair and swiped at the line of mascara she knew had ended up below her eyes. Her morning raccoon look, she called it.

Alex walked in, nearly catching her rubbing her finger back and forth across her front teeth.

As if that would sweeten up morning breath.

She lowered her eyes, feeling the color creep up her cheeks. Did she think the man was going to take her in his arms and ravage her right here on Ray's couch? Mentally, she cautioned herself to get a grip. But bad breath or not, the idea did have its merits.

Alex eased down on the sofa beside her, studying her face with a curious intensity. "Were you able to sleep last night?"

"Yes," Jordan lied. The truth was she hadn't stopped thinking about Derrick Young showing up at her apartment since she'd seen the security tape. It had been well after three when she'd finally drifted off.

"You're lying." He touched the soft area under her eyes. "The peepers always tell the true story. You don't get dark circles like these after a good night's sleep."

"Yesterday's mascara," she mumbled, embarrassed she hadn't had time to wash her face yet.

"What do you take in your coffee, Alex?" Ray interrupted, giving Jordan a much needed reprieve from the scrutiny.

"Just black."

Ray snorted. "Now I know you're a real cop."

When Ray returned with the steaming cup, Alex settled back to take a drink, allowing Jordan a few minutes to study him discreetly. With olive skin that contrasted nicely with his dark blond hair still slightly damp from his morning shower and eyes that belonged in a bedroom, Alex Moreland leapfrogged up her sex-appeal meter. Even faster now that she no longer thought of him as a bad guy.

He turned to her, catching her giving him the once-over, and his eyes flickered with mischief. "Hold that thought," he said simply. "I have to run into Dallas today to brief my boss about the operation. I've already been assigned to another case, and I'm heading out early Monday morning. But for tonight, I see you, me, and a home-cooked dinner with candles." He paused before adding, "That's if you say yes."

"Unless you like bologna du jour, I'd say that scenario ain't happening anytime soon," Ray interjected, shaking his head and grinning.

Both Jordan and Alex laughed. "If Jordan agrees, I'm going to show her how an Italian boy like me can razzle-dazzle her with a tray of lasagna."

"You're Italian?" Jordan asked, surprised. "Moreland sounds English."

"My dad's a Brit," he explained. "But my mom's a second-generation Sicilian. My nana was born in Palermo and only came to the States as a teenager."

"In that case, I can't wait to taste your lasagna," Jordan said. She stopped herself from admitting she wouldn't mind getting a taste of him, too. "I'll bring the bread."

Glancing at his watch, Alex's face suddenly turned serious. "I only have a few minutes, but I wanted to let you know both Roger Mason and his chef, Aaron Daniels, are in custody downtown. After I interrogated them for several hours, Daniels gave it up. By early morning, my counterpart in Canada had already executed a search warrant at the meatpacking plant and discovered more than ten million dollars' worth of blood diamonds waiting to be transferred."

"Did Mason admit he killed J. T.?" Jordan prayed the answer was yes.

"Said he had nothing to do with it, even though the bloody knife found across the street in your neighbor's yard definitely came from Longhorn Prime Rib. Mason can deny it all day long, but the evidence against him is too strong."

Jordan would have preferred it if Alex had been more convincing about J. T.'s killer and had shot down her anxiety over Derrick Young's visit last night. She decided when Alex returned from Dallas, she'd tell him about her suspicions over dinner. He'd probably laugh at her paranoia and convince her there was no doubt Mason was the killer.

He stood and walked to the kitchen to put his empty coffee cop in the sink. "Gotta run." On the way to the door, he stopped by the couch and bent down to kiss Jordan on the forehead. "Wear something sexy tonight. I've got a special dessert planned."

Jordan loved his attempt at humor but decided the joke would be on him. She had just enough time to run out to the mall and pick up something that would have him thinking twice about leaving Ranchero. Maybe even get a pedicure while she was at it. She'd show him all about special desserts. After all, didn't they call her the culinary queen of Ranchero?

Of course, she'd have to eat beans and weenies all week, but it'd be worth it. Remembering the way his Levi's hugged his butt on the way out the door only confirmed her decision to blow this week's paycheck on what might turn out to be a wise investment or, at the very least, a fun one.

After he was gone, she helped Lola clean up the kitchen before heading back to her apartment. Crumpling on her own couch, Derrick Young completely forgotten, she decided she'd better sneak in a power nap.

Alex apparently had a big night planned—and so did she!

The shrill ring roused Jordan from her much-needed nap. Shooting up off the couch, she grabbed the phone, not even bothering to check caller ID.

"Hello."

"Miss McAllister," the unfamiliar voice started. "I need to talk to you."

"Who is this?" She glanced at the clock. Almost five. She'd been asleep for two hours. So much for the ten-minute quickie and her trip to the mall to pick up something to wear tonight.

"Derrick Young."

She froze, her eyes darting to the door to make sure the chain latch was in place. She knew it was silly, but she couldn't stop the fine hairs on her arms from prickling at the sound of his voice.

"I don't have much time. I'm here at the stadium cleaning out my locker. If you get here in the next hour, I have something you really need to hear."

Jordan laughed more from nervousness than anything else. "What kind of fool do you think I am? Remember, I saw the bruises on Brittney's arm. I also know what happened in San Antonio, why you came to Grayson County College instead of going to a bigger school."

She heard him gasp.

"Those records are sealed."

"Yeah, well, let's just say I have friends who can be very persuasive." She took a deep breath, making it up as she went. "I know you get off on hurting defenseless women half your size."

"I've changed," he muttered. "I've been talking to the school chaplain about it."

"That's all well and good, Derrick, and I'm glad for your sake, but it still doesn't make me dumb enough to come over there right now. Whatever you want to tell me, I'd suggest you do it over the phone."

"Can't." He lowered his voice. "What I have to say is worth it, but I don't have time to argue with you. I'm leaving town in a few hours. It's now or never."

Talking to him gave her the creeps, and she swallowed hard. It would be idiotic to even remotely consider facing him by herself. Every instinct in her body told her to hang up and let him ride out of town like the abuser he was, yet she hesitated. What if she went with a hidden tape recorder and got him to admit to killing J. T.?

"I'll be there in forty-five minutes," she said, slapping her head with her hand the minute the words left her mouth. Visions of stupid people in movies who went down a dark stairway to the cellar after hearing a noise, or who opened the door to check out a scary sound, popped into Jordan's subconscious. Watching them, she'd always wanted to scream, "Can't you hear the music, you moron?"

After hanging up the phone, she ran into the bathroom and brushed her teeth, then ran a comb through her hair. A two-minute change of clothes and she was ready in less than ten minutes. Now all she had to do was grab Ray and get him to go with her to the college. She could only imagine the lecture she was in for on the ride over. But as Derrick had said, it was now or never.

Almost out the door, she remembered the voice-activated recorder she'd used when she and Brett interviewed the Texas Longhorn athletes back in the day, and she ran back in to retrieve it. She was determined to trip Derrick up and capture his confession on tape. Glancing at her watch and noting there were only thirty minutes left on the deadline Derrick had imposed, she pounded on Ray's door.

When Lola answered, Jordan burst through the entrance. "Where's Ray?"

"He's not here, sweetie. Can I help you with something?"

"Where is he?"

"He left about an hour ago to run into Dallas to return the security camera to his friend. I don't expect him back until right around dinnertime. You know how Dallas traffic can be, even on a Sunday."

"Crap!" Jordan slammed her fist on the door.

The smile on Lola's face faded. "What is it, child? You look really upset."

Jordan sucked in a gulp of air, trying to calm down. Okay, so Ray wasn't there to go with her. She could either forget about what Derrick had said or go by herself. She winced, hearing the *Jaws* music playing in her head. She didn't want to be *that woman*, who was too stupid to live, answering the door at midnight to find a psychopath on her doorstep.

"I got a call from Derrick Young," she explained to Lola, who was now patting her on the back, trying to comfort her. "He's leaving town and he wants to tell me something before he heads out. I don't have time to wait on Ray." She turned and kissed Lola's forehead. "Tell him I'll explain everything when I get back. It's probably nothing, anyway."

"Who's Derrick Young?"

Jordan stopped in her tracks, realizing no one but Victor knew about the quarterback, and absolutely no one knew he had shown up to her apartment the night before.

"I can't tell you now, but suffice it to say he might be someone with important information about who killed J. T." She failed to mention he might even be the killer himself.

"I thought Mason did it."

Jordan sighed. "I have to be sure. Tell Ray I'll fill him in when I get back."

"I saw Michael go out the front door about a half hour ago, but I think Victor is home," Lola offered.

That was it! Jordan was determined not to miss out on an opportunity to find out if Derrick was behind J. T.'s murder. She'd have to settle for Victor. "Thanks, Lola. I'll see you in a bit." She turned and headed down the hallway.

"Oh, no you don't," Lola hollered. "No way you're going to meet him by yourself. If Ray can't be by your side, then you're stuck with me." She grabbed a sweater from the rack and slammed the door behind her.

Jordan hesitated. but only briefly. If she couldn't have

Alex or Ray, it was probably wise to bring a crowd. There was that safety-in-numbers thing her mother had always preached when Jordan and her high school friend and cohort in crime, Sally Winters, went anywhere.

"Okay, come on. Let's go get Victor." She grabbed Lola's arm and dragged her down the hall.

After several frantic knocks, the door swung open and Jordan had to bite her lower lip to hide the smile. Victor had on a pair of striped cargo pants that stopped below the knee and matching knee-highs that came almost to the edge of the britches. His flaming red Hawaiian shirt make him look like he'd just stepped out of a fifties golf tournament—for cross-dressers.

"Don't ask," he said, before Jordan could say a word.

"Is Michael home yet?"

When Victor shook his head, Jordan made a snap decision. "I need you to come with Lola and me to Grayson County College to meet with Derrick Young. He's leaving and he might have some valuable information for me."

"About what?"

"Victor, I don't have time to explain. Will you come with us or not?"

"Where's Ray?"

Lola and Jordan spoke in unison, "In Dallas."

"What in the world could Derrick possibly have to tell you that's important enough for you to rush down there on a Sunday afternoon to hear?"

Jordan grabbed Lola's arm. "Come on. We have to go."

"Wait," Victor said, shaking his head. "I'll probably regret this, but if you give me a few minutes to change clothes, I'm in."

"No time," Jordan said, reaching in and grabbing him by the collar. "Maybe nobody will notice what you're wearing."

He let her pull him out into the hall before shrugging and slamming the door to his apartment. "We'll just say I'm Jack Nicklaus Senior if anyone asks," he deadpanned, wiggling his eyebrows.

Jordan couldn't resist. "Or Jacqueline Senior."

"You're a real comedian, Jordan. Now gimme the keys. I might be dressed funny, but I don't have a death wish. I'm driving."

Another door opened and Rosie stuck her head out. "How's a girl supposed to get her beauty sleep with all the racket out here?"

"Sorry, Rosie," Jordan said. "We're on a mission."

The older woman's eyes lit up. "Where are Ray and Michael?"

"It's a dangerous mission and we can't wait on them," Victor said. "Tell Michael I went out for a minute with Lola and Jordan, but don't tell him about the dangerous part."

"Hello! There's no way you guys are going without me. I love danger." She slammed the door before asking. "Do I need my purse?"

"No," they all said in unison, heading to the parking lot, where they piled into Jordan's Toyota. Five minutes later, they were crossing the Connor-Ranchero border and heading for the college.

Once again the scary music blared in Jordan's head.

CHAPTER 21

"Tell me again why I'm driving like a madman to get to the football field before"—Victor glanced down at his watch—"five forty-five?"

"I need to talk to Derrick."

"We get that, sweetie, but don't you think you should tell us why? That way we might be able to help when you find out what he wants."

Jordan turned slightly so Lola and Rosie could hear. "I need you all to stay in the car. Derrick might not open up if he sees all four of us. Don't worry, I've got my recorder and I'm hoping he'll slip up and confess—" The three friends gasped in chorus, effectively cutting her off.

"Confess what?" Rosie's escalated voice from the back seat seemed to reverberate across the entire interior of the car.

Jordan did a quick time check, hoping to buy time before answering. They were almost there, even had a few minutes to spare. She decided telling everybody what she suspected was definitely not the right thing to do, even though it was probably the smarter thing. For sure, they'd try to stop her.

She turned again so both Lola and Rosie could hear her from the back. "Okay, here it is. I found out Derrick Young . . ." She looked directly at Rosie, remembering Rosie had no idea who she was talking about. "He's the quarterback at the college. Anyway, he's been beating up on his girlfriend. She just happens to be the younger sister of J. T.'s best friend, Eric, who's in College Station at A&M."

"Holy crapola!" Rosie exclaimed before Lola shushed her.

"Let Jordan finish before we jump to any conclusions."

"Thank you, Lola. Anyway, one of the waiters at Longhorn Prime Rib told me Derrick came to the restaurant the night J. T. was killed and caused a big ruckus. Apparently, J. T. found out about the abuse and threatened to tell Brittney's parents or something. The waiter wasn't sure exactly what the commotion was about, but he said it involved the girl."

"Oh, good grief! Tell me you're not planning to meet a football player who beats up on women without having about six squad cars nearby?" Victor slammed the steering wheel with his flattened hand before glancing her way. "Jordan?"

She looked away, ready to fold under his scrutiny. If he was this riled up over Derrick beating up his girlfriend, he'd pop a cork knowing she suspected the man might be much more than a bully. She decided to keep that thought to herself for the moment.

"Think about it, Victor. He called because he's on his way out of town, and he thinks I need to hear something. He has no possible reason to hurt me."

Unless I get him to admit he killed J. T.

"It's Sunday. The place will be deserted. No way you're walking into that locker room without us," Lola proclaimed.

Jordan snorted. "Yeah, a lot of protection that would be. An adorable psychic, a chic fiftyish jewelry maker, and an antiques dealer dressed like . . ." Jordan smiled. "Trust me, my friends, I ran track in college. I can get out of there in a hurry if the interview goes south." She blew out a long breath, trying to make herself believe her own words. The truth was, despite her long legs, even she couldn't outrun a bullet.

After a few minutes of silence that made Jordan wonder if everyone else was thinking the same thing, Lola leaned forward, touching her forehead to the back of Jordan's headrest. "So, do we have a plan? I may be old but I can still do some damage to the crotch area if the situation calls for it." She chuckled. "Ask my self-defense instructor. He found out the hard way."

Jordan turned slightly and kissed her forehead. "Here's what I'd like to do." She took her phone out of her shirt pocket. "Right before I go down under the bleachers to the locker room, I'll call you, Victor, and leave my phone on. That way you guys can hear every word we say. If things start to get ugly, call the cops."

Victor shrugged. "I still don't like it, but I know there's no talking you out of something when you've set your mind to it."

"Thataboy! Think of us as *Charlie's Angels*." Rosie slapped Victor on the back, nearly causing him to swerve.

"Although with that outfit, darling, I'm not sure which one you'd be."

"Another freakin' comedian!" Victor pulled into the lot at the stadium and parked up close. "Call me, Jordan, so we can be sure it will work."

Convinced the connection was good, Jordan got out of the car, waving back at her friends as she walked toward the entrance. Although she no longer heard the how-stupid-are-you music in her head, she couldn't ignore the niggling thought that she was making a terrible mistake.

She shook off the feeling, hesitating in front of the door one last time. She wanted to turn back, but she had to do this for J. T. If he had been coming to her apartment to warn her about Mason, she owed him.

"What's the matter?" Victor's voice boomed loud enough to be heard even though the phone was in her hand.

She turned and waved again, pasting a fake smile on her face. "Everything's cool. I'm going in."

Blowing out a breath and secretly making the sign of the cross, a carry-over from her Catholic school days, Jordan entered the stadium, going directly to the area under the bleachers.

Walking down the same hallway the players used on game day, Jordan felt the chill sweep across her body, not so much because of the temperature in the concrete hallway, but because it was so eerily quiet with only the sound of her footsteps echoing in the tunnel. She darted her eyes back and forth, turning 180 degrees to see behind her, half expecting a vampire or something just as sinister to materialize.

Sheesh! She had to stop watching so much TV.

Spotting the door with COUGARS PERSONNEL ONLY etched in big black letters, she knocked, touching the phone in her shirt pocket one more time to make sure it was still there. If she could hear Victor while she held the phone in her hand, surely, she'd hear him from her pocket.

"So far, so good," she said into her shirt, opening the door a few minutes later when no one responded. Derrick had mentioned he was cleaning out his locker, so he probably hadn't heard her knock.

"Derrick," she hollered, making her way through the front office toward the locker room.

She opened the door and stepped in, and immediately, the lights went out. Turning back toward the door to run, she brushed against someone. The scream bubbled in her throat, hearing the unmistakable click of the door being locked.

Yanking her shirt up to her mouth, she shouted "Victor, call the cops," before she took off in a dead run toward the line of lockers. She could barely make them out in the soft red light of the security system keypad on the wall, now blinking furiously to signal a power outage.

"Victor," she hollered again. "Did you hear me? Call the cops."

She had no idea if she was running into a trap, but she prayed the police would arrive before she found out. Suddenly, she tripped and fell hard on top of something in the middle of the aisle between the two rows of lockers.

Lifting her body up, she screamed as she touched a human hand. Her terror turned to horror when she realized she was lying on top of a body.

CHAPTER 22

Alex closed the receiver on his cell phone and headed out the main entrance of Empire Apartments. He'd been trying to reach Jordan for over an hour. He still had to make a quick stop at the grocery store before rushing home to clean up and throw the lasagna together. Since the casserole had to cook for an hour, it would give them enough time to chill out with the wine he'd picked up in Dallas before he wowed her with his mom's recipe.

Assuming he ever reached her to firm up dinner plans.

The fact that he even wanted to impress her was so out of character for him considering he hadn't had a real date in over a year. He always figured his life was too complicated, not to mention too busy to toss romance into the mix. What woman wanted to date someone who lived a lie, mingling daily with some of the most heinous criminals on the planet?

He tried to believe tonight would be nothing more than a farewell dinner with a friend, but it didn't work. Ever since Jordan had agreed to this date, he'd had a hard time wiping the perpetual smile off his face. If he wasn't careful, someone might accuse him of having feelings for the girl, beyond his obvious physical attraction to her.

He glanced one last time at her window, checking for any movement before deciding she must have run out at the last minute to pick up something. He chortled to himself, hoping *that* something was a sexy new outfit to wear tonight. He'd been teasing when he'd mentioned it earlier, but he wouldn't be a bit upset if she followed up on the broad hint.

Heading down Main Street, he tried to focus on the earlier debriefing at central headquarters in downtown Dallas.

Things had gone well in that respect. Everyone had been pleased with the outcome, especially his partner who had fingered Mason from the start but had been forced to step back when he'd been made. After calling Rocco and updating him about the arrests, Alex had even weaseled a free celebratory steak dinner out of the guy for when he finally made it back to Houston. He knew exactly where he'd take his partner, his mouth watering, remembering the juiciness of the thick steaks, exactly the reason the prices weren't listed on the menu.

But that would have to wait. The head of DEA had called his boss and requested undercover assistance with an ongoing drug investigation. Seems a major player was a gang leader also being investigated by the FBI for interstate trafficking, and both agencies felt a joint effort was the best way to bring him down. Alex was already booked on a morning flight to El Paso, a known entry point where the Mexican cartel war was spilling over the border into Texas. Rocco was flying in from Houston and the two of them planned to infiltrate a local drug operation. If they were able to flush out the big fish and remove them from the picture, it might slow the massive flood of prime-grade heroin crossing the border.

But knowing he was leaving Ranchero after a successful wrap on his case brought more than a twinge of regret. He would have liked the opportunity to hang around longer to see if his friendship with Jordan might develop into an actual relationship.

That meant tonight was make-or-break time, and it was small consolation that Dallas was only an hour's flight from El Paso. He'd liked the way his pulse had quickened when she'd promptly agreed to have dinner with him.

A few blocks from his apartment, he dialed the Ranchero Police Station and was transferred to Sheriff Delaney, his contact in the small town. "Just thought I'd check in before I head out of town tomorrow," he said. "The bureau chief asked me to convey his gratitude for all your help."

"I appreciate that, Alex, but I can't talk right now. I'm right in the middle of a potential problem. Can I call you back?"

The cop in Alex took over. "Anything I can help with?"

"It's probably nothing," Delaney responded. "A 911 call came in from some guy who says his friend might be in trouble at the college stadium. I sent a couple of uniforms over to check it out. It's imperative I keep all lines clear in case they need backup."

"All right, then, I'll let you go. Again, thanks for everything."

"You said you're heading out tonight?"

"Tomorrow morning. You'll be happy to hear I actually have a date tonight since you're always giving me grief about that. You remember the girl who had diamonds in her fishbowl?" Alex had no idea why he spilled that information. "Anyway, I'll keep in touch."

The sheriff interrupted, "Jordan McAllister?"

Alex laughed. "Yeah, that's the one."

After a pause, Delaney cleared his throat. "Jordan is the girl who might be in trouble out at the college."

Alex didn't even bother to disconnect. He was only a few miles from the stadium. Slamming on the brakes, he made a U-turn and pressed his foot all the way to the floorboard, racing toward the college.

Jordan clamped her hand over her mouth to stifle the scream that threatened. It would be foolish to give away her position, maybe even deadly.

She slid off the body and braced her hands on the concrete floor to help push herself up, freaking out when she felt something sticky. The sound of footsteps coming her way then stopping abruptly very close to where she was sprawled across the floor shot her heart rate up another ten points.

"Derrick, listen to me," shc started. "I can help you.

Whoever this is on the floor needs help now." She bit back tears, searching for something, anything, to say to stay alive.

She prayed her friends were still listening and picked up on the fact they needed an ambulance. Hearing the footsteps walking away, she forced herself to believe Derrick had gone for help.

"I'd bet my hard-earned money it's a mite too late to help him, Jordan."

She was confused. The voice was familiar, but it didn't sound like Derrick's.

Suddenly the lights came on, blinding her for an instant before she snapped her focus on the body lying beside her.

It was Derrick Young.

Startled, she jerked her head up and stared at the man standing in the center of the room pointing a gun directly at her.

"You thought you were so smart and had this all figured out, didn't you?" Larry Trevelli spat out the words, his eyes filled with rage. "So did Derrick."

Jordan inched closer to the body and the knife, even though she knew that even if she could reach it, she and a knife didn't stand a chance against the gun he held. "What happened here, Coach?" she asked, hoping to keep him talking long enough for . . .

Oh please! Let someone get here soon.

"Obviously, you're not the sharpest pencil in the drawer." He laughed sarcastically. "A little reporter humor." He stepped out of the shadow, allowing her to see his face. Despite the smile, his eyes remained hard, hateful.

Unadulterated fear swept through her. She struggled

into a sitting position, staring at the blood covering her hands and the front of her shirt, knowing she had to try to diffuse his ticking bomb.

"I'm sure it was an accident, Coach. No one would ever believe you'd hurt your star quarterback." She was desperate to keep him talking as she rubbed her fingers down the side of her jeans to get rid of the sticky feeling.

Trevelli snorted. "Star quarterback? Let me tell you something, Jordan. *I* was the one who made him a star. I flew down to San Antonio a number of times to personally recruit him for Grayson County when every other coach in the conference—hell, in the entire state—shunned him like a homeless man with a nasty cough after he put the coach's daughter in the hospital for two weeks, so badly broken she had to drop out of school for a year. Derrick owed me everything. Did he appreciate it?"

He shook his head. "Hell, no, and after all I did for him. Even kept his sorry butt out of jail three or four more times after he arrived in Ranchero. Then he turns and betrays me like a damn snake."

"It's not too late, Coach. I'll say he was trying to hurt you."

"He did hurt me." He touched his knee, still covered with the brace from the mugging.

"He did that to you?" For some reason, she felt a little satisfaction knowing her original suspicion that Derrick had beaten up his coach was true.

"Might as well have. All I ever asked of him was to throw a game once in a while. Except for the division championship last year, it never really affected our win–loss record. How hard was that? He was so good, and it was only a couple of times.

"The boy owed me, and what did I get in return? A visit from a couple of Quincy Dozerly's tough guys who roughed me up pretty good and came close to ruining my career forever." He raked his free hand across his chin before he zeroed in on Jordan with the gun.

Instinctively, she reached for the knife beside Derrick's body, cutting her fingertip on the razor-sharp blade.

Trevelli's sadistic laugh caught her off guard, and she jerked her head up. "Like I said, not the sharpest pencil. Now your blood as well as your fingerprints are all over the murder weapon."

She held the knife in front of her, knowing it was asinine to think she had a chance against a bullet. "And what possible reason would I have for killing Derrick?"

"Never play with the big boys, Jordan. You're out of your league here. With your prints on that knife, I can say I was forced to kill you after you attacked Derrick, then came after me."

"Again, why would I attack him?"

Trevelli stepped closer, stooping down to backhand her. "Because he beat you up just like he did every other woman he's ever known who was unfortunate enough to fall for his charm."

Thankfully, Jordan was still on her knees and took the blow without falling backward. Stunned, she reached up to touch the area that burned down her entire left cheek, the spot already sensitive from the manhandling Mason had given her the night before.

"Perfect!" Trevelli exclaimed. "Now you've got his blood on your face as well." He moved quickly and kicked the knife out of her hand, sending it flying across the room.

The sound of metal against metal as it slammed into the locker caused Jordan's entire body to convulse with fear.

"My friends are out in the parking lot listening to every word you've said. The cops are on their way."

This time Trevelli threw his head back and laughed out loud, a sick, evil cackle that made Jordan wish Mason was here instead of the coach. She understood his kind of evil, but not this man's.

"Checked that phone lately, smart lady? This building is solid concrete. I guarantee not even a cell tower in the parking lot could pick up a signal down here."

Jordan inhaled sharply, tempted to pull the phone out of her pocket to check but able to restrain herself. She realized way too late he was probably right.

Why hadn't she thought of that? She had to come up with another strategy and quickly. Although she prayed her friends were already looking for her, she couldn't let them walk into a trap set by this madman.

"Why did Derrick kill J. T.?" She knew the answer to that one, but hoped it would distract him from thinking about the others coming for her.

"Wrong again. Derrick didn't kill J. T., you ignoramus. He was a coward who only picked on young girls. I followed Derrick that night, saw him have a meltdown at the restaurant, and knew I had to talk some sense into the waiter before he ruined everything I'd worked for. I only grabbed the knife from the table to scare him."

Jordan stared incredulously, her hope of seeing another day fading fast with the newfound revelation Trevelli hadn't killed Derrick in the heat of the moment. The man had a calculated plan. "You killed J. T.?"

"Had to. Somehow he found out about me and Derrick throwing the Division II championship game." He paused, a slight grin tipping the corner of his lips. "I made twenty-five big ones on that game. Got me out of the doghouse with Dozerly. At least until my luck went south again at the track." His face hardened again. "Anyway, the loser must have told his teenybopper girlfriend before he used her to practice his right hook. I can only assume she told J. T., and he'd threatened to go to the newspaper and expose all of us if Derrick didn't stay away from the girl."

Jordan lowered her head. So that was the reason J. T. wanted to see her that night. He knew she was a reporter, and he was coming to tell her about the point-fixing scam. She wondered if he'd even suspected diamond smuggling was going on right under his nose at the restaurant.

"So you killed him for money?"

Trevelli slammed the gun against the side of the locker closest to him, and Jordan flinched before catapulting to her feet and backpedaling.

"Only one way out of here, Jordan, but you can quit worrying. I have no intentions of shooting you, at least not with a Saturday night special I bought on the street after Dozerly's goons worked me over. That would be kind of hard to explain to the cops." He sneered. "You and me are going to take a little walk up the back stairway to the press box. Unfortunately, you, being clumsy, are going to have a really bad fall running from me when I confront you about killing Derrick. Poor girl! You'll probably break your neck when you land on the hard surface behind the bleachers."

He cocked the gun and jerked it toward the door. "No more talking. It's showtime."

Reluctantly, Jordan stepped toward him, her mind racing for something, anything, to stay alive. Slowly as possible, she made her way to the door, feeling the unmistakable pressure of the gun barrel pressed into the small of her back.

For the second time in two days, she looked to the sky for help, hoping the Big Guy up there believed she was worth saving.

Just one more time.

Skidding into the parking lot balanced on two wheels, the car nearly tipped over after Alex jerked the wheel, spotting Jordan's car. He regained control enough to screech to a halt and jump out of the vehicle, leaving the motor running and bounding from the front seat to race to the Camry.

He looked inside, his gut grumbling like a volcano on the verge of rupturing.

It was empty!

Alarm sent his pulse into overdrive, and he rushed back to his own car. He turned off the engine and reached inside the glove compartment for the Glock he kept stashed there. The uneasy feeling inside him snowballing, he galloped to the stadium entrance.

What possible reason could Jordan have for being here?

Touching the weapon now tucked into his waistband, he pushed open the door.

"Move," Trevelli growled, jabbing her harder with the gun. "The cops will be here soon, assuming you really do have friends out there. I can't take that chance."

Jordan scanned both walls of the empty corridor for something to use to defend herself as she reluctantly stepped up the pace Trevelli demanded.

Seeing the stairs ahead tucked into a hidden nook away from the hallway, she slowed her steps, tempering her voice. “You don’t have to do this, Coach. Everyone thinks Roger Mason killed J. T. and I’ll say whatever you want about Derrick—that he attacked me and I had to kill him in self-defense.” Trying to reason with him was the only weapon she possessed.

Trevelli snorted. “And you expect me to believe that line of crap? I bet the minute the cops get here, assuming they’re really on the way, you’d give me up before they even asked.” He shoved her forward. “Go, Jordan. I don’t want to shoot you, but I will. I can always say the gun is yours and went off when I tried to take it away from you.”

Panic like she’d never known before clogged her throat. She could hardly breathe, but she had to think of something to distract him long enough to make a run for it. If he got her all the way up to the press box, perched above the top row of bleachers, there was no way she’d survive a fall to the asphalt.

At the top of the stairs, they stopped in front of a door marked PRESS ONLY. Jordan felt a stab of irony that her lifelong dream had always been to sit in a press box like this one and report on anything athletic. Now she’d finally made it, and it was about to kill her.

CHAPTER 23

"It should be open," Trevelli said, his voice tight with tension. "I unlocked it earlier." He shoved again, nearly knocking her over. "Hurry up."

Jordan turned, trying once more to reason with him, this time using a more personal touch. "Larry . . ."

He slammed the butt of his gun against her temple, totally catching her off guard, and she groaned. Pitching forward, she fought to stay conscious, as the room began spinning in a vortex.

"Get up," he screamed.

Trevelli's voice was distant, echoing in her ears. Disoriented and sick to her stomach from the pain in her head, she tried to stand but teetered, falling back before finally lifting to her feet. Stunned, she saw him twirl his gun then motion for her to move toward the other side of the room.

Praying for the strength to make it there, she headed in that direction.

"This way," he said gruffly, when her knees buckled and she reached for a nearby chair to steady herself. When they made it to the opposite door of the press box, he reached around and flung it open.

Stepping out onto the top row of bleachers, she noticed right off how beautiful the sun looked making its descent toward the horizon. For some unexplained reason, the beautiful orange ball gave her hope. A whiff of fresh air, heavy with the smell of newly cut grass, reached her nostrils, and she closed her eyes, breathing deeply.

"Jordan!"

When she recognized Victor's voice, her eyes snapped open. "Up here," she shouted.

Trevelli stopped in his tracks. "What the—"

Victor stood on the bottom row of the bleachers with Lola and Rosie close behind him. With the distraction, Jordan spun halfway around and karate-chopped her fist against Trevelli's wrist, the one holding the gun. The weapon flew out of his hand and clattered across the aluminum bleachers. She completed the turn to face him and took aim.

His scream when her foot connected with his bad knee was a welcome sound, and she took advantage of his pain to leap down the steps two at a time, nearly pitching forward several times. Before reaching the bottom, she heard another familiar voice call her name, and she looked down to see Alex. He was racing up the steps, his gun pointed directly at Trevelli, who lay sprawled on the upper steps, his face twisted in agony.

"You all right?" he asked, his eyes darting to the side of her head where she knew her hair must be matted with blood.

Tears welled up. Unable to speak, she nodded.

"Who is this guy, Jordan?"

"Football coach," she whispered before clearing her throat and finding her voice. "He killed J. T." Then she remembered Derrick. "There's another body downstairs."

Alex left her to run up to Trevelli, and she continued down, the sounds of the sirens coming closer to the stadium giving her strength. Reaching her friends, she was immediately cradled in a three-man cocoon. Safe in the warmth of their embrace, she lost the battle with her pent-up emotions. Tears of joy flowed down her bloodstained cheeks.

Victor touched her head gently. "We need to get you to the emergency room. No arguments."

Jordan barely managed to nod, her head hurt so badly. Glancing up the steps and seeing Alex standing over Trevelli, she attempted a smile. His return stare was filled with so much concern, she forced herself to give him a thumbs-up before he focused back to Trevelli.

Glancing toward the parking lot, she saw the police units blazing across the asphalt, their flashing lights illuminating the area in a weird disco light way. Within minutes, a horde of cops ran past her, one of them radioing for the EMTs and backup as he grabbed her arm. "You need to sit, ma'am. That looks like a nasty cut you have there."

Exhausted, she slumped in Victor's arms, and he lowered her to the bleachers.

Rosie plucked a lock of hair that was glued to the blood

on her forehead and leaned in to kiss her cheek. "It's over, sweetie. He can't hurt you now."

"We were lucky we didn't have to shave too much of your hair," the doctor said, putting the bandage in place over the gash on her head. "You'll need to stay in the hospital overnight for observation, Ms. McAllister. If all goes well you can leave in the morning. Of course, you'll still have to take it easy for a week or so until we get these staples out."

Jordan nodded, already feeling the effects of the painkiller the nurse had given her. "Can my friends come in now?"

"I'll have the desk clerk call back to the waiting room and give them the okay."

He washed his hands before disappearing, leaving Jordan alone to reflect on the past two days. She'd nearly died, not once but twice. The nurse had mentioned her mom and brothers were on their way to the metroplex. She expected a full-court press when they arrived, knowing they would play on every one of her emotions to convince her to move back to Amarillo. Being Catholic, guilt would be their trump card.

But Ranchero was no longer a job stop up the career ladder for her. It was her home now. As much as she loved her parents and her siblings, holidays and an occasional vacation day worked fine as a family fix when she needed it. She just didn't want to live across town from them or, heaven forbid, in the same house.

Her brothers still treated her like she was a teenager, bossing her around and telling her how to live her life.

She thought about Brett's offer to put in a good word for her at his news station. As tempting as it was to get into sports reporting, it would mean leaving the people she had come to love as much as her biological family.

"I'm gonna kick your cute little butt if you ever try that again, young lady."

She glanced up to see Ray charge into the room. The concern in his eyes canceled out the gruff in his voice.

"Don't worry, I'm holding on to my other seven lives with both hands."

He bent to kiss her cheek. "What kind of animal does this to a face like yours?" he asked, staring at the bruise under her eye, now a mixture of purple and yellow.

"A coward," Victor chimed in, squeezing between Ray and Lola to grab Jordan's hand. "My God, girl, you nearly gave me a heart attack."

"Have you looked in the mirror lately, Victor? That outfit alone would stop a healthy heart." Ray laughed. "What were you thinking when you got up this morning? That you were going to a class reunion . . . for your great-grandfather?"

Everyone laughed, including Victor. "Some guy came into the store yesterday with a box of old clothes he found in his grandmother's attic. Thought I could use them in the antiques store. I was trying this on when Jordan knocked at my door insisting we leave immediately for the stadium."

Ray turned and nailed Jordan with a stare. "Speaking of the college, I saw a picture of the dead kid on TV this morning. He bears an uncanny resemblance to the guy we saw on the surveillance video at your door last night. You know, the guy you swore you didn't recognize." He shook his finger at her. "I'm a cop, Jordan. Why didn't you tell me what you suspected? I would have gone with you."

"I was planning to tell both you and Alex about him tonight. I thought I was being paranoid."

"So why didn't you tell me when he called?"

"I tried, Ray, but you were already on your way to Dallas. Derrick gave me a deadline."

"So, instead of a retired cop, you took the next best thing—Victor, Lola, and Rosie?" He threw up his hands. "I'll bet that scared the bejesus out of Trevelli."

"Hey, watch it, you old codger," Rosie cautioned, playfully. "I'll have you know it was because of us Jordan was able to get away from that madman." She giggled. "That was the most fun I've had in a long time. Well, since I broke up with Quincy, anyway."

At the mention of the lawyer's name, Jordan drew in a breath. "I have something to tell you, Rosie. Trevelli implied Quincy Dozerly was running some kind of gambling ring that was bigger than everyone thought."

"Oh, he definitely was," Michael said. "Remember me telling you about the old guy upstairs who made a killing when the Cougars won big their season opener?"

"No, Michael, I mean a really big gambling ring," Jordan said, suppressing a yawn. "Big like connected to the mob."

"That's true."

They all turned toward the door as Alex came in. "As soon as Trevelli told us about his connection to Dozerly, we got a federal warrant and raided Terlinga's Laundry. Although Quincy wasn't a big fish, he had ties to a couple of real sharks. The DA is working out a plea bargain with him as we speak."

"That slimeball," Rosie said before turning to Jordan. "You know he tipped off the cops that you had a knife missing, don't you?"

"I suspected as much. He got there two minutes after the police showed up."

"The jerk let it slip the other night, then tried to say he only did it because he wanted to impress me when he got the charges against you dropped." Rosie sighed. "I was such a damn fool."

"Oh, honey, I'm so sorry. Even though I never warmed up to the man, he did make you happy."

Rosie huffed. "Don't lose any sleep over it, Jordan. I was about to dump him, anyway. His idea of romance was a six-pack and a smack on my butt on the way to the bedroom."

"Do we need to stop at Wal-Mart today?" Jordan joked before mouthing *I love you* when Rosie looked her way.

"Me too, kiddo," Rosie said, her eyes twinkling with mischief. "And I'm good on the battery front, thank you."

"Geez! I'm invoking the 'too much information' rule, ladies," Victor said over the laughter of the others.

Alex raised his eyebrows comically. "I suppose I don't really want to know what that's about, do I, Rosie?"

"Trust me, you don't," Lola said. "Hey, Alex, did Trevelli say why he killed J. T.?"

"The kid was apparently going to tell Jordan about the point-fixing scam Derrick and his coach were involved in with Dozerly."

"Point fixing?"

"It's a way to make a bundle on the odds even when a really good team plays a team they're expected to beat." When Lola still looked confused, Alex continued, "Let's say a great team like Grayson County plays Waco Christian, a team far inferior to them. The oddsmakers will slap a spread on the game, for example, giving Waco a thirteen-point advantage. That means Grayson County would have to win by more than thirteen points for the people who bet on them to collect."

Lola moved closer to the bed. "How did Derrick fit into the scam?"

Ray took over. "A lot of people would bet on Grayson County even with the big point advantage because they're so potent on offense and should clean up on a team like Waco. Trevelli would get his quarterback to flub a pass or two so that the final score was, let's say, twenty to fourteen. Although the Cougars would actually win the game and keep their first-place standing in the conference, they wouldn't beat the spread. That means everyone who bet on them would lose money."

"According to the spreadsheets they picked up in the back room of the laundry when they served the warrant, sometimes that amount hit six figures," Alex interjected.

"Is that why Dozerly sent his thugs after Trevelli with a can of whup-ass?" Michael asked.

"Exactly," Jordan said. "Derrick was supposed to screw up the last play at one of the games, and at the last second, he threw a touchdown pass instead. Both Trevelli and Dozerly lost a bucket load of money. Probably the mob guys, too." She sighed. "I think that's what Derrick was going to tell me."

"That's right," Alex said. "Trevelli admitted he and the kid had a blowup earlier that day, and he followed him to the locker room to talk him out of leaving school. When he heard him on the phone with you, he knew something was up. He figured he had no choice but to kill him and pin it on you."

Seeing Jordan yawn, Alex turned to her friends. "Would you all mind if I talk to Jordan alone for a minute?"

"You got it," Ray said, huddling the group and nudging them toward the door. He turned and winked at Jordan before he closed the door.

Left alone, Alex bent down and kissed her tenderly. Not an I-want-to-jump-your-bones kind of kiss but more like an I'm-so-glad-you're-still-alive one.

"You're still leaving Ranchero tomorrow, aren't you?" she asked when the kiss ended.

"Have to. They want my partner and me working on our cover as soon as we get there," he replied, his eyes solemn. "I was going to talk about it over lasagna tonight."

She looked up at him, her eyes drooping. She struggled to stay awake with the heavy drugs now working their magic. "The one time I get an offer for a home-cooked meal, and I have to go and darn near get killed."

His eyes narrowed. "Don't joke about that, Jordan. I hate to think what might have happened if Victor and the others hadn't shown up when they did."

"Shh." She touched her finger to his lips. "I make jokes when I'm nervous."

The beginning of a smile tipped his lips. "I make you nervous?"

"Yes."

"That's good, because I'm like a quivering idiot around you. I was really looking forward to getting to know you better."

"Who says you can't?"

"I leave for El Paso at o'dark thirty tomorrow morning."

"I love El Paso. Maybe I can hop on a—"

He silenced her with his lips, and this time it was a bone-jumping one. After a moment he pulled back and smiled.

"Hold that thought."

"She's not coming back? Ever?"

Dwayne Egan shifted in the chair and leaned forward to put his elbows on the desk. "Nope. Ran off with her physical therapist. Heard she was in Vegas, walker and all, spending that wad of cash she's already collected on the first installment of her settlement from the personal watercraft manufacturer."

Jordan glared at her editor, not sure she totally comprehended what he meant. "So, are you saying my job writing the Kitchen Kupboard is now permanent?"

"Yup." Egan leaned back and propped his feet on the desk. "There would be a pay increase, of course."

"How much?"

He rubbed his head before meeting her glare. "You do realize the economy is in a slump, right?" Seeing her nod, he continued, "Newspapers are getting hit pretty hard with all the online readers canceling their paid subscriptions."

"Get to the point, please. I've got an inbox full of e-mails to answer."

"That is my point. You've become an icon in Ranchero because of the column."

"Don't kid a kidder, Mr. Egan." Jordan shrugged. "How much?"

"An extra hundred a week."

She bit back a snippy remark and settled for, "I'm sure Loretta Mosley got more than that."

"She did, but that's because her mama and the man who signs your paycheck are siblings. You have an extra perk with the job that she didn't. This gig gave you a fan base Loretta never even came close to having."

Jordan sighed. Though she hated to admit it, Egan was right. People were starting to recognize her on the street, wanting to chat about recipes. Truth be told, she was proud of the way she'd pulled it off so far, given her undeniable lack of culinary talent. She'd tried one of her own recipes the other day, thinking she would surprise Alex when he was able to sneak away from El Paso. She cringed remembering how miserably she'd failed. Writing about food was way easier than actually cooking it.

"Okay," she said, finally. She hated that she'd caved so easily, wishing she could have held out for another fifty bucks, but the lure of extra income was too strong to turn down. "Then it's settled. I'll write exclusively for the Kitchen Kupboard now."

She saw the tips of his ears pink up.

"Not exactly."

"What do you mean not exactly?"

He cleared his throat. "I can't afford to pay someone else to write the personals."

She mulled that around in her head, fixing her gaze on a picture of downtown Ranchero behind Egan's desk.

"What if I sweeten the offer?" he asked, apparently taking her silence for a negative response.

"I'm listening."

"What if you keep on writing both the culinary column and the personals, and I arrange for you to sit in the press box with Jim Westerville for a couple of the Cougar games next season?"

Even memories of her nearly fatal escapade the last time she'd been in the press box couldn't dampen her excitement over this opportunity. She stared at Egan, trying to pull off a pensive look. In reality, he had her with the extra hundred bucks.

"You've got a deal." She stood. "Unless there's something else, I have a column to write."

A column I should have finished last night, she thought, instead of spending two hours on the phone with Alex. His new assignment had him in deep cover, and it was the first time he'd found more than ten minutes at a time to call her in the three weeks since he'd left Ranchero.

"There is one more thing, Jordan," Egan said, motioning for her to sit back down. "Ever hear of Lucas Santana?"

She shook her head, slowly lowering herself into the seat. She had a sinking feeling she wasn't going to like this. Why else would he save it until after she'd agreed to his terms?

"He owns Santana Circle Ranch, the biggest beef-producing property in the area and one that spends a lot of advertising dollars at the *Globe*. Anyway, he called yesterday. Seems it's time for the annual Cattlemen's Ball at the Pavilion Hotel in downtown Fort Worth. He thought it would be good for business if you went this year and talked it up in your column. Thinks it might boost the beef market and be a good incentive for people who are watching their budgets and eating less steak right now."

"Mr. Egan, I've never been to Fort Worth in my life. There's no way I can drive there by myself at night."

The editor's eyes twinkled. "Already on top of that. His ranch foreman, who I've been told is not only very handsome but also very single, will take you there."

"You're hooking me up with a date?"

"Not really a date per se. Let's call Rusty Morales an escort." He smiled. "It never hurts to be seen with a good-looking cowboy, if you know what I mean."

"Unfortunately, I do," she said, thinking about her non-existent social life. "Is this mandatory for my job?"

"If you want to look at it that way, then yes. I prefer to think of it as an opportunity to mix with the social upper crust in the county. And don't forget, this yearly hullabaloo raises a lot of money for cancer research."

She narrowed her eyes. "Did you just make that up to guilt me into going?"

He laughed out loud. "Hell no, but it's good to know you can be guilted." He shook his finger in her direction, reminding her of her high school English teacher Sister Catherine when she was about to blow a gasket. "Trust me when I tell you the Cattlemen's Association is the biggest supporter of the American Cancer Society in the entire country, and most of the research money stays in Dallas at Southwestern."

When he saw her wavering, he continued, "What do you have to lose except a few hours spent dining and dancing? Despite your recent penchant for getting into trouble, how dangerous could it be to have a steak dinner with a bunch of beefcakes wearing spurs?"

She blew out a breath. She didn't even want to imagine.

RECIPES

LONGHORN PRIME RIB'S STRAWBERRY-MANDARIN SALAD

Yields 4–6 servings

SALAD

1 bunch of red-leaf lettuce, rinsed and torn
1 cup sliced strawberries
1 can (11 ounces) mandarin oranges, drained
1 cup red onion, sliced in strips
½ cup slivered almonds, toasted
3 crisp bacon strips, crumbled

DRESSING

⅓ cup sugar (can use sweetner)
⅓ cup red wine vinegar
⅓ cup extra-virgin olive oil

To make the salad, place all of the salad ingredients in a large bowl. To make the dressing, in a small bowl whisk the sugar in vinegar and oil until the sugar is dissolved. Allow this to sit at room temperature for several hours. You can use sweetener instead of sugar. Drizzle salad with dressing. Toss the salad gently to coat before serving.

• • •

ROSIE'S PORK CHOP CASSEROLE

Côte de Porc á la Cocotte

Yields 6 servings

1 tablespoon cooking oil
1 16-ounce package frozen grated (not the chunks) hash browns, thawed
1 can (10 ¾ ounces) cream of mushroom soup
½ cup milk
6 thin boneless pork chops, fat trimmed
2½ cups grated cheddar cheese
1 can (2.8 ounces) French-fried onions

Preheat the oven to 350° F. Grease a 9 × 13 baking dish with a tablespoon of oil. Mix the hash browns, soup, and milk and pour the mixture into the pan. Place the pork chops in a large sauté pan over medium heat and brown them on both sides, 3–5 minutes each side. Lay the pork chops on top of the hash brown mixture (Each pork chop will be a serving.). Cover tightly with foil and bake for 40 minutes. Remove the dish from the oven and sprinkle the top with the cheddar cheese and French-fried onions. Return to the oven and bake uncovered for 10 more minutes, or until the top is browned and cheese is melted.

• • •

LONGHORN PRIME RIB'S CHOCOLATE DECADENCE CAKE

2½ cups cake flour
½ teaspoon baking soda
1 teaspoon salt
¾ cup (1½ sticks) unsalted butter, softened
2 cups sugar
3½ ounces semisweet or bittersweet dark chocolate, melted and cooled
1 teaspoon vanilla extract
2 large eggs
1½ cups cold water
Nonstick cooking oil
Raspberry liqueur, for drizzling

Chocolate-Chip Butter Cream Frosting (recipe follows)
Dark chocolate shavings, for decoration
Raspberry Sauce, for decoration (optional; recipe follows)

Preheat the oven to 350° F. In a large bowl sift together the flour, baking soda, and salt; set aside. In another large bowl use a hand mixer on medium speed to cream the butter and sugar until light and fluffy, 3–5 minutes. Add the chocolate and vanilla and beat for 3 minutes on medium speed. Beat in the eggs one at a time. Beat for another 3 minutes. Gradually mix in the dry ingredients, alternating with the water. Beat 1 minute after each addition. Mix until batter is smooth.

Spray two 9-inch round cake pans with nonstick cooking oil. Cut two circles of parchment paper (I use waxed paper) to fit the pan bottoms and place them inside the pans. Spray the paper for added nonstick insurance. Pour equal amounts of the batter into each of the prepared pans and smooth the surface with a spatula; the pans should be about two-thirds full. Bake 30–35 minutes, or until toothpick inserted near the center comes out clean.

Cool for 40 minutes. Place one of the layers on a cake dish and remove the paper. Drizzle with a few tablespoons of the raspberry liqueur. Spread ½ cup of the butter cream frosting over the first layer of cake. Carefully place the second layer on top of the first and repeat what you did for the first one. Smooth the sides with the frosting and then spread the rest over the top so that the cake is completely covered. Refrigerate for 5 minutes before decorating or cutting. Scatter chocolate shavings over cake. Drizzle Raspberry Sauce, if using, on the plate before adding a slice of cake. Serve with a scoop of vanilla ice cream. (This is really a rich cake and the ice cream cuts the sweetness.)

CHOCOLATE-CHIP BUTTER CREAM FROSTING

4½ cups confectioners' sugar
10 tablespoons hot water
6 ounces semisweet dark chocolate, melted and cooled
2½ teaspoons vanilla
6 tablespoons (¾ stick) unsalted butter, softened
½ cup (4 ounces) semisweet dark chocolate, finely chopped

In a medium large bowl use a hand mixer on low speed to dissolve the sugar and water. Beat in the dark chocolate and vanilla. Add the butter gradually. Continue mixing on low speed. Mix until everything is completely incorporated. Using a spatula, fold in the semisweet chocolate bits.

RASPBERRY SAUCE

1 10-ounce package frozen raspberries
1 tablespoon freshly squeezed lemon juice
1 tablespoon orange liqueur (optional)

Put the raspberries in a food processor and puree until smooth. You can strain to remove seeds or not. Add the lemon juice and, if using, the orange liqueur.

ROSIE'S POTATO CHIP CHICKEN

Budin de Papitas Fritas con Pollo

Yields 6 servings

4 boneless, skinless chicken breasts, rinsed and cut up into bite-sized pieces
4 stalks celery, chopped
1 package (10 ounces) sliced almonds
1 cup (2 sticks) butter, melted (or for low-fat version, use ¼ cup butter and ¾ cup low-fat mayonnaise)
1 tablespoon dried onion flakes
1 tablespoon freshly ground black pepper
Nonstick cooking oil
10 ounces grated cheddar cheese (about 2½ cups)
1 (7.5-ounce) bag of potato chips, crumbled

Preheat the oven to 350° F. In a large bowl mix the chicken, celery, almonds, butter, onion flakes. and pepper. Spray a 9 × 13 baking dish with nonstick cooking oil and add the chicken mixture to the dish. Top with the cheese and then the chips. Bake uncovered 45 minutes, or until filling is bubbly and chips are golden brown.

RAY'S PUMPKIN PIE CRUNCH

1 (15-ounce) can solid pack pumpkin
1 (12-ounce) can evaporated milk
3 large eggs
1½ cups sugar
4 teaspoons pumpkin pie spice
½ teaspoon salt
1 package Duncan Hines classic yellow cake mix
1 cup chopped pecans
1 cup (2 sticks) butter, melted
Whipped topping

Preheat the oven to 350° F. In a large bowl combine the pumpkin, milk, eggs, sugar, pumpkin pie spice, and salt. Pour the pumpkin mixture into a greased 9 × 13 pan. Sprinkle the cake mix evenly over the pumpkin mixture and top with pecans. Drizzle the melted butter over the top. Bake 50–55 minutes, or until golden brown. Cool for fifteen minutes. Serve warm with a dollop of whipped topping. Refrigerate the leftovers and reheat in the microwave before serving. You will never eat regular pumpkin pie again!

MYRTLE'S MANDARIN ORANGE CAKE

CAKE

1 package yellow cake mix
1 can (11 ounces) mandarin oranges with juices
½ cup cooking oil
4 large eggs, beaten

TOPPING

1 large (16-ounce) container Cool Whip
1 small can (8 ounces) crushed pineapple and juices
1 small box (1.4 ounces) vanilla instant pudding, dry

Preheat the oven to 350° F. Grease and flour a 9 × 13 baking pan. To make the cake, combine all the cake ingredients and mix by hand, then pour the batter into the pan. Bake as indicated on box. Cake is done when toothpick inserted in center comes out clean. Allow cake to cool completely (approximately 30 minutes). To make the topping, combine all of the topping ingredients and mix well. Spread the topping on top of the cake and store in the refrigerator until ready for serving.

ALEX'S TEX-MEX BREAKFAST CASSEROLE

Tejano Casserole Desayuno

6 slices of any kind of bread
Butter or margarine for bread
1 teaspoon cooking oil
1-pound tube hot breakfast sausage
12 ounces grated cheddar cheese (about 3 cups)
6 ounces pepper jack cheese (about 1½ cups)
6 large eggs, beaten
2 cups whole or 2% milk

Trim the crust off of the bread and butter one side of each slice. Grease an 8 × 11 baking pan with cooking oil and line the bottom with the bread, butter side down.

In a small skillet, brown the sausage, crumble, and drain. Layer the sausage over the bread slices. Top with the cheddar and pepper jack cheeses.

In a small bowl beat together the eggs and milk and pour over the cheese. Cover and refrigerate overnight.

Preheat oven to 350° F. Bake covered for 35 minutes. Uncover and bake another 15–20 minutes, or until the cheese is golden brown.

MYRTLE'S CHOCOLATE-CHIP COFFEE CAKE

Yields 1 9 x 13 pan

2½ cups all-purpose flour
1½ teaspoons baking powder
1 teaspoon baking soda
½ cup (1 stick) unsalted butter, softened
1½ cups sugar
2 large eggs
1 cup sour cream (can use low fat)
1 teaspoon vanilla
1½ cups semisweet chocolate chips
1 teaspoon cinnamon

Preheat oven to 350° F. Grease and flour a 9 × 13 pan.

Combine the flour, baking powder, and baking soda in a medium bowl and set aside.

In a large bowl use a hand mixer to cream the butter and 1 cup of the sugar. Add the eggs, sour cream, and vanilla and mix well. Gradually add in the flour mixture. Batter will be thick.

In a small bowl combine the chocolate chips, the remaining ½ cup of sugar, and the cinnamon. Set aside.

Spread half the batter in the pan. This is tough, so sprinkle a little flour on your hands and spread like pizza dough. Sprinkle half the chocolate chip mixture over the batter. Spread the remaining batter on top. (This is also going to require a lot of patience. Don't worry if you aren't able to cover the entire first layer. It will still be delicious and look good.) Top this off with the remaining chocolate-chip mixture.

Bake 25–30 minutes. Allow the cake to completely cool before cutting or the chocolate will be messy.

• • •

LONGHORN PRIME RIB'S RATTLESNAKE PASTA

1 pound bow-tie pasta
5 tablespoons cooking oil
¼ cup sliced onions
½ medium yellow squash, cut diagonally into ¼ inch slices then cut in half (about 3/4 cup)
½ medium zucchini, cut diagonally into ¼-inch-thick slices (about 3/4 cup)
¾ cup sliced mushrooms (optional)
1¼ cups heavy cream
1 jalapeño pepper, seeded and minced (or ½ small can minced jalapeño)
1 teaspoon minced garlic
1 tablespoon Dijon mustard
1 tablespoon Cajun seasoning
2 ounces freshly grated Parmesan cheese (about ½ cup)
1 can (14½ ounces) fire-roasted diced tomatoes

Salt and pepper to taste
3 boneless, skinless chicken breasts, rinsed and cut up into bite-sized pieces
All-purpose flour and Cajun seasoning, for dredging

Cook the pasta according to package instructions. Meanwhile, heat 2 tablespoons of the oil in a large skillet over medium heat. Add the onions, yellow squash, zucchini, and mushrooms (if using) and cook for 5 minutes, or until the vegetables are heated through but still firm.

Pour in the cream and the cooked pasta and simmer for 4 minutes. Mix in the jalapeño, garlic, mustard, and Cajun seasoning and cook for 1 minute. Stir in the cheese and the tomatoes. Reduce heat to low.

In another large skillet, preheat the remaining 3 tablespoons of oil over high heat. Shake the Cajun seasoning over the chicken pieces and then dredge in the flour. Pan fry for 5 minutes on each side, or until brown. Add the chicken to vegetable pasta mixture and stir a few times to incorporate. This casserole has a bite (that's why it's called Rattlesnake Pasta), so if you don't like spicy food, go easy on the jalapeño.

JORDAN'S CHOCOLATE HO HO CAKE

CAKE

1 package chocolate cake mix

FILLING

8 tablespoons (1 stick) margarine
½ cup Crisco
1 cup sugar
⅓ cup lukewarm milk

ICING

8 tablespoons (1 stick) margarine
½ cup of cocoa
1 1-pound box confectioners' sugar (or a little less to make less sweet)
¼ cup cold milk

Preheat the oven to 350° F. To make the cake, prepare the cake mix according to the package instructions. Divide the batter into two greased and floured 9-inch cake pans and bake 10–20 minutes, or until toothpick inserted in center comes out clean. Let cool.

To make the filling, in a medium bowl use a hand mixer to beat together the margarine, Crisco, and sugar until fluffy (5–7 minutes). Pour in the milk and beat until smooth (taste until sugar crystals are gone). If the filling is too thick, add a little more milk, a tablespoon at a time, to thin it. Place one layer of cake on a plate and spread the filling over the first layer. Place the second layer of cake on top of the first.

To make the icing, in a large bowl use a hand mixer on medium high speed to beat the margarine, cocoa, sugar, and milk until fluffy (5–7 minutes). If the icing is too thick, add more milk, a tablespoon at a time, to thin. Spread the icing on the top and sides of the cake.